ELLE GRAY | K.S. GRAY

OLIVIA KNIGHT
FBI MYSTERY THRILLER

THE
LOCKED
BOX

The Locked Box
Copyright © 2022 by Elle Gray | K.S. Gray

All rights reserved. Without limiting the rights under copyright reserved above, no part of this publication may be reproduced, stored in or intro-duced into retrieval system, or transmitted, in any form, or by any means (electronic, mechanical, photocopying, recording, or otherwise) without the prior written permission of both the copyright owner and the above publisher of this book.

This is a work of fiction. Names, characters, places, brands, media, and in-cidents are either the products of the author's imagination or are used fic-titiously. The author acknowledges the trademarked status and trademark owners of various products referenced in this work of fiction, which have been used without permission. The publication/use of these trademarks is not authorized, associated with, or sponsored by the trademark owners.

PROLOGUE

B‍ROCK WAS SURE HIS LIFE COULD GET MUCH WORSE, BUT being handcuffed to a pole and kept alone in a room with no food or water wasn't exactly how he'd choose to spend his day. His back still throbbed from where he'd been sliced open, all for the benefit of the video sent to the FBI. He wondered if Olivia had seen it yet. If she had, he was sure she was already chasing down the ends of the earth to find him. He didn't know if that was a good thing or not.

He should have seen it coming. He knew something wasn't right on this mission. He could feel the scales tipping, about to throw him into the deep end at any moment. He should have known better than to re-establish contact with the same old informants after all this time and pretend like nothing had changed. There had been signs of something wrong, and he'd ignored them. And that was exactly how he'd landed up in trouble with the wrong kind of people.

Still, at least he had a view outside the ship. The small window in his cell provided him with the sight of endless blue waves, gently bobbing the ship up and down to take them to their new destination. He had no idea where that would be, though he had a few guesses. He knew the nooks and crannies of the organization like the back of his hand—he'd followed them for long enough—but it still wasn't enough to keep out of their clutches.

The door to his cell opened, and a little light streamed in, causing an ache behind his eyes. Someone was holding a tray of food for him and a big glass of water. He didn't recognize the man who was holding the goods, but then again, he didn't expect anyone from the big leagues to serve him. He was their prisoner, and they weren't exactly trying to make him feel welcome.

"This is luxurious," Brock quipped as the tray was placed just within the reach of his cuffed hands. He couldn't help himself from making a joke, even though the situation was far from funny. The man serving him kept a straight face and said nothing.

"Such a conversationalist."

The man's eyes flared in anger. He clenched a fist, ready to strike Brock across the face, but he took a breath to calm himself instead.

"If you want to keep that smug smile of yours, you'd better talk," the man said bluntly before leaving the room. Brock sighed.

"Nice talking to you too…"

Brock picked at the food that had been left for him, but despite his grumbling stomach, he couldn't eat it. Not that the gruel looked very appetizing to begin with. He'd been in bad situations before, but this topped them all. He knew he was in real trouble from the moment his cover was blown.

He recalled the gun pressing into his back in a back alley in New York. In that instant, he knew that his life was never going to be the same again, and everything was about to go wrong.

"Do as you're told or everyone you love will die," his captor—the man who'd once been his ally—had told him. And when Brock's mind immediately drifted to Olivia, he knew he'd do whatever

CHAPTER ONE

Olivia couldn't stop staring at the screen in front of her, frozen on the image of Brock being beaten, somewhere she couldn't reach him. She didn't understand. How had this happened? How had he been burned? Had he known the danger he was in?

None of that mattered, she knew that. The only thing that did was getting him back, and it was up to her to get him back.

Olivia forced herself to watch the video a second time. Then a third, then a fourth, then a fifth. It wrenched her heart to do so, but she had to keep herself steady. She had to focus on anything but Brock and his anguished cries. She was hoping she could find some clue as to where he might be based on his surroundings,

THE **LOCKED BOX**

they wanted him to. He couldn't bear to live if they tried to hurt her.

No matter the cost to himself.

despite how dark the video was. She strained her eyes, looking in every nook and cranny of the screen for something of interest.

"Come on, come on…" she murmured. And then she glimpsed something behind Brock's helpless frame. A circular window. It was dark outside the window, but the closer she looked, she realized she could see waves thrashing against it.

Not just a window. A porthole.

So, Brock was on a ship. They were taking him somewhere far away from her. It felt as if her heart were sinking to the bottom of the ocean as she thought about him already being thousands of miles away from her. She knew that trying to find him at sea would be like trying to find a needle in a haystack. It was nearly impossible.

But not completely.

Immediately, her adrenaline kicked in and her mind began racing with possibilities. Despite the early hour, she already knew she had to get to work. As she called Jonathan back, she took a steadying breath. He picked up immediately.

This time, even his brisk introduction wasn't fast enough. Olivia said it before he could even get a word out.

"I want to work the case."

He sighed on the other end of the line. She could perfectly picture him rubbing the bridge of his nose in frustration.

"No. You're too close to this, Knight. I've already got a team in the lab analyzing the video."

"He's on a ship somewhere," she pressed. "They've got him out at sea."

"The team will tell us more when they can," he countered. "Jesus, it's not even four in the morning."

"So what? Are we just supposed to sit around and wait?" she thundered. "Every second counts, sir!" She barely appended the 'sir' at the last minute, as if suddenly remembering that he was her direct superior.

"Once we get a fix on the location, we'll dispatch a squad to retrieve him," Jonathan said.

"Let me do it," she demanded.

"Olivia," he warned sternly. He must have been seriously pissed to use her first name. Jonathan never used first names.

"I can handle this. This is what I do best. And I work best under pressure."

"You know that's not wise. He's your partner."

"And if it was the other way around, I know he'd be doing everything in his power to find me," Olivia fired back. "I'm not leaving this to someone else. I have to know that the most is being done to get him home safe. And who knows him better than I do? If there's even a slight chance of finding him alive, then I'm going to be the one to make it happen."

Jonathan was quiet for a moment, and Olivia held her breath. As much as she needed this case, she couldn't just fly off the handle and try to handle it on her own. She needed Bureau resources and approval to find Brock, or they both might be dead before she got anywhere. Jonathan had to see her side of things, didn't he? How could he drop this bombshell on her and then expect her not to want to be a part of it?

After a while, he let out a long sigh. "Alright. I'll put you in charge. But if I see any inkling that you can't handle this, that you're too emotionally attached… you're off the case. In a heartbeat. Understood?"

"Completely," Olivia said firmly. There was no chance she was screwing up this opportunity. She couldn't afford for him to put her on the back burner when the person she cared for most was relying on her. She knew that wherever Brock was, he'd be thinking of her—he would know that she was looking for him. It would give him hope, and that meant she couldn't let him down.

Jonathan cleared his throat. "I can already tell you won't just wait around for the office to open, so I'll have the video analysts reach out to you. If you need anything, you know where to find me."

"Thank you, sir."

"And Knight? I… I hope you can find something. And quickly. Time's ticking."

"I know."

THE **LOCKED BOX**

They hung up, and Olivia immediately went to work. The first thing that flitted across her mind was the unusual demand for ransom. Two million dollars was a lot of money, but certainly it would be chump change to a massive international organization like this. This had to be a trap—and, of course, these things always were traps, but why bother with the ransom at all? Why not just kill Brock?

She had no doubt in her mind that Brock was in danger, even if they did somehow get the ransom money together to save him. As she hung up the call, she returned to look at the video they'd been sent. It was the only thing she had to start with, and she needed something solid. Some direction to follow.

What did she know so far? Well, it made sense that Brock was on a ship. From what little she knew about his mission, he'd been investigating an international drug and weapons trafficking organization, so they had to have a way to transport their goods overseas. But how did they do it without being caught? And now that they had live cargo, how had they smuggled a man onboard without raising suspicions?

She needed more. She watched the video several more times, muting the sound so that she didn't have to hear Brock's cries of anguish. It was almost too much for her to bear. But she kept her focus on the video, desperate to find something of use.

There was one thing she kept coming back to. Barely poking out from one corner of the video was the barest edge of something—a blue symbol printed on the wall. The only problem was that it was only a few pixels in size. The majority of the symbol was off-camera. The more Olivia tried to decipher it, the more frustrated she became. It might be the key to everything, and even though it was right in front of her, it was just out of her reach…

She keyed up an email to the video analysis team, but they hadn't had much more luck than she had. She brought the blue logo to their attention, and they confirmed that they'd seen it and were working on matching it to any number of possibilities. Of course, they were the ones with the manpower and resources to match the tiny piece with a bigger picture. All Olivia could do was wait.

And that was about all she could find. There were no other clues. No hints or signs of where he could possibly be, except for somewhere in the middle of the ocean.

Olivia took several calming breaths. She had to stay focused and calm. Getting worked up wouldn't save Brock. It might even sign his death certificate. She closed her eyes for a single moment to collect herself, and when she opened them again, she had calmed the storm inside her.

"Alright, think," she murmured to herself. "Where is he headed?"

She watched the video again, this time turning the sound back on and gritting her teeth through Brock's pained cries so she could listen to the captor's voice. They wanted the ransom money to be dropped off in the UK. They'd given the location of a small town that Olivia had never heard of, but she was sure that Brock wouldn't be there. They wouldn't take him there until they were certain they'd been paid, and maybe then they still wouldn't hand him over.

But it did raise a question: Why would they have a drop-off location in the UK? Was that one of the places where they traded? It had to be important for some reason. And if the ship Brock was on was at sea, wasn't it entirely possible that he was already headed toward the UK?

It was a place to start, at least. She didn't want to consider the fact that Brock could be anywhere in the world by now. She told herself that her theory made perfect sense and that she wasn't just grasping at straws.

Sinking back against the wall, she considered how to approach finding him. She had limited time, but she had to take advantage of Bureau resources. That meant that she could likely have someone monitoring each of the major ports in the UK, looking for any suspicious shipments that might come in. A quick online search revealed the list of major ports she needed to research. She called up a map on her computer and marked each of them: Felixstowe, Southampton, London, Immingham, and Liverpool. If this organization masqueraded as a shipping company, it made sense that they'd try to hide in plain sight while surrounded by other ships.

But she knew she had to cast a wider net. It was also entirely possible that the reason Brock's captors had been slipping under the radar was because they were using smaller ports to smuggle their goods. Olivia knew it was unlikely those were being as heavily monitored for criminal activity, given that they were small and unassuming. She'd need to do further research and find ports of ingress that wouldn't have the same large international security systems in place.

Olivia's head was already beginning to ache, but she tried to ignore the sensation. She didn't have time for it. Besides, she was used to working late at night. All she needed was a cup of coffee, and she'd be ready for anything.

Olivia headed into Emily's kitchen as quietly as she could and started up the coffee maker. She tried not to think about the fact that everything was riding on her. Brock's life was in her hands now. She hadn't thought that through so much when she'd begged to take on the case. All she'd known was that he was in danger and she wanted to help.

But now, the weight of the situation was beginning to hit her. She leaned against the kitchen counter, her head spinning. Her mouth was dry, and her heart was thumping hard against her chest. What would happen if she couldn't get to him in time? Would they really kill him for the money? She felt sick at the idea that she could be the reason he didn't come home. She felt sick at the idea of a life without him in it.

Things had finally been looking up for the two of them. There had been a distinct feeling that when he came home, they were going to pick things up where they'd left off months before. That spark between them was just waiting to be reignited. Now, Olivia wished she had told him what she was feeling sooner. Now she was scared she might never get the chance.

She got a sudden bout of nausea and hung her head over the sink. The stress was just too much.

"Olivia?"

Olivia looked up to see Emily standing in the doorway to her bedroom, watching her in concern. Emily moved to her side and cupped her cheeks.

"What's going on? You look so pale right now," Emily said urgently, her doting manner kicking in. "Are you sick?"

Olivia took a deep breath. "No, I'm not sick. I *feel* sick…"

"What's going on?"

Olivia swallowed down the lump in her throat. "It's Brock. He's been taken hostage."

Realization took over Emily's face. She knew, as any agent would, that having your cover blown was akin to a death sentence. Emily pulled Olivia in close, gripping her tightly as Olivia tried to remember how to breathe.

"It's going to be okay," Emily whispered. "You'll find him, I know it. Don't start doubting yourself now. You have come through so many times before. This time will be no different."

Olivia took a deep breath. "Thank you. I think I needed to hear that."

Emily pulled away from her with a tight smile. "You're going to be fine, I promise. Sit down. I'll bring your coffee to you."

Olivia sat down on the sofa, feeling her heart finally starting to slow down. She was reminded once again of what a good friend Emily was to her. She always seemed to know what to say when she was at her lowest. When Emily pressed the mug of coffee into her hands, she immediately felt a little better. She took a long sip then let out a long sigh.

"I'm under the pressure of time here," Olivia told Emily. "His captors have issued a ransom. The drop-off point is in the UK, so I think that might be where Brock is being held. He seems to be on a ship, so I'm trying to figure out a way to intercept him as he comes into the dock, before things get any worse. But that's the problem. He could be on any of the thousands of ships crossing the Atlantic on any given day. If that even is where he is, at all."

Emily nodded, considering what she'd been told. "Do you know anything about the ship itself? If you find a particular model or type you can track active ships and try to narrow it down."

THE **LOCKED BOX**

Olivia chewed her lip. "Jonathan has a team of video analysts trying to pull data from the ransom video. There's the tiniest corner of a logo in the back that could lead to something, but so far, nothing."

"Can I see?"

Olivia handed her phone to Emily and called up the video. She couldn't bear to watch it again, so she averted her eyes while it played.

"Jesus," Emily muttered. "I'm so sorry, Olivia…"

Olivia nodded, sinking a little farther into her seat. "This is just insane. I knew it would be dangerous for him; I knew there were risks involved… but I never anticipated this. I wonder if he knew just how bad this could go?"

"I don't think he would have agreed to go if he did. Going undercover is never safe, but even Jonathan wouldn't have sent him out if he thought he might get burned. Brock would probably have run for the hills if someone told him this was going to be the outcome."

Olivia laughed quietly. "Oh, I don't know. He does love an adventure. I just… I can't help thinking that there's something I'm missing. I feel like he would have prepared for something like this. Brock puts on a big front of being some big, dumb lunkhead, but he's pretty crafty. If he thought there was a slight possibility that something could go wrong, he'd have made arrangements."

"Like what?"

Olivia shook her head slowly. "I don't know, but I'm going to find out." She stood up suddenly, pacing the room. "I need to go back to his apartment in Belle Grove. If there are any clues at all, they'll be there. And even if not, he will surely have notes for the case there. It's a place to start."

"You're going now?"

"I have to," Olivia replied gravely. She didn't have a second to waste. "I don't want to leave anything to chance."

Emily folded her arms over her chest, like she was hugging herself. She was watching her friend with such concern on her face that it made Olivia's heart ache.

"Let me come with you. Let me help."

"No. I don't want to drag you into this. You've already done so much for me." Olivia offered her friend a smile. "Thank you. For everything. But I have to do this on my own now. I can't risk losing you too."

Emily pulled her in for one last hug. "If you change your mind, you know where to find me. I'll be here, day and night. You just call me, okay?"

"I know," Olivia murmured. "Thank you."

There was no more time to waste. Olivia threw on a coat over her pajamas and grabbed her car keys. There was no time to pack or prepare. She had to get back to Belle Grove. She had to find something that would save Brock.

Before it was too late.

CHAPTER TWO

O**N THE DRIVE BACK TO BELLE GROVE, OLIVIA'S MUSCLES** were tight, and the air inside the car felt stale, like she couldn't really breathe. It had been a long time since she'd felt so completely at a loss. Over the past few months, she finally felt like she'd been taking control of her life, growing in confidence after everything she'd been through. Even though her home being ransacked had knocked the wind out of her, she thought she was finally recovering. But now, it felt like she was hurtling back to square one—like someone was out to get her, to make her life miserable when she was about to find happiness.

Brock meant so much more to her than just her work partner. He was more than just a friend, and more than just someone she was falling hard for. He was a huge part of her life, always there when she needed him. He was the person who made her laugh when she was sure she was about to cry. He lifted her spirits when the world around her seemed like such a dark place to be. He showed her good in a world full of bad people.

She'd felt his absence since he'd gone away, but now, knowing that she might never see him again, made her feel sick to her stomach.

But she couldn't afford to think that way. Until she knew his fate, she had to work tirelessly to get him back. She was willing to have sleepless nights, to work herself to the bone, to keep pushing until the end if it meant she could have him back with her. Whatever it took, she would do it.

Despite it still being dark outside, sleep was the last thing on Olivia's mind. How was she supposed to ever sleep again when she wasn't sure that Brock was safe? She thought about the video and the way his captors had brutally hit him, their whip slicing through his back. It made her shudder to think about it. She knew when she did sleep next, she would have nightmares.

To get this done right, she had to work fast, and she had to work smart. If she was going to make sense of any of this, then she had to look where no one else would think to look. She had to take control of the situation before it was too late.

As she closed in on Belle Grove, Olivia cracked a window, feeling as though she couldn't get enough air to her lungs. It felt strange to be in the place that she associated so strongly with Brock when she knew he wasn't there. He'd created her entire experience in Belle Grove. Before he showed up, she felt alone there. Because she was. She didn't know anyone in the town very well, and she was miles away from her friends and family. It had been a place to escape her troubles, but she hadn't realized she was escaping the people she cared for too. It had made her feel like the world was just a little too quiet.

And then Brock had arrived on the scene. And suddenly, she had reasons to smile again. Suddenly, she was laughing at the jokes he told, even when she tried her hardest to keep a straight face. She was taken in by his spell, and it hadn't been broken since.

THE **LOCKED BOX**

The feeling he gave her was one that couldn't be replaced. She knew that now. If she couldn't have Brock, she didn't want anyone. She pulled up in front of his apartment, her heart beating faster than it should. She had to get him back. Not just for his sake, but for her own.

Nothing would be the same without him.

Olivia locked up her car and then slipped her hand inside Brock's mailbox, feeling around for the key he'd promised to leave for her. She hadn't thought she'd need to use it, but now, she was glad it was there. Her fingers found the cold metal, but there was something else in there too. She brushed against a piece of paper and frowned. She thought at first that it might be unopened mail, but the paper felt too flimsy to be an envelope.

She pulled out the key and the paper with it. It was a note, written in Brock's untidy scrawl. Olivia felt her heart tug at the sight of something so personal, a reminder of how desperate the situation was, but she forced herself to read the note.

Stay safe, Olivia. I'll be home before you know it, and we'll have a nice cup of instant coffee, just the way you like it.

Olivia read the note several times, feeling deflated. Somehow, she was expecting something more. Why would Brock leave her a note about coffee? He'd made her switch to proper coffee months ago, so the joke landed with her, but it made her feel empty. Why would he insist on her drinking the old instant coffee that she used to swear by?

He was probably just teasing her. It was his specialty, after all. He probably left her a dumb note thinking that he'd be home in a few weeks and it wouldn't matter. Maybe he felt no need to watch his back. He was always so sure of himself. Maybe he never expected to land himself in trouble.

But Olivia knew him better than that. She knew the man beyond the surface persona he put on. Brock might be cocky, but he was also smart. He knew how dangerous his mission was going to be. There was no way that he wouldn't have some sort of contingency plan in place in case he didn't return. Olivia just had to figure out where his mind had gone before he left. If she could think like him, then maybe she could understand what she needed to do to find him.

She turned the key and let herself into Brock's apartment, feeling distinctly uncomfortable about how quiet the place was. It was usually filled with Brock's chatter and raucous laughter. Now, it was silent, like even the apartment itself was aware of what had happened and had gone into shock. Olivia took a deep breath and looked around. The place felt different in other ways too. Like it wasn't exactly as she had left it. It made her question whether she was the first person who had come snooping here…

It would make sense if the people who took Brock had been here, rooting around and hoping for more than they had already taken. Perhaps they had come looking for clues, just as she had. If he was refusing to talk to the people who had captured him, then perhaps they thought they could find something in his apartment.

But where? The place wasn't exactly big, and Olivia had lived there for long enough to be sure that she knew every nook and cranny of the place. Was it possible that there were things that Brock had hidden even from her? That he had hiding places that she would never have dreamed of searching? She chewed her thumb. It did seem like him to keep something right under her nose.

She wasn't even sure where to begin. Where would Brock hide something? She moved aimlessly through the apartment, flicking through books on his shelves, delving under his bed, even checking in his dresser. She couldn't find anything out of the ordinary at first glance, but in her experience, she knew that didn't always mean there was nothing to find. Only an amateur would hide something important in a sock drawer, and Brock was far from an amateur.

She felt tiredness gripping her mind again, and she absentmindedly headed into the kitchen to start up the coffee maker. It was only when her hand brushed the jar of gourmet grounds that Brock kept on the counter that her heart froze and her mind began to whir.

We'll have a nice cup of instant coffee, just the way you like it…

THE **LOCKED BOX**

Olivia frowned. Was she insane to think that maybe that comment meant more than just a silly joke? Was there something about the note that was important?

Olivia yanked open the pantry and reached up to the top shelf where the long-abandoned jar of instant coffee had rested for months. Ever since she'd effectively moved into Brock's place, she'd been forced to admit that the real stuff really was better. She was surprised he even still had this around.

With zero hesitation, she opened up the jar and tipped its contents onto the counter. Coffee granules scattered everywhere, covering the floor and filling the room with its earthy scent. Olivia found herself scrabbling through the pile of granules on the counter, looking for something—*anything*—to prove her theory. She thought she might find a scrap of paper in there, or a secret key, or at least *something*.

But perhaps she was going crazy after all, because there was nothing hidden in the coffee. She sighed, shaking her head. She had wanted to find answers so badly that she was reading between the lines way too much. That wasn't going to get her anywhere.

She was about to clean up the mess she'd made when, from the corner of her eye, she saw the discarded lid of the jar sitting on the counter. Her heart froze. There was something written on the underside of the lid in thick, black marker. There was no way it was a coincidence. There was no way it was just something that the manufacturers had inscribed.

Brock had left her a clue.

Olivia snatched up the lid and examined the lettering inside. She read it several times, trying to make sense of it.

ROT 13 ENIRA.

It was obvious to Olivia that it had more meaning to it than a few random digits and letters, but if she was meant to know the significance, she was still drawing a blank. Was it a reference to something she had forgotten? She tried to think of a time when she had heard that sequence of letters and numbers, but it was completely foreign to her. What was Brock doing leaving such a cryptic clue behind? It was such a strange thing to write that Olivia wondered if it only had meaning to him.

But Brock had written it for a reason, that much was clear. Maybe not for her, but for someone. His note had led *her* here, though, and she was sure this clue was for her. Now, all she had to do was decipher the meaning.

Taking a stab in the dark, Olivia typed the sequence into her phone and decided to see what came up. Her heart thumped a little faster when an explanation came up right before her eyes.

ROT 13 is a simple substitution cipher that dates back to Ancient Rome. The cipher takes any letter in the twenty-six-letter alphabet and replaces it with the thirteenth letter that follows it. For example, A translates to N, and each letter that follows it translates to the next letter in the alphabet. The simple yet effective code can be used to keep secrets and hide clues in online forums and within books.

Olivia read the information several times and then she grabbed a pen and paper from the coffee table. *ENIRA.* Whatever ENIRA translated to had to be of some importance. Olivia chewed her lip while she worked on cracking the code, swapping each letter out for the thirteenth following it. Slowly, the word she was looking for revealed itself.

RAVEN.

Olivia sighed. Another puzzle. She had no idea what relevance the word RAVEN had. It wasn't something that had any significance to either her or Brock, as far as she knew. She had never once heard him take an interest in birds. So, what was it all about? Was it symbolism? She doubted that Brock was the type of guy to put symbolism in a clue, though her bookish heart liked the idea of it. No, she thought it was likely to be something much more literal. Something she could find physically.

Now she really did need a cup of coffee. She quickly swept up the kitchen as the coffee maker bubbled, then poured herself a cup of the nice stuff and cupped it in her hands as she strolled around the apartment, looking for inspiration about what it might mean. She couldn't see any symbols or ornaments that related to the bird, so she was starting to really feel confused…

Until she laid her eyes on the bookshelf.

Most of the books on the shelf actually belonged to her, which is why it was obvious to her which books were Brock's. He didn't have many at all, claiming not to be much of a reader. Most of what he read consisted of spy novels and non-fiction.

…which is why one book stood out among the rest.

Edgar Allen Poe's *The Tell-Tale Heart*.

And suddenly, the word RAVEN made all the sense in the world. Olivia didn't consider herself a particular fan of Poe's work, but she knew what his most famous poem was called.

The Raven.

Olivia rushed to the shelf and snatched up the book. She'd been on the right track earlier without even knowing it. She felt a rush of warmth for Brock, burying clues for her in a bunch of books. He knew her so well that he was even trying to amuse her while she was fighting to save his life.

As she opened up the book, she almost laughed. As the pages fell open, she found that the middle of them had been hollowed out, leaving behind yet another piece of the puzzle.

A silver key.

Olivia picked up the key and examined it. It was small; much too small to belong to a real door. Olivia was also certain that none of the doors in the apartment had locks other than the front door. So, that begged the question… what was the key for?

Olivia chewed her lip. There had to be something in the apartment that she could use the key on. She was sure that whatever it was used for would give her the answers she so desperately needed.

Olivia remembered that she'd seen a safe in the closet several times and felt a rush of excitement. She rushed to test out her theory, but she found that the safe required both a code and a larger key than the one she'd found. As soon as that theory had failed, she realized that the safe probably wasn't where Brock would leave a clue anyway. Not when his life might depend on it. It was too obvious, almost like a red herring for anyone who might come snooping.

And so, her search continued. She hunted high and low in the apartment, hoping to find something that would aid her search. But hours in, as the sun was beginning to peek over the horizon, she still hadn't found anywhere for the key to fit into.

She'd tried every cupboard, slotted the key in every lock she came across, and looked behind, inside, under, and over every item in the apartment.

But there was nothing.

Olivia cursed Brock for being so clever. Who'd have thought he was even capable? Any other person would have just told her these secrets before he left. But Brock was used to being a pain in Olivia's ass, and it seemed that he was still succeeding, even while he was captured hundreds of miles away. Olivia gripped the key hard, feeling it jabbing into her palm. She needed answers, and she needed them an hour ago when her search began.

Olivia picked up the book where she'd found the key, flipping through the disemboweled pages. She had hoped that maybe there would be another note from Brock inside it, but he hadn't written a single word on the sliced-up pages.

She studied the book for a long time. She had never read it, and she was sure it wasn't Brock's kind of thing either. She doubted he would even give the book the time of day.

But he'd picked that book in particular to hide the key. Maybe it was simply because he could use the cipher code to point Olivia in the right direction…

But what if there was more to it? What if the book itself was a clue, and there was something there in the story that might lead her in the right direction?

Olivia wasn't one for reading on the job, even if it was her favorite pastime, but she suddenly knew what she needed to do. She needed to read the story, or at least get the gist of it.

It was a short story, but Olivia knew that if she was going to save time, she should at least research the synopsis. She hated the idea of ignoring the artist's work and reading a summary, but this wasn't the time for appreciating good writing. She simply needed to know what happened in the tale.

And what she found made her heart beat a little faster.

It was a tale of murder. A tale of an old man being killed and then hidden beneath the floorboards beneath his bed…

Olivia was on her feet in an instant. She rushed into the bedroom and began to desperately shove the bed out of the way, the posts of the furniture leaving deep grooves in the carpet. There was nothing under the bed, but Olivia knew that if Brock had committed to the mystery this far, then what she needed was under the carpet and buried in the floorboards.

It took Olivia a while to rip up the carpet from the corners of the room. It was a good thing Brock didn't have any neighbors—just the diner beneath him—because she was making a hell of a lot of noise. She'd have a hard time explaining to anyone else why she was in someone else's apartment in the early hours of the morning, ripping up their carpet. But it was necessary. Her heart was pulsing hard, knowing she was getting closer and closer to her answers.

By the time she had managed to get the carpet up, she was out of breath, but she didn't stop to catch it. She got on her hands and knees and began to poke at the floorboards, trying to find one that might be loose, one that might have unknown treasures hidden beneath it.

"Come on, come on," Olivia muttered to herself, feeling insanity tugging at her. She knew that what she was doing was crazy, but if it got her answers, she didn't care at all. She knew now that Brock had made a cry for help before he was even captured. He'd been preparing for this for a long time, and she wasn't going to let him down now.

All the floorboards under where the bed had been were firmly nailed down, except for one. Instantly, she knew that was it. All she needed to do was dig her fingernails into the side and lift it up. Without hesitation, she ripped it up and delved her hand into the dusty crevice underneath. She fumbled around blindly, unable to feel anything at first.

And then her hand closed on something.

Something hard and wooden—a box, perhaps. She tried to grab it with one hand and pull it up, but to her surprise, it was quite heavy. She lay flat on her stomach and slid her other hand under the floorboards, lifting the box out with some effort. It was small, but it definitely felt like it contained a treasure trove.

And all of a sudden, she had answers in front of her. Whatever was inside the box, she knew it was going to point her in the direction she needed to go. She ran back into the living room to get the key and slid it easily into the padlock on the box. The satisfying click of it opening made Olivia feel relieved. She was getting a little warmer in her investigation, and that was all she needed to know.

"What do you have for me, Brock?" she whispered as she opened the lid of the box.

And the pieces began to come together.

CHAPTER THREE

OLIVIA FELT LIKE A PIRATE UNCOVERING AN ANCIENT buried treasure as she marveled at the box's contents.

Brock really had been prepared for what was to come. It was like he'd gotten far too close to the truth and that's why he had been made to disappear…

Inside the box was a treasure trove of documents—most notably, the itinerary for a number of ships that were coming and going from Howland Hook Port in New York. It was almost as though he knew that he was going to get burned and sent across the sea. Olivia frowned, scanning over the papers he'd left behind. How had he been so ahead of the game? Brock had told her that it was one of the hardest cases he'd ever worked, and yet it seemed like he knew so much.

It didn't matter how he'd come across the information or whether he'd ever intended to use it. It was a lead. If she could narrow down the place of his capture to this one port, then she would possibly be able to figure out which boat had taken him. She might even be able to figure out where the ship would moor in the UK or consult with the port authority to find some footage of Brock being taken away.

She had to start by reviewing what was in front of her. Greedily, she snatched the papers out of the box and sat cross-legged on the floor to review them. The wooden floor was uncomfortable and cold, but she didn't care about that. She wasn't there to be comfortable. She was there to solve the mystery.

Olivia could see that several of the ships on the sheet were highlighted in yellow marker, and she checked those out first. They were obviously of importance to Brock, so that meant they were important to her. She took note of the names of the ships, trying to find a correlation between them, but she soon realized their names weren't what they had in common.

Each ship was registered under the same company name. They all belonged to a shipping logistics company called ANH. Their company wordmark was in a bright blue. Olivia thought back to the barest hint of blue on the video she had seen and called up the screenshot she'd taken to send the video analysis team. Her lips twisted into a smile.

"Bingo."

It was definitely the start she needed. It was pointing her in a real direction now, not just generally guiding her. She picked up the phone and dialed Jonathan's number.

He answered quickly, but his voice was groggy like he'd just woken up.

"Knight. Have you found anything?"

Olivia scowled. She couldn't believe he was sleeping when Brock had gone missing. Still, she didn't have time to address that. She needed his help.

"I've found a lead," Olivia told him. "I went to Brock's apartment and he had left a series of clues for me. They led to a lockbox containing some information about a bunch of ships.

THE **LOCKED BOX**

I think he was on to the people who did this to him. He was investigating one particular port in New York, Howland Hook, and he was keeping an eye on the ships that docked there under the company name ANH. I want to contact the port and see if there's any security footage."

"You work fast," Jonathan replied, his voice still tinged with sleepiness. "I can get you what you need in the morning."

"This can't wait until the morning."

"Knight, you shouldn't even be awake. Get some sleep, and I'll send you what you need in a couple hours."

"In a couple hours, everything might have changed. In a couple hours, Brock could be one step closer to being killed. Is that what you want?"

"*Enough*, Agent Knight," he snapped. "A team is already working on analyzing the evidence we have, and we can't do anything until we know what we're up against."

"But sir—"

"And that means your well-being too, Knight. You're human, as much as you'd like to pretend you're not. You need to sleep if you're going to keep working in the morning. Take a few hours. I'll get in touch with the port and request what we need. I promise you, you can start up again in a few hours. This isn't a negotiation."

Jonathan ended the call before Olivia could protest. She let out a furious sigh, but she didn't call back. She knew that her boss was much more stubborn than she was, which was saying a lot, and she didn't want to give him any reason to kick her off the case. He was already unsure about whether she should be involved, and she didn't need something else hanging over her head too. She had to play this strategically.

She gathered up the papers Brock had left for her and took them to the living room, putting them on the coffee table so that they were just within her reach as she settled on the sofa. She knew that Jonathan was right—a few hours of sleep would do her a world of good. She lay down on the sofa, and it felt familiar to her from all the nights she'd spent there before. It was almost molded around her body, and it lured her into a false sense of security.

With her eyes closed, she could almost pretend that things were back to the way they were.

With her eyes closed, she could imagine that Brock was sleeping soundly in the next room over, his snores echoing through the apartment. He always slept like he didn't have a single thing on his mind, while Olivia often lay awake and worried about each and every thing.

And now, she had so much to worry about that it weighed down on her eyelids. She felt more tired than she had in a long time. She couldn't help it when the heaviness of her eyes dragged her into sleep and locked her down in a fitful slumber.

∞

It was three hours later when Olivia woke up to the sound of her phone receiving an email. She sat up immediately, knowing that it must be Jonathan with the security footage she had asked for. She blinked her eyes awake and set to work, grabbing her laptop and getting ready to trawl through the videos Jonathan had sent.

She didn't know what she was expecting to find. She needed to search through all of the footage from the nights that he might have gone missing since they didn't know for sure how long he'd been at sea. Then, she needed to see if there was anything suspicious going on at all. But that could take hours, so she grabbed a snack and settled down for the long haul, putting the footage at double speed to see what she might come across.

Hours passed of finding nothing. Olivia checked the footage from several different cameras, keeping a close eye on the ships that Brock had highlighted in his port notes, but she saw nothing out of the ordinary. She was beginning to worry that she was wasting her time, wondering if there was something more active she could be doing to find him. It felt wrong, sitting still and watching hours of videos when she could be out there, doing *something*.

THE **LOCKED BOX**

But she stuck with it. Brock had saved those notes for her for a reason, and she couldn't just ignore that. For his sake, she had to follow this lead through to the end.

Her eyes were beginning to hurt and blur from staring at her screen for so long. But when she finally spotted something, she felt a jolt of excitement in her heart. She paused the footage for a moment and squinted to see if her eyes were playing tricks on her.

No, they weren't. There he was. Brock. She'd know him anywhere. He was walking onto a ship, followed by several men dressed in black. He had a backpack on his back, and he wasn't cuffed or being forced aboard. Olivia frowned. He didn't look like a prisoner at all. It was almost as though he was complying of his own free will.

That couldn't be true though. Why would Brock willingly go with these people, knowing that they were going to torture him and make his life miserable? Why would he go with them so casually when they were the very people he'd been working to take down? It didn't make any sense. Could it have been part of his cover identity? Had he posed as an ally to them and then agreed to board the ship, only to be betrayed with nowhere to escape once on board?

It was a possibility, but it still didn't seem right. Even in the grainy security footage, she could clearly see that Brock was unlike himself. His trademark grin was gone, and he had a cold light in his eyes.

Again—it could well have been part of his cover identity. Or maybe he had decided to work with them after all…

But Olivia shook her head to clear that thought away. She knew Brock. Sure, he could be secretive and hard to read, but he was no criminal. And as much as she struggled to get him to let her in, she knew that he cared for her as much as she cared for him. There was no way he would betray her to join some criminal organization, no matter what they'd offered him.

No. He was their prisoner, she was sure of it. Just because they were letting him walk on his own two feet without cuffs, it didn't mean there wasn't a threat, and it didn't mean he was with them voluntarily. They had whipped him, for goodness' sake. Why would they do that to one of their own?

Had he known when he got on that ship what they planned to do with him? Or was it only when he got onboard that he realized he'd been busted? That seemed like a probable explanation, but Brock wasn't stupid. He knew that these people were dangerous.

And yet he looked so casual as he boarded the ship. Olivia resumed the footage and watched him walk onto the ship without even looking back. It made her heart ache to watch him go, to watch him walking into his horrible fate.

And now he was somewhere at sea, being treated terribly by the men who had lured him there. Olivia felt sick just looking at the video.

But there was one very key piece of evidence in the video that would help her track him down. On the side of the ship, Olivia could see the name of the boat that had taken Brock out of her life.

The *Dynamic Dawn*.

Olivia shuffled through the papers on the coffee table, looking for evidence of the ship in Brock's notes. She found a mention of the *Dynamic Dawn* and scanned the information about it. She felt a smile forming on her lips.

The ship was listed as going between the port in New York and a port in the UK. Newhaven, to be exact. It was another strong connection to the UK, and Olivia knew they couldn't ignore it now. That's where they were most likely going to take Brock, and they clearly had a base of operations there. It seemed more important than ever to follow that lead to the end. She needed to get over there and start searching for him on a closer level.

But before Olivia could snatch up her phone to call Jonathan back, she spotted something else. Something she'd overlooked before.

Olivia picked up the piece of paper that had caught her eye, reading it through slowly. There was something familiar on the page that she couldn't put her finger on at first. But then she realized that she was looking at information she'd been told before…

The page was highlighted, but in pink, not in yellow. It was like Brock had wanted to separate it from the rest of his notes, to point out that it was different and important.

The ship that he'd highlighted also belonged to ANH, but it didn't moor at the New York dock. It was also detailed as a passenger ship, not a container ship. Brock had made a single note above the name of the ship.

Trafficking?

Olivia's heart began to beat a little faster. She knew of one person who had been tracking down a trafficking ring for years. One person who had almost died during her investigations. One person who refused to give up on the case until she had finished what she started…

Her mother.

Olivia felt breathless. If Brock's theory about the passenger ship was correct, then maybe there was a link between his case and her mother's. And if that was the case, then Brock was in even more danger than she had ever imagined.

She didn't know how or why he believed that ANH was trafficking, but she had to find out. Just as soon as she'd found him safe and sound, she would make sure that ANH paid for what they had done. She had a million puzzle pieces to put together before she could paint a clear picture of what the hell was going on, but once she did, she would make sure that ANH went down for it.

But first, she was going to get Brock the hell out of there.

CHAPTER FOUR

"We need to get on British soil if we are going to get anywhere with this. I'm not just going to sit around here and try to investigate when he's thousands of miles away by now."

Jonathan nodded as Olivia presented her case to him. It was just past 9 a.m., and she'd driven up to Washington to speak to Jonathan in person. He seemed to be suffering from his lack of sleep, but Olivia was buzzing like a bee, driven by caffeine and adrenaline. He rubbed at his temple.

"I think you're right about the British connection. And given the drop-off location for the ransom money, it makes sense that they're operating there. But it's not our territory. We'll have to liaise with MI5."

"Do we have a contact?" she pressed. "We need to tell them—"

Jonathan held his palm out in a gesture that told her to calm down. "I will get in touch to make sure we can coordinate operations. MI5 already has a team working to take down ANH—they have for years."

"Are they aware that Brock suspected—"

"Yes, they're aware," he sighed. "This has been a major interagency case for years."

"So, it should be simple to just pop over there and get to work, right?"

At that, Jonathan gave her a troubled look. "It's their territory; they'll be taking the lead. I'm still not sure I made the right decision letting you work this case, given your circumstances."

Olivia raised an eyebrow. "Even though I've got a lead several hours into the investigation? I know that you think I'm too close to this whole thing, but if I wasn't, we wouldn't even have this evidence right now. Brock left those clues for me and *only* for me," she pointed out. "He knew that if he was in danger, he'd be able to rely on me to find him and save him. I'm not just going to put my trust in a bunch of foreign agents that I don't know. Besides... they clearly aren't doing their jobs properly if they're still trying to take them down. They've had their shot. Now it's my turn."

"You know it's more complicated than that, Knight," he bristled.

"Well, I don't know what you expect me to do from the FBI then, if you just want to let them take over!"

Jonathan rubbed the bridge of his nose. "Look at you, Olivia. You've been up all night. You're running on empty. You're no good to us like this."

"Don't try to tell me what I can and can't do. I know what I'm capable of," Olivia said through gritted teeth. It wasn't like her to talk back to her boss like this, and yet she found that she couldn't help herself. "I've been through a lot in my career, and you know that. You know that I'm not some damsel in distress. This is my job, and I'm good at it. So, I don't want to hear anything more about me not being prepared for this. You and I both know that if this was the other way around, if Brock was in my shoes, you'd send him off to England in a heartbeat."

Jonathan raised an eyebrow. "That so?"

"Yes. You wouldn't accuse him of being too emotional to handle this case. I think it's a little insulting. I'd like to be treated like an agent and nothing else."

"I happen to think that you're handling this a lot better than Tanner would have. Believe it or not, you're one of his only weaknesses. It made me regret pairing you up in the first place," Jonathan replied coolly. "And if the tables were turned, I'd be telling him the exact same thing. It's not easy knowing that your partner is in danger. Especially when the agents involved are very close."

Olivia blushed a little. She had no idea that Jonathan was aware of how close they were. They didn't spend a lot of time around him in person, but she guessed that over time, their connection had become obvious to everyone they knew. Jonathan sat back in his seat with a knowing look.

"I know you're pretty determined to get over there, Knight, and I understand. But this is a delicate operation. We can't just charge in like a bull in a china shop. They're demanding money for his release, but you and I both know it's not about the money. We should think this through before we go in all guns blazing."

"Sure. So, why don't I think this through on British soil? The place that our leads are taking us? You know it makes sense."

Jonathan's lips quirked into a small smile. "You don't give up, do you?"

Olivia folded her arms. "Not where Brock is involved."

Jonathan wasn't one to laugh often, but he let out a quiet chuckle, shaking his head. "Say I let you go over there… do you promise to be cooperative with MI5?"

"Of course, I do."

"And you will allow them to lead the way? Will you stay out of the way when it's their jurisdiction? Brock was the only US operative on the job, and he's out of commission now. You need to trust them."

THE **LOCKED BOX**

Olivia bit the inside of her cheek. She didn't see the sense in trusting anyone she didn't know. Not even agents who were supposed to be on her side. She had been burned plenty of times before, and it didn't make her keen to work with anyone else. Brock was the exception. She would much rather be on her own than in an unsteady alliance with another agent.

She didn't want to make a promise she couldn't keep by promising to get along with the MI5 agent. And yet she knew it was the only way that Jonathan was going to let her go over there. She took a deep breath and fixed a small smile on her face.

"I can do that."

Jonathan let out a tired sigh of relief. "Alright, then, it's settled. We'll fly you into London, and then I'll have someone at MI5 pick you up. You can head straight to Newhaven and see what you can find there. In the meantime, I'll send over whatever information they'll need to have operatives monitoring the port. If this is the only lead we have to work with, then we'll have to make sure it's worth chasing."

Olivia nodded and stood up, ready for action. She already had her passport in hand and she felt prepared for anything.

"And Knight?"

Olivia turned around at the sound of Jonathan's voice. He looked world-weary as he offered her an encouraging smile.

"I hope you know that I do believe in you. If anyone is going to get this mess solved, it's you. Just be careful. And bring our guy home."

It was the most emotion she'd ever heard in his voice, and she didn't miss it.

"I intend to," Olivia replied.

∽

Her flight wouldn't leave for another few hours, so she killed some time packing up and putting everything in order. But even as she prepared to leave, there was one place that she knew she had to go. The one place where she might be able to get some answers about the whole mess she'd landed herself in. She set off for her parent's home, feeling as though she needed to speak to her mother before she left.

Things had been complicated with her mom for a long time. They had fought so much that the raw wounds they'd inflicted on each other felt as though they might never heal. But time was making things a little better. In recent months, her mother had made up for her mistakes with apologies and promises to change.

Olivia hadn't been sure that her mom had it in her, but Jean proved her wrong. And now that they were on speaking terms again, Olivia knew that her mother was the one person she could trust to make her feel better about everything that was going on. As an FBI agent herself, and as someone who had been through so much during her own career, Olivia knew that she'd have some sage advice for how to get through the whole ordeal alive.

When she pulled up in front of her parents' house, her mother was out gardening in the front of the house. Seeing her mother look so domestic surprised Olivia. Even before she'd discovered that she was a secret FBI agent, she had never really seen her getting into the role that some mothers did. Jean Knight had never been one for sitting still and cuddling her kids; she didn't really cook or clean either, and she certainly didn't garden. Olivia had always liked that about her—the fact that she never once complied with motherly stereotypes. Sure, she'd been a bad mother at times, but at least she was always true to who she was. She didn't give her entire self over to motherhood. She was still her own person.

Her mom looked shocked to see Olivia pulling up in front of the house, and Olivia was a little shocked that she'd come on her own accord too. After all the lies and betrayal, it took a lot for her to visit her family home. There was a point in time, not too long ago, when she'd been certain that she'd never step foot in her parents' house again. But now, it was starting to feel like a place where she could be safe once again. As she got out of the car, she headed straight for her mother.

"Olivia, darling!" Jean said, straightening up. "What are you doing—"

Olivia cut her off by hugging her mom hard. Jean almost recoiled in surprise, but then she wrapped her arms around Olivia tight and rested her chin on top of her head. They stayed that way for a short while, and Olivia felt all of her caged emotions threatening to spill out. That was the last thing she needed when she was supposed to be holding things together for the sake of finding and saving Brock. Still, it felt good to hold her mom and be held back. It was a rare occurrence, and it felt nice to just indulge in it in that moment. Plus, she didn't know how long she would be in England. It might be a long while before she got to see her parents again.

When they pulled apart, Jean cupped Olivia's face in her hands, examining her for signs of emotion. In other words, she was looking for an explanation for what had happened to make her drive over there in the first place. Olivia swallowed down the lump in her throat.

"It's Brock, Mom. He's been taken."

"Taken?" she asked. Then her face fell as though in realization. Did she know more about Brock and his case than she was letting on?

"Oh, Olivia. I'm so sorry. You must be worried sick."

Olivia didn't know what to say now. She'd been drawn to her mother for a reason, but now that she was standing in front of her, she couldn't form the words to say why she needed her. Jean put an arm around her daughter and steered her toward the house.

"Let's get you sat down…"

"I can't stay long. I have a flight to catch. I'm going to England to find him."

Jean nodded as though that made sense to her. "You should be there. If anyone is going to find him, it's you. But you need to sit. Rehydrate. Take some calming breaths. Then we'll talk."

For once, Olivia didn't argue with her mother. She didn't need to be babied, but it almost felt nice to have someone fussing over her. It had been so long since she'd had this kind of relationship with her mom that she'd been worried she would never get it back. Now, Olivia knew that their relationship had never really ended, but simply paused, ready for them to come back to it when they were ready.

Jean pressed a cup of tea into Olivia's hand, and she sipped it gratefully. Caffeine was definitely what she needed. Jean sat down beside her on the sofa and watched her daughter thoughtfully.

"I'm sorry that you're going through this. Again," she told her. "You've been through so much. You've been so unlucky. But... I'm not sure I can help you with what you're here for."

Olivia looked up at her mom, frowning a little. "What is it that you think I'm here for?"

Jean wavered. "I think you're looking for a connection between the people who took Brock and the case I've been working on all these years. I think that because Brock being taken feels like my disappearance in nature... you're looking for links between the two. And if I'm being honest, you might be right. I have been briefed on Brock's case several times in the past, and there have been some... crossovers."

Somehow it didn't surprise Olivia in the least that Jean knew what had been going on without her having to explain. She always felt like the last one to know anything. But she didn't press the issue. Instead, she asked: "Crossovers?"

Jean gave Olivia a warning look. "There's not much more that I can say. You know I'd tell you more about it if I could, but talking about this with you could put both of our jobs on the line. It might even risk my case being exposed."

"I don't care about that if it leads me to Brock."

"Darling, you won't even be able to work his case if I divulge details about my own. I've already told you more than I should since coming home. It's supposed to be confidential. You know how one little slip-up can change the course of a case."

Olivia opened her mouth to continue arguing, but she stopped herself. She knew that there was no sense in pushing when her mother was even more stubborn than she was. Besides, she had a point. Neither of them wanted to lose the jobs they had put so much hard work and care into, and Olivia certainly didn't want to be cut off from Brock's case. She knew that she had to be

THE **LOCKED BOX**

the one to find him, even if it cost her, but there was nothing she could do if she was dismissed from the FBI.

"Then what do I do? Where do I... where do I begin?"

Jean shook her head at Olivia.

"Darling... why are you asking me that question?"

Olivia blinked several times. "Because... because I'm scared? Because I feel lost?"

"You've felt those things before, a thousand times over. This is nothing new. You can get through it."

"But it's different this time. Because I can have some control over what happens next. And it's... it's Brock. There's so much at stake here. I... I can't lose him."

"He means a lot to you, doesn't he?"

Olivia thought about Brock and the impact he'd had on her life. She couldn't stop the small smile that came to her face. "Brock is everything to me. He's been with me through some of the hardest times in my life. He was there when you were gone. He was there when I thought I was going to die at the waterfall last year. And he was there to help me through every single case we've cracked this year... until now. He knows me better than anyone. He treats me differently too. He doesn't treat me like I'm broken. He knows that all I ever needed was a little help to get back on my feet. Brock is the reason that I'm healing. And without him, I don't know what I'd do. If he dies... I'll be right back to square one, and I'll have even less than I started out with. It makes me feel vulnerable. It makes me feel like... like I'm not ready."

Jean took Olivia's hand in hers. "You're not going to lose him. I know you're scared... but how many times have you used that to propel you forward? I know you, Olivia. I know the lengths that you'll go to to succeed, even if it puts you in danger. There's nothing you can't do if you put your mind to it. I know you came here looking for me to offer you solutions. If this was any other scenario, I would. But I can't help you with this, and it doesn't matter. You don't need me to. Because at the end of the day, you are your own superhero. You'll figure this out, just like you always do. You don't need me, or anyone else, for that matter. And when

Brock is home safe, you'll see that it was you that got him back. I have faith in you. I just wish you'd have faith in yourself."

Olivia felt tears filling her eyes. It had been so long since she'd heard such praise from her mom. For months they'd been keeping everything at surface level, never diving deeper into their emotions because they both knew that neither of them was prepared for it. But hearing those words soothed Olivia's shattered heart a little. Those words prepared her for what was to come. The past didn't matter anymore. Jean was pointing Olivia toward her future, and that was where she needed to look.

"Thank you," Olivia whispered to her mom. She clasped Olivia's hand in hers.

"Of course."

Olivia checked her watch. She had to be at the airport soon. It had been a quick visit, but it was all she needed. She turned to her mom.

"I… I have to go."

"I know. It's okay."

Olivia stood up, and Jean did too. They hugged one last time, Jean's arms tight around Olivia's body. She closed her eyes for a moment, savoring the feeling. She didn't know when she'd feel so at home again.

"Good luck. Not that you'll need it," Jean said with an affirming nod at Olivia. Olivia took a deep breath and began to head for the door, but then Jean grabbed her wrist to stop her.

She looked at Olivia with a war of emotion in her eyes. The veil slipped, and all of a sudden, she wasn't thinking of this as the detached FBI agent, but as a mother.

"And one last thing… *Aurora Nova*."

Olivia frowned. What was that supposed to mean? She looked at her mom for confirmation, but Jean's face made it clear that she'd said more than enough. She ushered Olivia out of the house, not unkindly, but firmly, pushing her toward her destiny. Olivia headed to the car in a daze, not knowing what to make of her mother's strange last words.

Olivia knew she needed to set off for the airport, but first, she wanted to know if there was any meaning to her mother's words. She typed *Aurora Nova* into a search engine, waiting for the answers to be revealed to her. It was Latin. She read over the results several times.

A new dawn.

CHAPTER FIVE

BEFORE SHE BOARDED THE FLIGHT, JONATHAN HAD TOLD her to report to Headquarters for briefing. She found him in his office, reading contemplatively over a file that was laid out neatly on his desk. He looked up as Olivia entered. He looked a little surprised when he saw how at ease she seemed. Talking to her mother had made her feel much better and eased much of the trepidation she felt. She kept her chin up as she sat down in front of Jonathan.

"Here's everything you'll need," he started as he pushed the files he'd been reading across the table toward her. "Look these over and then destroy them. We can't risk this information falling into the wrong hands."

THE **LOCKED BOX**

Olivia looked up at Jonathan and tried to read his expression. After her mother's hints that her case might be linked to Brock's, she wanted to know whether Jonathan was about to divulge that information to her. But he remained quiet, clearly not interested in exploring that vein of thought.

But why not? Surely it might be important to finding Brock? Jean had been working on her case for many years, and she had mined so much useful information. If that was connected to Brock's case in any way, then why wasn't she being told about it?

Still, Jonathan said nothing, and Olivia knew she couldn't bring it up with him. She didn't want to get her mother in trouble, and he wouldn't tell her anything he didn't want her to know anyway. If he thought it was important, she'd know about it already.

"You'll be partnered with Henry Caine. He's MI5's lead investigator on the ANH case. He's been following some of the same leads Brock has over the last three years," Jonathan told her as she flipped through the file.

Olivia quickly scanned the profile of the man. He was in his mid-thirties, just like Brock, and according to his profile, he was a highly skilled investigator with advanced combat training, and fluent in English, German, and Spanish—and he even dabbled in Chinese. The information regarding his specific case history was much sparser, of course, but Olivia already surmised that having such a skill set meant he must work internationally. He tended to work alone on his cases, and yet he had more under his belt than most. His repertoire impressed Olivia, though she would never admit that to him.

Olivia took one look at the man's picture and took a dislike to him. There was something about his cold features and hard stare that made her uncomfortable. She already knew he was a lone wolf, and despite the fact that she often was, too, it didn't bode well for them working together. After working with Emily for her last case and Brock for months before that, the last thing she wanted was to work with a stranger that didn't like to play on a team.

But that was the deal. If she wanted to be involved in the case, then she'd just have to get used to Henry being around. She also knew there was a high likelihood that she'd be taking orders from him, which made her stomach twist uncomfortably. Even when she was working with Brock, she didn't often let him tell her what to do. She valued her independence too much to let anyone order her around.

She took a deep breath and told herself that this wasn't about her. If being ordered around by some cocky British agent got her closer to saving Brock, then she was more than willing to make that sacrifice. The sooner they found him and got him out alive, the sooner she'd be able to breathe again.

"Seems charming," she remarked.

"Caine is a bit of a lone wolf, from what I've heard. It's not ideal, but I've been told he's the best in the business."

"So, I should follow his lead is what you're saying?"

"We don't have much choice in the matter. This operation is his, and he's the only partner you're getting. You'll have to learn to get along with him."

Olivia didn't respond. She didn't like the idea of relinquishing control. No FBI agent did, really. Their jobs relied heavily on teamwork, but if you couldn't trust your partner, you had to be able to trust yourself. Olivia had no idea who this British operative was or what he was going to be like, but she was certain from what Jonathan had mentioned that he was going to be the complete opposite of Brock.

"You're not selling him to me. And I can imagine that his brief about me is going in a similar manner. You said he usually works solo. Why is that?"

"His choice, apparently. As for his brief about you… well, I gave you a stellar recommendation. You don't need to worry about that."

Olivia felt a little flattered, she had to admit, but that didn't prevent her from feeling as though her new partner was already dismissing her the way she was dismissing him. She'd never worked with an operative abroad before, and she was intrigued, to say the least, but it also made her nervous. She didn't know how she was going to adapt to such a daunting situation when she was already under so much pressure.

But she didn't have a choice, so she told herself to suck it up and stop being a child about it. Jonathan seemed to be thinking along the same lines, eyeing her with an amused smile.

"Don't get so in your head about it. You're not there to make a new best friend. You're there to find Brock and get him out. Now, MI5 told me that all of their resources will be at your disposal, so anything you need will be provided to you there. Should you need a team for the extraction, they will be the ones to provide it... which means you need to trust your partner."

"Yes, sir," Olivia said firmly. Whatever her feelings were about working with someone new, she wasn't going to allow them to get in the way of saving Brock. Nothing was more important in the world.

"And lastly... stay on task. ANH's network runs deep. But your mission is not to take them down. You are *not* to compromise any leads that Caine has established. You're there for Brock and only Brock. Once you've found a way to get him out, the two of you can come back home. There's no need to stick around and see this one through when it's not your case. Am I clear?"

Olivia nodded. Jonathan was warning her for a good reason. He was fully aware that Olivia wasn't one to leave a mystery unsolved. The temptation to bring the whole network down would be hard to resist.

Except this time was different. There was too much on the line, and any distractions could cost her dearly. She was determined to bring Brock home, and the rest didn't matter to her. Her only investment in the case was him, and she didn't need to take it any farther than that.

"Are you ready?" Jonathan asked her. Olivia tucked the file into her bag, feeling its weight. At least she'd have some reading for her journey to England.

"Yes. I'm prepared."

"Good. Now, remember, you're representing the FBI when you head over there. Do me proud."

"Of course, I will. I wouldn't dream of embarrassing you."

"And what are you going to do while you're there?"

Olivia sighed. "Focus. I'll get Brock out and then be out of there."

"Excellent. Now, enjoy your flight. I'll be on standby for remote support."

Olivia stood up and was about to leave when Jonathan reached out to shake her hand. She smiled a little as she took the handshake. He didn't give them out very freely, and she felt honored to have been awarded one. He gave her a long, hard look, his features solemn.

"Good luck," he said. "Bring him home to us."

∞

It was late afternoon by the time Olivia settled into her seat for the eight-hour flight to London. The aircraft was cramped and stuffy, making it even harder for Olivia to breathe. She was anxious to get to London, but she had plenty of work to do on the way. She knew that she should try to sleep while she could, especially when jet lag was likely to hit her like a ton of bricks, but the thought of rest wasn't appealing to her. Not when she felt like with every second that passed, Brock was in more danger.

She hadn't proposed her theory about the connection between ANH and her mother's case yet. Brock clearly thought he was on to something when he wrote about the trafficking in his notes, but Olivia still didn't know what had led him to that conclusion. For now, the connection was flimsy at best, and she needed something solid before she started on a wild goose chase. Besides, she felt like she was on thin ice. Jonathan already believed she was letting her emotions influence her work, and she didn't want him to think that she was losing her mind by throwing in some baseless theories. Once she found Brock, perhaps he could enlighten them further about the connection. Then, they could take down all of ANH's operations.

THE **LOCKED BOX**

Besides, Brock was her priority. It wasn't that she didn't care about the possible dark connections she'd uncovered. She didn't even dare to think of the horrors of human trafficking, and the idea that people were suffering at the hands of ANH was sickening. So, of course, it wasn't that she didn't care. It was just that nothing mattered more to her in the world than getting Brock home safe. Maybe that was wrong of her when there were so many people likely in pain because of ANH, but they had made it personal when they took the most important person in her life away from her. They probably didn't even know or care who she was, but now that they were on her radar, she wouldn't stop until she'd buried them entirely.

As the plane took off, most people on the flight got settled in to watch movies or take a nap, but Olivia's work was only just beginning. She opened the first file that she'd packed and let her eyes scan the pages.

It quickly became clear to Olivia that she was dealing with an absolute beast. ANH had been under investigation for years by several agencies, but nobody had been able to quite nail them down just yet. ANH was a multi-billion-dollar shipping and logistics company with plenty of contracts all over the globe; but according to Brock's notes, there was a lot more to them than the legal front that they put on. In fact, it had been him who'd alerted the US government to their illicit activities: their supposed drug trafficking, their weapon trading, and potentially more. But despite years on the case, he had yet to dig up any hard proof to disrupt their operations, and it seemed like the British operatives were fresh out of luck too.

Olivia knew that if Brock was struggling to catch these guys, then they had to be pretty good. He was one of the most seasoned agents she knew, even at his young age. All those years of training overseas and working on complex cases had made him a threat to any criminal organization. She couldn't even begin to imagine how many criminals he'd taken down over his career, and she knew that he never stopped until he got to the bottom of a case.

And yet this was where he'd gotten stuck, and now he was paying the price for his digging. It should have made Olivia nervous, knowing that trouble followed anyone who tried to mess with ANH, but she was in too deep already. Her goal was to rescue Brock, and if she couldn't, then what was the point of anything?

What stumped her was how they'd managed to evade capture for so long. Both the US and UK had fairly robust customs procedures, and with dedicated agents like Brock or Caine looking into ANH, they must have had a seriously good network to stay in the shadows for so long.

And then there was the human trafficking. There was a single page at the back of Brock's folder that suggested that there might be something to look into, but he didn't leave Olivia with enough details to work with. Either Brock didn't have a solid lead himself, or the information was too sensitive to leave lying around in random files. Olivia wasn't sure which was preferable.

There was so much left unanswered. By the time she was two hours into the flight, Olivia had read through all the notes, yet she had no clue where to begin her investigations. She sighed, closing her eyes and leaning back in her seat. She would have to hope that Newhaven would have some answers for her. But how was she supposed to start when she didn't know what to start looking for?

She didn't allow the thought to cross her mind that he might already be dead. She didn't want to think that way. But he was the man who had spent years of his life trying to take them down. He was the one who'd found out their dark secrets in the first place. What use did they have for him? Sure, they'd asked for ransom money, but what did a multi-billion-dollar company need with government money? It was simply a way of manipulating the FBI, a way to show them who had the power.

And it was working.

Which begged the question… what use did they have for Brock? Maybe they would try to torture him for information, try to squeeze him for something juicy… but then what? The longer they waited to rescue him, the less value his life had to them. What was to stop them from putting a bullet in his brain and throwing him overboard?

Olivia shuddered. She was scaring herself. She had to believe that he was going to make it. It was the only thing keeping her sane. She closed her eyes and wished for sleep, but her mind was whirring with dark thoughts, the kind that can derail a person entirely. With five hours to go before her touchdown in London, Olivia fell into a desperate sleep, dreaming only of Brock and the fear she felt for him.

When she opened her eyes again, it was to the sight of everyone getting off the plane. She quickly gathered her things and followed the crowd of people off the aircraft.

She'd never been to England before, and the air felt different here. Not just the bitter chill of it, but like she could feel the heaviness of the clouds above her weighing her down. She moved through the airport feeling like she'd been transported to another world, one that she couldn't navigate quite so easily.

And when she saw Henry Caine waiting for her, with a sign bearing her name held snarkily above his head, she knew she was truly a fish out of water. There he was, a Brit dripping with sarcasm, not understanding the weight of their situation at all. There she was, a woman who desperately wanted to bring her friend home.

They had nothing in common.

When she approached him, he gave her a once-over and didn't look pleased with what he saw. He offered her a hand to shake, and though she didn't want to, she took it. She had to. He was the one who was responsible for the case being a success or a disaster.

"Welcome to England, Agent Knight," he said.

CHAPTER SIX

THE DRIVE TO NEWHAVEN FROM LONDON WAS ONLY A couple of hours, but it felt like a lot longer to Olivia. As she sat in the passenger side with Henry driving, she felt distinctly uncomfortable. He had barely said a word since her arrival, clearly not happy with having to pick her up so early in the morning. She didn't exactly want to spend time with him either, but she had expected a slightly warmer welcome.

How was she supposed to trust this guy when they barely knew a thing about one another? Olivia had tried to analyze him since getting in the car, but it was nearly impossible since the only words that had come out of his mouth had been sarcastic and cutting. It didn't make it easy to ask questions and get to know him.

THE **LOCKED BOX**

She could see how that attitude worked for him. He was handsome, she had to admit, and he had a smug, cocky attitude that might earn him the favor of some women. But to her, he just seemed rude and standoffish. She could look past his handsome features, with his dark eyes and close shaved beard, to his stony interior with ease.

She had tried hard to make conversation at first, asking him about his time in MI5, trying to get him to talk about the case, but he shut down the conversation each time with one-word answers. And, of course, he hadn't asked a single question in response. It was like he was simply her taxi driver and wasn't interested in getting to know her at all. Eventually, she'd given up and taken to staring out the window, taking in the British countryside that lined the motorway.

By the time they reached Newhaven, the sun was finally starting to come up, and Olivia didn't feel quite as cold toward England. Despite the dismal weather, Newhaven was beautiful, with a collection of colorful houses on the waterfront and quaint little shops lined along the cobblestone streets. The fishermen were already out, cheerfully ragging on each other as they unmoored their boats and began the day's work. It was a far cry from Belle Grove, but Olivia didn't mind the change. Being at home was the last place she wanted to be without Brock there.

Henry cracked a window and cold air seeped into the car. Olivia shuddered, wrapping her arms around herself. Henry snorted.

"What? You can't handle a little fresh air?" he asked. Olivia scowled.

"I wouldn't call it fresh air. It's freezing cold, not fresh."

"You Americans. You wouldn't survive a year in England. You don't have thick enough skin."

Olivia had to bite her tongue to keep from firing back a response that would have singed his eyebrows. She had to keep things diplomatic, she reminded herself.

They pulled up in front of a small bed and breakfast on the edge of town, a little cottage with white paint and a shingle roof. It was cute, if a bit unassuming. Olivia thought that perhaps Henry would just drop her off there and that would be the last she'd see of him for a while, but he turned to her, his face like stone and one eyebrow perpetually raised.

"Alright. Time to go over the rules," he started. "As far as I'm concerned, you shouldn't even be here."

"Excuse me?"

"You're too involved in this case. I know that the man we're looking for is your partner. And to add to the issue, you're coming in fresh with no background. I've been working on this case for years, and I don't really appreciate some rookie coming in and messing with the status quo."

"I'm no rookie," Olivia growled. "I'm a seasoned FBI agent. How dare you!"

"I meant on this case. You think you can just walk in here and tie this thing up with a neat little bow? You're delusional. This case is hard, and you've just made it harder by showing up. But I'm willing to overlook that so long as you're ready to take orders and put your all into this."

Olivia was shaking with anger. She had already known that she'd be taking orders from Henry, but his attitude was making her determined to defy everything he said. She didn't like the way he was speaking to her as though she was some disobedient kid, and it only made her want to mess with him more. Who did he think he was?

Olivia took a deep breath in through her nose, trying to keep her cool. One wrong move and she'd be sent on a plane right back to Washington. She might not like Henry and his methods, but like it or not, she was under his thumb now.

But that didn't mean she had to like it.

"Of course, I'm going to put my all into this," Olivia said tightly. "I want to get my partner back more than anything."

Henry sighed, shaking his head. "Don't get your hopes up, American. You have no idea what these people are capable of."

"And you have no idea what *I'm* capable of," Olivia fired back, glaring him down. "I've been to hell and back these past few years. I've lost a lot, and it's only made me a better agent. If anyone is going to get to the bottom of this, it's me."

THE **LOCKED BOX**

Henry scoffed. "You think I didn't say that to myself when I started this case? You think I wasn't as confident as you are now? This case has been haunting me for a long time, long before your partner got himself caught. Don't expect much."

"Well, let's get started, and maybe I'll prove you wrong. Maybe I'll bring something to this investigation that you can't."

Henry rolled his eyes, but said nothing in response. He nodded toward the house.

"I've got us rooms here. We'll be staying in town until the case is closed, or we find somewhere more important to investigate. Drop off your things, and we can get to work. Unless you're too tired?"

"Absolutely not," Olivia replied, getting out of the car. "There's no need to baby me. I'm ready to go."

Ten minutes later, Olivia and Henry rejoined forces. Olivia found him waiting outside her room, checking his watch pointedly as though she were holding him up. She gritted her teeth in irritation. It was clear to her that he was going to be a thorn in her side the entire time she was there, and she was also certain he was getting some sort of enjoyment out of that fact. It was like he was on a power trip, glad to lord over Olivia and glad that he could get away with bossing her around. It made Olivia like him even less, but she told herself not to focus on her emotions. It was bad enough that she was so worried about Brock without Henry winding her up more.

The pair of them drove in silence down to the port. They had plans to liaise with the import and security team there to follow up on the *Dynamic Dawn*'s whereabouts. Olivia wasn't getting her hopes up though. The ransom video had been a good lead, but ANH had been in this game too long to simply allow the authorities to waltz straight in and bring him back. In the back of her mind, she worried that this would all turn out to be a trap, but she tried not to think about that. All she could do for now was to follow the leads they had until they had something better to follow up on.

"Let me do the talking," Henry told her when they arrived at the port. Olivia tried her best not to roll her eyes. Clearly, Henry was insecure, so desperate to prove himself that he constantly had to be in charge. It was never this way with Brock. Though Olivia often led the way in their cases, it wasn't her way of trying to assert dominance. It was simply the rhythm that she and Brock had fallen into, and it suited them both fine. She excelled in interviews while Brock tended to take a back seat, analyzing from afar. Neither of them was trying to show off or outdo the other. Henry, on the other hand, clearly wanted to prove himself—if not to Olivia, then to the entire world.

Still, in some ways, Olivia didn't mind. It was nice to take a backseat, to watch and observe for things that Henry might miss. It was nice to fill Brock's shoes, to work the way he so often did. It made her feel less alone and closer to finding him.

Henry managed to get them access to the video feeds at the dock, and Olivia followed him up to the security office. There was one seat at the desk in front of all of the video feeds, and Henry didn't offer it to Olivia; he sat down without a word. Olivia scoffed quietly to herself. Another way in which Henry was worse than Brock.

Still, he worked efficiently. He began to dredge through the video feeds, instructing Olivia on which screens to watch while he took the others. It was quicker than watching one security camera at a time, but it was also harder, splitting focus between all of them. Olivia was desperate to get a glimpse of Brock's face again, to see him walking off the boat again as though nothing had happened to him.

But that didn't happen. Even when Olivia spotted the *Dynamic Dawn* coming into the dock and pointed it out to Henry, there was no sign of Brock. While all the ships around unloaded their cargo, there was no sign of life on the *Dynamic Dawn*.

They watched for a long time, but no one appeared. It was as though the ship was commanded by ghosts they couldn't see. The port was alive with action, but the *Dynamic Dawn* was silent and still.

"He's on there. He has to be," Olivia said, but Henry hushed her before she could even finish speaking.

THE **LOCKED BOX**

"Shush. I'm watching," he said. Olivia was just about ready to scream in his face, but she kept her mouth closed. She needed Henry, and though he wouldn't admit it, he needed her too. There was a reason the case had been haunting him for so many years. He needed a fresh pair of eyes, an FBI agent willing to think outside the box. An FBI agent with everything to lose if she couldn't solve the case. Someone so desperate that failure wasn't an option.

She was going to be the one that finally got to the bottom of it all. That, she was sure of.

She kept her eyes on the ship, looking for any signs of life at all. It was odd, seeing the ship so still that it was like the video feed was on pause. And that's why the second something changed, she spotted it immediately.

The men in black that she'd seen at the other port were making their way off the boat in formation. Between them, they were carrying a single container. Olivia's heart sped up as she searched for signs of Brock among their ranks. She thought perhaps they'd put him to work, making him help carry their cargo.

But no. He wasn't with them. Olivia felt despair clinging to her heart. What did that mean? Surely, he wasn't still on the boat? Surely, they hadn't gotten rid of him at sea?

"Where is he?" Olivia asked, her voice cracking ever so slightly. She'd told herself that she wouldn't give Henry any more reasons to be aggravated with her, but she needed to know. She needed to see his face. She needed to know he was alive, that there was something worth fighting for.

She needed answers.

"I don't see him," Henry said quietly. But then he leaned forward and placed his finger over the container that the men were carrying. "I'm betting all my money that he's in that box."

Olivia paused to think about it. It might make sense. They needed to get Brock out of there without him being spotted. Besides, he was their prisoner. That box provided the perfect little prison cell for him.

And then there was the fact that he was better to them alive than dead. They wouldn't get their ransom money otherwise.

Besides, if Brock had information that they were interested in knowing, they couldn't get intel from a corpse.

"Where are they taking him?" Olivia thought aloud. Henry didn't respond to her, but he also didn't tell her to be quiet again. They both watched intently as the men disappeared from view on one camera and appeared on another. They followed their slow path until they reached a van in the parking lot. Trucks were being loaded all around them, and no one cast a second glance in their direction, but Olivia never let her eyes leave that box. If Brock was in there, then she'd chase that van to the ends of the Earth.

"We need to lift a license plate from the video," Olivia said. She knew she was stating the obvious, something that seemed to make Henry's face twitch, but he still paused the video and the pair of them tried to make out the blurred lettering on the back of the vehicle. Olivia shook her head.

"It's too fuzzy. Try another frame."

Henry's jaw was tight. Taking requests from Olivia clearly hadn't been on his mind when he agreed to work with her, but knowing she was right, he did as she had asked. He tried several times to get a better look at the license plate, but the camera was too far away to get a good look at it. Henry muttered something under his breath irritably.

"Well. That's that," Henry muttered.

In the video, the van was loaded up and the men dispersed as the van was driven away. Olivia shook her head, unwilling to give up.

"We need to look at the other cameras in the feed as the van is leaving. We might be able to catch the plate then."

But no matter how they tried, they couldn't get the angle right to pick up the license plate. It was so frustrating, watching their lead slip away right in front of their eyes. Olivia cursed, and Henry blinked in surprise at her sudden show of emotion.

"Look… it's probably not as big a deal as we think," Henry said, trying to balance the mood out. "Chances are, they'll ditch that license plate as soon as possible. I don't know that we'd get anything from that lead anyway."

THE **LOCKED BOX**

"But it was the only one we had," Olivia said through gritted teeth. Henry stared at the screen, his dark eyes seeming to be doing some sort of calculation.

"Perhaps not," he murmured. "That was a damn big ship. There must have been other precious cargo on it other than Brock. They'll be unloading it at some point. If we can get down onto the dock and stake it out, we might be able to figure out where it's going. Maybe it'll be the same place that Brock is going."

Olivia thought about that for a moment. She was sure that Henry was more interested in pursuing an ANH warehouse lead than actually finding Brock, but he was right. They might be headed to the same place. And if they were, then they needed to follow it up.

"You're right. Even if they use that ship for some of their legit business, they'll have to store it somewhere, right? They'll be taking some pretty big trucks to carry all that cargo. I'm sure we can get a lead on at least one of them."

"Then it's settled," Henry said with a decisive nod. "Let's do a stakeout."

CHAPTER SEVEN

THE DOCKS WERE COLD AND BUSY AS OLIVIA AND HENRY scouted them out. They'd changed their clothes in order to fit in with the other workers on the dock, but it was difficult to make it look like they were keeping busy, especially when they were trying to keep an eye on the *Dynamic Dawn*. While the other workers milled around, unloading cargo, barking orders and laughing with their friends, Henry and Olivia stuck to the shadows, trying their best to seem as though they belonged there.

"Something is coming off that ship. It has to be," Henry murmured in annoyance. He clearly wasn't happy about spending the day standing around in the cold. He rubbed his hands together. "I refuse to believe they just lugged a man across the sea with nothing else on board. And I really could use a lead on these guys."

"You mean you've never gotten this close before?" Olivia asked. Henry shot her a cold look.

"No, I haven't. It's a complex case, American. You think these are the kind of people you'll just see down at the pub on a Friday night? No. They're a huge organization, but they run things quietly. They don't make waves. All I know is that for years, they've been running my country into the ground. Getting more drugs on the street, selling illegal firearms, making people disappear."

"Disappear?"

Henry looked at her again and looked a little guilty this time. He could clearly tell that she had Brock on her mind. He sighed.

"When people go missing over here, we often blame ANH. Not always, of course, but they have a certain kind of target. The kind of people with nothing to lose. The kind of people that they can use and abuse, and it doesn't matter if they never make it home. People without family and friends. People who have lost everything, people who have been living on the streets." Henry shook his head. "We're almost certain ANH uses those kinds of people to do their dirtiest, most dangerous work. And a lot of the time, these people show up eventually. Dead, of course."

Olivia tried not to shiver. She didn't want to think of Brock receiving the same fate. He hadn't looked like he was in danger in that video of him on the docks, but she knew that likely meant very little. He was among dangerous people who liked to do dangerous things. They might have promised to hand him over if they paid them enough, but Olivia knew they couldn't really be trusted to even make good on their promises.

She forced herself to push Brock out of her mind. She had time to kill while they waited, and she supposed she should use it on something useful. She wanted to know more about Henry and his investigations to date.

"So, if you've never gotten this close before… then how do you know they're behind half of the things you're accusing them of?"

Henry glared at her. It seemed to be his default expression. Olivia backtracked a little.

"Let me rephrase that. What leads have you found over the years?"

Henry shook his head in irritation, casting his eyes back to the ship. There was still no sign of action from aboard, and they'd been nestled between a block of containers for at least an hour, waiting. It was no wonder he was impatient. Still, they had time to kill, so he may as well talk to her.

"I have some connections in the underworld. They whisper things to me," Henry said, his voice tinged with something close to boredom. "Sometimes, people on the inside are willing to loosen their lips for a favor. But it's usually a one-time interaction."

"Why?"

"Because snitches in ANH don't usually live to do it twice. You have no idea how many people I've met and never seen again. Maybe some of them will get away, find a way to outrun ANH, but not often. These people are brutal. They're not afraid to slit someone's throat over something small. You'll learn as we go along. To be honest, I'm surprised I've made it this far. I'm sure that ANH would love to see anyone investigating them wind up dead. But I'm careful. I fly under the radar. It's kept me alive so far."

Olivia wondered how that was even possible. She had no doubt that Henry was good at his job if they'd trusted him with such a big case, but that didn't make him invincible. How was it that he'd managed to evade these people for so many years, all the while poking around in their business? It made no sense.

But Olivia didn't get the chance to ask any more questions because she spotted movement aboard the *Dynamic Dawn*. She nodded subtly in the direction of the ship, and Henry shifted his focus over there. They both watched as several men aboard the ship made their way off, carrying boxes of goods between them. They set off across the port, and before Henry could say anything, Olivia began to slink through the crates toward the parking lot, keeping her eyes on the men at all times. She heard Henry curse behind her, but he followed her anyway. Olivia only hoped that they were being subtle enough not to get noticed.

THE **LOCKED BOX**

The men didn't seem to know they were being followed. They continued on their way, the boxes in their arms keeping them occupied. By the time they got to the parking lot, a truck was waiting for them to pick up the product. Olivia knew they'd need to get closer if they were going to get the license plate, but at least they had a lead to go off of now.

"Bingo," she murmured to herself. Henry had finally caught up, and he scowled at her.

"You're supposed to be following my orders. You can't just run off without me."

"Maybe you should be quicker then," Olivia replied irritably. The look that Henry gave her was so cold that she almost shivered. She knew she shouldn't have said anything, but she was already getting sick of the British operative. His negative attitude wasn't helping, and he wasn't moving fast enough for her liking. He was the one who hadn't been paying attention, the one who'd taken too long to respond. That wasn't on her.

But there would be no telling him that.

"Just stay close and do as I say," Henry growled. "We need to get closer to put a tracker on it, and then we'll get the hell out of here. Got it?"

"Fine," Olivia relented. She was more than happy to get out of that place. She let Henry take the lead as they walked casually toward the parking lot. Olivia kept her eyes on the plate, memorizing the numbers there as a backup. But it didn't matter because Henry managed to take a picture without Olivia even seeing him do it; and then before she could blink, he'd sidled up to the truck by dodging through the rest of the traffic and placed a small device on the underside of it. Somehow, he hadn't been seen at all. She was no fan of the man but had to admit he carried out his work pretty effectively. They snuck back into the shadows, and by the time they made it back to his car, he seemed pretty pleased with himself.

"That's cheered you up," Olivia murmured under her breath, but Henry didn't even react. He examined the plate in the picture he'd taken.

"This is good," Henry said with a pleased nod. "Let's get back to the B&B. You can get some rest while I run the tracker and see what I can come up with."

Olivia frowned. "I don't need to rest. I can help out."

Henry sighed as he strapped himself into his seat. "Agent Knight… I'm going to tell you the same thing that I told my bosses. They didn't listen, and I'm sure you won't either, but it's the truth. I don't need your help. I don't need you sticking your nose in where it doesn't belong. You're not adding anything to this case. If anything, you're just weighing me down."

"You don't mince your words, do you?"

Henry threw his hands up in frustration. "Why should I? You're a liability as far as I'm concerned. You're too emotionally charged to handle this thing with your partner, and I think it was a mistake having you sent over here."

"So, that's why you don't like me."

Henry rolled his eyes. "What are we, twelve-year-olds? I don't have an opinion of you either way. I really couldn't care less about you in any way, shape, or form. What I'm saying is that you can take a back seat and let me handle this. And since I'm leading this case, I suggest you listen to me and do just that."

Olivia was seething. Who did this guy think he was? Just because he was successful in his own right, just because he was leading the case, what gave him the right to be so disrespectful toward her?

But she'd never know because he drove off without another word, as though their conversation was over. Olivia didn't speak either, waiting until she was back at the B&B before she let out her frustration, punching a well-plumped pillow in her room and letting out a ragged, almost silent scream.

Perhaps Henry was right about one thing. She was emotional. How could she not be? But that didn't mean that she wasn't useful. She knew she could do anything she put her mind to. She was sick of being overlooked. She didn't know what made men like him doubt her from the moment they met, so confident in their own abilities that they felt she was unnecessary. Perhaps he was just

THE **LOCKED BOX**

a bog-standard misogynist, unable to believe that a woman was capable of doing as good a job as a man.

And hell, she was sure that anything Henry could do, she could do better. He wasn't the only successful one. She had plenty of experience in the field, and she'd done it all while being weighed down by emotional trauma. This dumb, grumpy Brit wasn't going to make her feel like some kind of rookie. She had come all this way to save her partner, and that was what she intended to do. She wasn't planning to allow Henry to do all the heavy lifting just because he thought he was better than she was.

She could do her own research too. While Henry was next door tracking down the truck, she decided that she would take a look into ANH. Brock had some information, but the case notes that Henry had stacked up over the years would likely be even more detailed. That was, if he was as good as he claimed to be...

Henry had handed her a brief file during their journey to Newhaven, and she decided it was time to take a look at it. It was very thick, possibly Henry's way of letting her know that she'd never catch up with him, but she was a quick study. She opened up the file, trying to let the anger inside her simmer down while she read.

From what she could see, ANH had a legal front that was almost impenetrable. Half of the reason that MI5 was having so many problems in taking them down was their lack of proof to assist their claims about the company. On the surface, they were simply a company trading goods overseas.

But from Henry's notes, it was clear there was more to it than that.

Contact Seven reports that ANH has begun distributing a new drug. In his words, it's not some party drug that the kids are after. It's something much more dangerous, and it comes at a cost: price-wise and health-wise.

Olivia wondered what that meant. Was this new drug killing people? It wasn't exactly uncommon for drugs to harm people, but Olivia knew that some drugs were more deadly than others. She thought back to the stash she'd found on Charlie Evans's yacht she'd raided only a few days before. She'd already seen those drugs become responsible for one woman's death, and she hadn't even taken a full dose.

And then there was the Grim Reaper and his reign of terror on her home soil. Was it possible that his operation was still going? That the drugs he'd peddled were still making it onto the streets, even overseas?

Olivia thought about it for a while. Even with the Reaper locked away, they had never managed to find what they believed to be all of his stock. It was entirely possible that his product was still being moved by someone else. If that stuff was making it to England, it was possible that ANH was using it.

But that didn't get her any closer to figuring out where Brock was or what they might want from him. Sure, it made sense that they'd capture someone that had been investigating them so closely, especially if he was getting too close to answers.

But if they were keeping him alive, then it had to be for a reason. Perhaps they wanted to know what information he had passed on to the Bureau, and they were grilling him for answers. Perhaps they really did want the ransom money for him, just to get the upper hand over the authorities.

And yet somehow, Olivia was sure there had to be more to it than that. A company like ANH was already swimming in money. They kept their secrets so tightly stored that it had taken years of hard work for the FBI and MI5 to get anywhere at all. Whoever was running ANH must know that they were still in a pretty safe position.

So why keep Brock around? What did he have to offer them that they needed? They didn't seem like the kind of people who were wanting for anything at all. But Brock must have something. Something that he'd never admitted to Olivia—a darker side to his life, perhaps. All of a sudden, she found herself questioning how well she knew him.

She had started to think that she knew him better than most. They'd lived together, worked together, and shared everything in their lives. Or so she'd thought. What if she was only seeing him on a surface level? What if all this time he'd been hiding things from her that she never expected from him?

He'd kept secrets from her before. He'd tried to hide his life from her many times in the past. At some point, she had accepted that there were things he wasn't willing to talk about with her. But now, she was questioning if there was something dangerous hidden among his secrets—something that had set this whole thing off and left her in the dark.

She wanted to believe he had nothing to hide. She wanted to believe he was the man she'd grown to care about so much. But she also knew that everyone has a darker side to them. And perhaps Brock's was going to change everything she thought about him.

A knock at Olivia's door brought her out of her thoughts. She got up and headed to the door, fixing Henry a cold glare for the second she opened it.

"Yes?" she asked, raising her eyebrow. He pushed past her into the room, and Olivia had to bite her tongue to stop herself from getting angry with him. When she'd met Brock, she'd found him infuriating, but with Henry, it was on a whole new level.

"I've tracked down the truck," Henry told her brusquely. "And it's led me to a warehouse about ten miles out from here—notably, one that is *not* listed by ANH in their official documents. I'm guessing it's a base for their operations."

"So, what now? We go and stake it out."

"Wrong. *I'm* going to stake it out."

Olivia felt her cheeks turning red with anger. "Excuse me?"

"You heard me. I'm not trying to leave you out of the loop, but you're too big of a target. If ANH has Brock, then they're likely waiting for you to storm in and make some kind of heroic rescue. You've got a target on your back, and if you go anywhere near their base, they're going to kill you. Simple as."

"But you'll be fine, I presume?" Olivia replied, rolling her eyes. She was getting sick of his high and mighty attitude. She wasn't sure why he thought he was so much better than she was, but he held his chin high as he spoke to her.

"They don't know who I am. I told you before, I keep a low profile. The only person who knows about me is a guy I have undercover in the company. Which means I can go in there without any consequences, but you can't."

Olivia knew that he was making sense, and yet it still annoyed her. She wanted to be useful. She wanted to help out. But with one look at Henry's face, she knew there was no way he'd let up on this one. He would knock her out before he let her go with him, she was sure of that much.

"So, what am I supposed to do while you're off on this little mission of yours? You're just leaving me here?"

"Oh, I don't know. Take a walk. Do a little shopping. Enjoy everything that Newhaven has to offer. I'm sure you'll think of something," Henry said sarcastically, already heading for the door again. "Just stay out of trouble, and we won't have an issue here. I'll be back by morning." As he shut the door behind him, Olivia sank onto the bed, feeling helpless. She had no control, and it was driving her crazy. In all of her time as an agent, she'd never felt so trapped. She felt farther from finding Brock than ever before, and the thought of him slipping away from her forever was too much to even think about.

But there was no way she was going to sit quietly twiddling her thumbs. She'd keep herself busy, keep studying the case. And when Henry returned, she'd show him just how useful she could be.

And she'd find Brock, one way or another.

CHAPTER EIGHT

"**G**ET UP. THE BOSS WANTS TO SEE YOU," THE GUARD sneered at Brock. He was a hulking, brutish man with a thick Cockney accent and a short shock of hair above his beet-red face. Brock wasn't even sure if the man had a neck.

He sat up slowly from his position on the floor, feeling his bones aching. He hated being cooped up, unable to move around much. Suddenly, the thought of walking through his own personal prison to speak with the big boss seemed almost appealing.

"Are we having tea and cake?" Brock asked sarcastically as he got to his feet. The guard paid him no attention, simply waiting for him to get up and follow him to the door. Brock wasn't cuffed any longer, but he knew there was no need. If he tried to run, they'd shoot him. And it wouldn't be a nice, clean shot to the head either. They'd probably shoot his legs first, to stop him from getting away. Then they'd leave him to suffer while still keeping him alive. After all, they still needed him.

The guard firmly poked the edge of his gun into Brock's back as he pushed him away from the safety of his cell down a series of dark concrete corridors. Brock knew his interrogation wouldn't be like in the movies. They wouldn't politely slap him around until he gave in to their demands and told them what they wanted to know. He knew a world of hell awaited him. He knew that the anxious beat of his heart was entirely justified. Brock had been in danger many times during his career, often putting his life on the line to get things done; but in that moment, he'd never been so close to touching death.

Or so he thought. He was led through the dark building that he'd arrived at several hours earlier in a crate. There wasn't much to see to help him figure out where his location was, but as he was taken outside and through a courtyard, he saw a warehouse ahead. People were milling in and out of it with boxes full of goods. Brock already knew what was contained within. Finally, after all this time, he was right in the center of it with all the evidence he could ever ask for, and yet he knew he wouldn't make it out of that warehouse with his life intact.

He thought of Olivia then. He prayed that she wouldn't try to avenge him. He didn't want her to get sucked into the dark world that he had become a part of. He didn't want her to meet the same fate that he was about to. He hoped she'd just be able to forget about him, to go on and live her life as though they'd never met.

But he knew if the roles were reversed, he'd never be able to manage that.

Despite the bitter cold outside, the warehouse was stuffy. A legion of workers in hazmat suits and protective gear formed a perfect little assembly line. The place was neatly organized: on one side of the warehouse, they were unpacking and organizing guns and ammunition; the other side consisted of packaging large pallets of drugs. It reminded him of a time long ago when he had been just like those warehouse workers, packing and shipping off important goods all over the world. Of course, what he'd been doing was legal. He knew already that ANH was breaking countless laws. Now, he was seeing it all firsthand.

The fact that he hadn't been blindfolded told him everything he needed to know. It didn't matter how much he saw. He was never going to be allowed to walk away with his life anyway.

His chest felt heavy. He had so much he still wanted to do, places he wanted to go... people he wanted to see. There was so much left unsaid, so much that he still needed to explore. He had words locked in his heart that he'd hidden away for months, always waiting for the right time. And now, that time would never come.

Brock was poked in the back to force him up a staircase which led to an overseer's office. His back throbbed from the place where the whip had struck him, but they hadn't touched him since. He could at least hope for a quick death at their hands. Perhaps that would be the only mercy they granted him.

When he entered the office, though, there was no gun resting on the desk. There was only a spindly white man in an impeccable suit sitting at the table. His desk was very neat, but he nudged a pen ever so slightly to neaten it further. He looked up at Brock through his thin glasses.

"It's good to see you, Mr. Tanner. I hope my men weren't too rough with you," the man said with a polite nod. Unlike the goon who'd escorted him here, the man's accent was very posh and cultured. "Please, take a seat. I'd like to talk."

Brock was frozen in place for a moment, but another poke in his back forced him to move and take a seat opposite the man. He didn't know the man, but the man clearly knew him... or *of* him. He didn't smile as he appraised Brock, but there was something in his eyes that told Brock that he was pleased to finally be sitting down with him. That meant several things.

First, this man was high on the list of ANH's operatives—if not the big boss himself.

Second, he'd been tracking Brock for a long time.

And third... he thought Brock could do something for him.

"I don't think you know why you're here, do you?" the man asked, cocking his head to the side. "Well, perhaps I can clear the air for you. You know someone that is of interest to us. This… contact of yours could be vital to the future workings here at ANH. I'm sure you can guess now who we're talking about."

Brock felt a sinking sensation in his chest. He knew exactly who they were referring to. And he knew already that he wasn't going to be able to help them.

"Walter would never make a deal with you. I'm sure he's told you that himself."

"Mr. McCall has mentioned that he has no desire to work with us, yes. But that was before we held something precious to him. I'm sure that he'll be a little more lenient now that you're in our company."

Brock offered up a tired smile. "You obviously don't know him very well if you think that I'm going to be able to budge him. There are things much more important to him than me."

"Such as?"

"I don't know. His pride, perhaps? His morals… however questionable I may think they are, he's certain that he's always right. He seems to believe he has a perfect moral compass. And I think that includes leaving me in your hands in order to remain legitimate."

The man leaned forward in interest, analyzing Brock's face like a difficult math equation. "Even if your life is in danger?"

Brock almost laughed. He leaned back in his chair. "*Especially* if my life is in danger. I hate to break this to you, but you may as well shoot me now. I'm not as important as you think I am. Walter isn't going to tell you a thing."

The man hummed in response, clearly interested in Brock's take.

"Well, perhaps it's time to test that theory. Let's call your grandfather for a little chat, shall we?"

Brock hung his head low.

CHAPTER NINE

Working from behind a desk in a quiet B&B in England didn't suit Olivia at all. The place was too quiet, and she found herself feeling like she was missing out on the action. She preferred to be out in the world, looking for clues and working toward answers, not sitting around and sifting her way through basic details.

But she didn't have much choice in the matter. She was alone in a country that she'd never been to before. She had no idea how to get around or where to start looking, especially without a car. Her temporary partner had gone off and left her, and she was in the midst of one of the most difficult and taxing cases of her career.

At least their modest lodgings had a nice view of the sea. It wasn't much, but it was something. Olivia sat out on the back porch, enjoying the mild breeze as she booted up her laptop. If she couldn't go anywhere, she could try to find what she could without moving at all.

She flipped through Henry's entire file, and then she hit the internet to look into crime statistics in England. She was interested to see how life in the UK differed from that in the US. When The Grim Reaper had been most active, she had seen a huge rise in drug-related deaths in the areas he'd hit. Olivia was sure that if there was a connection between him and the drugs that ANH were doling out, then she'd find it in statistics.

And not unsurprisingly, she found that there had been a spike in drug-related hospitalizations in many of the major cities: Manchester, London, Liverpool, Leeds, and Birmingham. It couldn't be a coincidence. Olivia thought back to Henry's notes and the fact that ANH had apparently been pushing some kind of new drug. Something dangerous and scary. If they were the ones responsible for the trail of horrific overdoses, then they were a force to be reckoned with. The sooner they were blown up, the better.

But of course, her priority was Brock. Still, Olivia knew that if she was going to find him, she needed first to infiltrate ANH. Finding them was one thing, but getting inside without getting herself and others killed was another. That was going to be the tricky part.

Tricky, but not impossible.

But first, she had to keep trying to understand the organization inside out. That was the key. The chances were, Henry might find one of their bases, but that didn't mean Brock would be there. They had to get smarter, get more informed. To find Brock, they had to think like ANH and almost become them…

Olivia continued her research through the afternoon, trying not to think too much about what Henry was up to. If he messed up, it would ruin their entire operation, but she wasn't in any position to do anything about that now. She just had to focus on the small role she was playing in the whole thing. Besides, as much as she didn't like the man, she knew that he was one of the best agents that MI5 had to offer. His heart was well and truly in the case, given how much of his life he'd dedicated to it. If anyone was going to succeed, it was the pair of them together. They had too much to lose to give up on it, even if the going got tough.

Her research took her down other avenues. News articles confirmed her suspicions that ANH was likely hitting all the big cities since there was a rise in gun crime throughout England. That in itself was hard to swallow, given that guns weren't even legal for civilians in this country. That meant that their organization had to be strictly and tightly controlled to avoid getting on the wrong side of the law. And it also meant they had their hooks deep into the criminal element, into the people who thought nothing of smuggling weapons to do their dirty work. Something of this scale could bring a country to its knees.

One thing was certain to Olivia: ANH's operations were not just contained to the British Isles. It was much bigger than that. It was like a weed, growing and spreading all over the world. And if Olivia had her guess, it had all originated right back home in the United States. While ANH was cooking up plans for making more money than they would ever need, someone was cooking up drugs to sell that would end lives. Someone was signing over firearms that would change the dynamic of an entire country.

And Olivia was sure she knew at least one of the people involved.

Olivia had sent plenty of people to jail, but some stuck out in her mind more than others. She couldn't stop thinking about the Grim Reaper and his lackeys. She couldn't get Charlie Evans out of her mind either. She had never confirmed that the Grim Reaper was his source of the drugs he'd imported, and yet now that she knew that they were almost identical substances, she was sure there was a connection. There were plenty of drugs capable of killing people out in the world, but this one… this one was special. It had a unique signature that differed from all others. There was no mistaking it for something else, and it all seemed connected.

And if her hunches were correct, then maybe Charlie could tell her something useful. Maybe she could wheedle something out of him that would help her find Brock. All she had to do, in theory, was set up a phone call and go from there.

Olivia was on the phone with Jonathan before she could change her mind. He picked up the call quickly, as if he had been waiting to hear from her.

"Any luck, Knight?"

"It could be going better," Olivia said bitterly, thinking about Henry and his little solo mission. "But I need something from you. I want to set up an interview with Charles Evans."

Jonathan was silent on the other end of the line for a moment. "What for?"

"I'm working on trying to figure out ANH. These particular drugs that they seem to be distributing in the UK seem all too familiar to me. I think it has something to do with the ones I found on the *Astoria*. And I think it might even connect back to The Grim Reaper."

"Alright… that I can understand. But how is this getting you closer to finding Tanner?"

"I don't think we can find him until we figure out what's going on within the company. Between Brock's notes and Henry's knowledge of them, they barely have anything. Maybe Brock got too close to the truth, and that's why they took him. But it's a mess over here. They hardly know who they're dealing with. But Charlie has already been arrested. He has nothing to lose by talking to me."

"You know that's not exactly true. If he's involved with ANH, we both know he'll wind up dead in his cell should he talk to you."

"Look, I know it's a shot in the dark. But I can't help thinking that he might be the key to getting just a little closer to the truth. And in all honesty, I don't know where else to turn. We've got a lead on a possible ANH stronghold, but until we confirm that, this is the only thing I can do to try and move things forward. If there's something—any information he can provide—I need to know it."

THE **LOCKED BOX**

Jonathan harrumphed. "I'll see what I can arrange. But in the meantime, try to stay focused. You know as well as I do that we don't have all the time in the world."

Olivia closed her eyes. "I know. I know that with every minute that passes, his life is more at risk. But I'm doing my best with what I have. I think this might get us on the right track."

"I'll be in touch."

As the call ended, Olivia did her best to stop the pressure on her shoulders from crushing her down and suffocating her. It was getting harder to breathe with each passing moment, but she didn't have time to break down. She had to get answers, and she had to get them as soon as possible.

Beside her on the desk, a ringtone sounded out that didn't belong to her. Olivia saw that it was Henry's phone. He'd left it behind, not wanting to take anything on his mission that might compromise him. Olivia leaned over to see who was calling, and her heart froze.

Contact Seven.

She'd seen that name mentioned before in Henry's notes. He was the undercover informant within ANH. Possibly the only one still alive. Olivia didn't know what to do. She wanted to pick up the call, but she knew that Henry would likely be furious with her if she did. Still, he had gone and left her on her own without a second thought, doing everything in his power to irritate her. Maybe this was her opportunity to give him a taste of his own medicine, and maybe get a new lead on the case.

Before she could tell herself it was a bad idea, Olivia picked up the phone.

"Hello?"

"Hello. Is this the phone of Henry Caine?"

"Yes, that's right. I'm his partner. Can I take a message?"

There was a pause on the other end of the line, and Olivia was certain she heard a police siren in the background. She frowned. What was going on?

"Well, Richard Greene had this number listed as his emergency contact… I figured that Henry should be informed.

He was shot dead an hour ago in front of his home. I'm sorry to be the person to relay this news…"

The woman's voice faded into the background as Olivia's mind whirled. If Richard, the undercover informant, was dead… did that mean he'd been discovered as a mole? If so, that made him a person of interest to her. The woman on the other end of the line was still talking, but Olivia knew that she had to get to the scene as soon as she could and get involved. Clearly, Richard had been killed for snitching to Henry, and that changed everything about their case.

If they'd just murdered Richard in cold blood, what would they do to Brock?

"Ma'am, like I mentioned, I'm Henry's partner," Olivia cut in. "I work for the FBI. I believe that Richard's death might be of interest in the case we are working together. Henry is not available right now, but I'd like to come to the scene and speak to the police."

"FBI? Really?" the woman on the other end of the line asked. She seemed shocked. Clearly, she hadn't been expecting the case to involve anyone higher up than the local police. "Um… sure. I can get you the address to come over here. Though we'll need to see some credentials before we pass over any information."

"Of course. I'll be there as soon as possible."

After she wrote down the address that the police officer gave her, she hung up the phone and grabbed the cottage keys. She wasn't about to sit around and wait for Henry to come home. She needed to deal with this right away. If his informant had been murdered, it was certainly her business. If she could somehow trace the killer back to ANH, she just might find Brock in the process.

Or so she hoped.

CHAPTER TEN

OLIVIA'S HEART WAS POUNDING AS SHE MADE HER WAY to the scene of the crime. She hadn't expected things to get so complicated when she'd landed in London. She had been planning to focus on finding Brock and nothing else. She didn't care about ANH or what they were up to. Her plan was to get her friend home safely, and that was all that mattered.

But she couldn't ignore what was unfolding right before her eyes, especially when Henry wasn't around to see it. A man was dead, and it could not have been a coincidence. Someone had shot their undercover contact in the head. Why? Because he knew something he shouldn't have known. And since he was one of the few undercover snitches still working for Henry, it made sense for

ANH to have ratted him out and bumped him off. That meant it was definitely her business to figure out what had gone wrong.

And since Olivia couldn't conclude that until she'd been to the scene and learned more, she took it upon herself to go there and investigate. Henry would be furious that she was going rogue, investigating on her own, but if he was allowed to do it, then so was she. There was no time to lose, and they still had so much to figure out if they were going to make it to Brock before ANH killed him.

When she arrived at the house, the garden was already cordoned off by police tape, and there were three cop cars parked along the road. The body of Richard Greene was still lying on the grass, the gaping hole in his head evident even from the car. The cab driver wavered as Olivia paid him for the ride.

"Are you sure this is where you want me to drop you off?" he asked anxiously. Olivia nodded.

"Yes. This is exactly where I need to be."

She got out of the car and surveyed the scene. On the porch, a woman wept quietly as she recounted her story to a police officer. Olivia could see a few neighbors anxiously watching the scene unfold from their windows, all of them too scared to come out of their houses. Unlike back home, gun crime was far from a common occurrence in England, especially in rural towns outside the big cities. She could see how something like this would shake up a neighborhood forever.

But that wasn't her concern. Her concern was finding who had done this and tracking them back down to ANH. If the killer truly had murdered Richard for his connections, they were dealing with a professional. But she was a professional too.

Olivia approached an officer who had been watching her since she got out of the cab.

"Are you Agent Knight? The agent I spoke to on the phone?" she asked. Olivia nodded and presented her badge.

"I have reason to believe that this wasn't a random assault," Olivia told her. "This man was part of an important investigation. If you don't mind, I'd like to speak to his wife and find out what she knows."

THE **LOCKED BOX**

"Of course. Anything you can find out would be great. We're not used to dealing with things like this around here. We spoke to a few of the neighbors already, and none of them have come forward with anything useful. They all said it happened too fast for them to notice anything out of the ordinary, and everyone was indoors when it happened. So, for now, we have no witnesses to work with." The officer shook her head. "To be honest, I've never worked a case like this before. Not involving gun crime. It's not exactly what the people of this town expect to happen."

Olivia nodded in understanding. A quaint town such as this one would be shaken to the core by a murder case. She only prayed that she could provide them with some closure on the matter.

Before walking up to the porch, Olivia took a moment to check out the body. The bullet wound was clean and precise, like someone who was used to firing a gun had handled the murder. There didn't appear to be any other signs of a struggle. He had fallen just beside the driveway, where his car was parked with the door still open. It was like he had just gotten out of the vehicle, turned, and been met with a shot to the forehead.

It seemed like expert work to Olivia. A hitman, perhaps, who had been hired to rid ANH of their traitor. It all seemed logical, like a story she could write herself without any complications. And yet Olivia had been in her line of work long enough to know that there were *always* complications, no matter what.

Richard's wife was still talking to one of the officers, so Olivia waited patiently, turning the case over and over in her mind. If this was in fact an assassination, then ANH was pretty bold. There were plenty of ways to kill a man, and yet they'd opted for something so old-fashioned, so classic. It was an easy way to kill someone, but not subtle in the slightest. If a man dies in his home, slowly killed by poison, then the neighbors might never find out that foul play is involved. But if you kill a man in broad daylight, on the lawn in front of his home with an illegal weapon… then you really have people's attention.

Were they really so cocky? Did they simply not care anymore? Perhaps they knew that they were already being hunted by both the FBI and MI5, and they figured they had nothing to lose. But it still struck Olivia as a little odd. Henry had practically sung their praises, impressed by their ability to lay low despite the huge operation they were running. So, in what world did it make sense for them to get sloppy now? If anything, they should be trying their hardest to become more incognito, and yet they were broadcasting themselves to the entire town.

Richard's wife was finally freed from her conversation with the officer, so Olivia made her move to speak with her. The wife spotted her right away and stared at her warily, unsure of what she was about to be bombarded with. She was a frail-looking woman in her mid-fifties with a beaky nose and thin hair. She wrapped her arms around herself like she was trying to protect herself from Olivia.

"Are you a reporter?" she asked, taking in Olivia's plain clothes. "I don't want to speak to the papers right now."

"I'm not a reporter, ma'am. I'm with the FBI, and I'd like to ask you a few very important questions."

The woman frowned. "What could the FBI possibly want out here? You're in the wrong country."

Olivia nodded. "I'm sorry, ma'am. I understand that this may be hard to hear, but your husband may be a person of interest in a case we've been working."

Richard's wife looked around her, as though she was looking out for eavesdroppers. Then, wiping a tear from her cheek, she ushered Olivia towards her home. "Come inside. We can talk there."

Olivia wiped her feet as she stepped into Richard's home. She always felt strange stepping into the life of someone who she knew was no longer living. This time was no exception. She glanced at the photographs that lined the hallway—pictures of his wedding day, of friends and family, of him and his wife when they were younger. Now he was gone, and a gaping hole was left where he once was. Olivia felt a tug on her heartstrings for the wife. He never should have been involved in the first place, but the fact was, he had been. Now, all Olivia could do was pick up the pieces for the people he had left behind.

THE **LOCKED BOX**

Richard's wife offered Olivia a seat on a plush sofa, and Olivia sat down, leaning forward to begin the interview. But Richard's wife held up a hand before Olivia could say anything.

"What's your name, dear?"

"Olivia. Olivia Knight."

"Thank you for coming. My name's Rebecca," she said politely. "I know what you're about to say. I knew about his undercover work. I know that he agreed to inform for MI5, and I know that's why he's lying dead right now. I told him so many times… your life is worth more than this. I told him as soon as he figured out that they were corrupt. I said he should leave and never look back." She took a deep, shuddering breath and dabbed at the tears in the corner of her eyes. "He could've taken an early retirement, even if it meant living off their damn blood money. But he wouldn't listen. He wanted to do what he called the 'right thing.' He wanted to make up for the years they'd had him under their thumb. And now look at what's happened."

Olivia nodded in understanding. It was a story she was familiar with. Good people who got punished for doing the right thing… while the evil ones got off scot-free. Rebecca sighed and shook her head.

"Not that any of it matters now. Men will do what they're going to do, even if it kills them in the end. What is it that you'd like to know? I'll do my best to help you out."

Olivia leaned forward a little further. "Truthfully, I'm new to this case. ANH has taken someone very close to me, and I'm trying to find ways to expose them and bring them down for good. Your husband was our man on the inside, and now he's dead, and the only explanation seems to be that he was found out. I want to know if there's anything you can tell us about today that might have changed things for Richard. Why today of all days? Did he seem on edge? Was he worried that he was about to be found out?"

Rebecca shook her head. "I couldn't tell you. Lately, things have been tense, of course… we both knew that what he was doing was dangerous. I let it fly because I knew he was doing a good thing. So, yes, things have been a bit strange around here for a while. But there was no major shift today, or yesterday… I wasn't expecting my husband to be shot on his way home from work."

She sniffled, and Olivia waited patiently as she fetched a tissue to blot her tears. She put on her best sympathetic face.

"I'm so sorry this happened to you."

Rebecca shook her head. "It's hardly of your concern, is it? His company's people were the ones who were rotten to the core. But in answer to your question… no, today didn't feel different. It just seemed like any ordinary day to me. I was in the kitchen when it happened. I always like to have dinner ready when he gets home from work. I know I'm old-fashioned. I heard the car pull up and was about to dish up our meal. But seconds later, I heard the gunshot. It was two minutes after six. I'd glanced at the clock almost exactly when the shot happened. It was almost a running joke of mine, that Richard was always so damn punctual. And I think someone knew that. How else would they know what time he gets home, what time he would step out of his car, what time he would turn around so they could… so they could…"

Rebecca finally seemed to break, and she doubled over in an open sob. Olivia reached a hand to her shoulder and squeezed it gently. She watched Richard's widow shaking as she withdrew the tissue from her face, leaving it red and blotchy.

"As soon as I heard the shot, I ran to him," she whispered. "Somehow, I knew he was dead. When I heard the shot, it's like I felt that bullet go right through my heart. I knew he wasn't going to come out of it alive, and I knew it had to be connected with his damn job. He was always so determined to provide for us, to give me the life he thought I deserved… but I wish he had just quit. He'd still be here now if he had. We could have bought ourselves more time. And now what am I left with?"

Olivia fumbled for words to comfort the widow, but she held up a hand again to stop her.

"I don't need your sympathies. I need answers. But I'm not sure how much I can help you, agent."

"Every little bit helps," Olivia tried. "What did he do in his day-to-day?"

THE **LOCKED BOX**

"I was always spared the details of what he did exactly. His official title was a shipping and logistics manager, but I don't even know what that meant, really. I suspect they had him doing more than a normal company would, perhaps some jobs on the side. But he used to come home from work completely drained… sometimes, recently, he's skipped dinner entirely and headed up to his study with a bottle of whiskey. That place… it took a toll on him. And I still don't understand why—not fully, anyway—but I got the feeling that Richie was close to a breakthrough. He kept telling me that things would get better, that soon we would be okay… but now that day won't ever come. I married a fool."

Olivia offered her a sympathetic look. "He thought he was doing the right thing. And he was. He was trying to help us take down bad people. I am truly sorry that this was the outcome."

"Me too. Me too," Rebecca sighed heavily. "I hope that you're able to find who did this to him. I'm sure that no one directly linked to the company would get their filthy hands any dirtier. I'm sure they hired someone to hurt my poor Richie. But I want the bastard taken down. Any man who is willing to kill my man for no good reason doesn't deserve to be walking these streets."

"I promise… I'll make sure to find the person who did this."

Rebecca nodded sadly. "Thank you. All I want is for this nightmare to have some kind of solution. Richie would have wanted that."

Olivia stayed for a while, talking to the woman about what she knew, but she wasn't able to give Olivia much more than she had already shared. She'd explained that Richard only told her what he was doing because she had suspected him of cheating, with long nights at work and his withdrawn attitude. Now, she knew better, and though she had tried to wheedle information out of him plenty of times, he always kept her in the dark.

"He was trying to keep me safe. But no one was keeping him safe, were they?"

Olivia thanked Rebecca for speaking to her and offered her sympathies, then headed out into the front yard to talk with the police once again. It was dark outside now, and the neighbors had retreated behind their curtains. It was easier for them to hide there than face what was just outside their windows. Olivia knew that life would never be the same for the residents on that street.

Olivia took another look at the body that was still being pored over by the crime scene unit. Richard was flat on his back, his arms and legs spread as though he'd fallen from a great height, his limbs flailing out. She could see the sweat stains on his worn shirt, like in life he'd been constantly too stressed to control his perspiration. Olivia wondered if he'd known that he was about to die. Had he known that ANH was on to him, that they were going to end his life without a second thought?

"Did you find anything on his person that could give us any information? Anything in his pockets?" she asked the officer who was meticulously cataloging every detail.

The man donned a fresh pair of gloves and checked. "Just a bit of fluff," he reported back.

She sighed. Of course, it couldn't be that easy. She squatted low and stared closely at what was left of Richard Greene's face. He looked so completely ordinary, but she knew that he'd died with a thousand secrets. She needed to know what those were. She needed to know everything he knew about ANH and what they were up to.

She still couldn't understand the dilemma she was faced with: a man killed in the daytime and a killer who got away without a trace. The neighbors hadn't seen a thing, and the killer was gone by the time Rebecca had made it to Richard. Olivia couldn't understand how it had happened. The person must have been crazy fast, crazy prepared, and crazy desperate to get it done. It made a shiver run down her spine.

"Learn anything useful?" the officer Olivia had spoken to earlier asked. She shook her head.

"Not yet. I was hoping for something more. The person who did this… I believe he was some kind of hit man for the company that Richard worked for. We're investigating them for all kinds of illicit activity, and Richard was our man on the inside. I guess he knew too much."

THE **LOCKED BOX**

The officer whistled. "Damn… well, I wasn't expecting that. He seems so average. I suppose you never can tell what's going on in people's lives."

Olivia nodded. It was true. Looking at Richard, you'd never suspect that he was a mole for MI5. He just seemed so meek and unassuming. Maybe he'd known that, and he'd thought it would keep him safe. Maybe he'd believed it would stop him from being found out.

But apparently not.

Olivia tried to make sense of how this affected their case. If they knew Richard was an informant, then they knew about Henry. If they knew about Henry, then his position was certainly compromised. Olivia wondered whether she should be worried that she hadn't heard from him.

But then again…

Olivia felt nausea clinging to her stomach. It suddenly seemed like a coincidence to her that this man had wound up dead just as Henry had insisted on going on his little solo mission. Olivia wasn't usually one for conspiracy theories, and yet she didn't trust Henry one bit. He had seemed so angry when she showed up, as though she had turned up specifically to ruin things for him. Was that because he was actually up to something he shouldn't be?

Maybe it was because she was in a strange, new land around strange new people, but Olivia was feeling wary of everyone she met—even more than usual. Maybe it was because she was working with someone as hardened as Henry after working with Brock for so long… but she was becoming more suspicious of him by the minute.

Henry hated the fact that she'd shown up. Had he been an ANH agent all along? Was she ruining his plans? Had he thought she was going to get in the way of him finishing Richard off?

Olivia knew that the idea was likely absurd, but she couldn't shake it off. It was crazy, but it would explain why they seemed to have found more leads in one day than he had in three whole years. It would explain why his so-called informants kept winding up dead, why Richard now had a bullet in his brain, and why

Henry was still MIA. Was she crazy, or was her theory starting to make some form of sense?

Was he really trying to solve the case, or was he trying to derail it even further?

Olivia knew she couldn't afford to accuse him of these things. No matter what, he was her only link to Brock, to ANH, and to the answers she needed. She couldn't turn on him without solid evidence.

But that didn't mean she couldn't keep an eye on him. That didn't mean she couldn't dig deeper while he was sure that she was being kept in the dark. One way or another, she was going to find answers. One way or another, she was going to get to the bottom of the case.

Even if it meant taking everyone down with her in the process.

CHAPTER ELEVEN

Night had fallen by the time Olivia made it back to the B&B. There was still no sign of Henry, and Olivia couldn't decide whether she was glad or not. On one hand, she was desperate to figure out if her hunches about him were true. But on the other hand, he could be a dangerous individual. If he was really working against her, then making him aware that she was suspicious of him was the last thing she wanted to do.

Perhaps being around him was the last thing she needed, especially if she hoped to find Brock alive. If he was working with ANH, anything she said could make it back to them. If she stepped a toe out of line or got far too close for his liking, then she ran the risk of getting Brock deeper into trouble than he already was.

She knew that it was entirely possible that she was overreacting and looking for enemies where she had a solid ally, but she didn't intend to risk it. There was too much at stake. She would rather be overly wary of Henry than not wary enough. Besides, he was still out there somewhere doing God only knew what. If he came back empty-handed, then putting her faith in him was certainly going to be misplaced. She could only truly rely on herself from that moment forward, and the thought didn't worry her. She'd always come through for herself in the past, and this time would be no exception.

About an hour later, she heard footsteps in the hallway. Her ears perked up as she realized that it had to be Henry. She found it interesting that he hadn't come to her first instead of heading to his room. Surely that wasn't a good sign? They were supposed to be a team, and all he'd done so far was keep his distance from her. Did he have some reason to completely freeze her out like this?

She was about to march right over to his room and grill him about what he knew, but then she heard the muffled sound of voices. Or rather, just one voice—Henry's. She pressed her ear to the wall, but she couldn't make out what he was saying. There didn't appear to be anyone with him, because there were long stretches between his speech. Which could only mean one thing: he was speaking on the phone with someone.

Which was interesting, considering that Olivia had his phone right there in her room.

Olivia frowned. It wasn't too uncommon for people to have personal phones to separate from their work lives. She knew that wasn't necessarily a suspicious thing. But her heightened nerves and her desperation to find Brock had made her even more untrusting than usual. She wasn't willing to let it slide when Henry had already spent half his time sneaking around since she'd arrived... which begged the question: Who was he calling at eleven o'clock at night? And why?

Olivia wasn't interested in waiting around any longer. She needed to find out where Henry had been and what he'd been up to. Perhaps it was his alibi for the time of Richard's murder. She grabbed Henry's phone and burst out of her room, rapping loudly on Henry's door.

She heard a very definite sigh from inside his room, and he murmured to whomever he was speaking that he'd call them back. When Henry opened the door, he looked disgruntled and tired. It didn't stop Olivia from entering his room as casually as he'd entered hers before, not waiting for an invitation.

She had hoped that she might get some clues about the man she was working with from the state of the room, but there was nothing to work with. The room looked as though it had barely been touched. The bed was neatly made and no personal items could be seen anywhere. Not even a comb or a book or a set of toiletries.

In particular, Olivia was irked by the lack of a book on the nightstand. She didn't tend to trust people who left the house without a book. What were they supposed to do when they had a spare ten minutes? Stare into space?

"I thought you'd let me know when you got back from your little trip," Olivia said pointedly. Henry raised an eyebrow at her.

"I got back five minutes ago."

"I noticed."

"I had a call to make."

"I noticed that too."

She'd only been in the room for a few moments, and they were already losing patience with one another. Olivia knew that it wasn't a good start to their working relationship, but considering that she was secretly suspecting him of being a double agent, she felt that her coldness to him was almost justified.

"Well? Did you find anything?"

Henry sighed. "Not so much. I followed up the lead on the lorry, but it was pretty much a bust. I didn't find anything of interest at the location that it traveled to. I can keep track of the lorry a little while longer, but I'm pretty sure the trail will go cold. ANH isn't sloppy enough to keep using the same vehicles over and over."

Olivia folded her arms. "So, you're saying that you've been there this entire time? Scouting that location?"

Henry scowled at her, rolling up his sleeves. "Where did you think I was? Day tripping to London? I had a job to do. It just didn't get me where I hoped it would."

"So, I guess you know nothing about your dead informant then?"

Olivia studied his face as he reacted to the news. If he was pretending not to know, then he was a damn good actor. He blinked several times, his hand still hovering on his half-rolled sleeve.

"What? How do you know?"

"I picked up a call from your phone while you were gone. I would have contacted you, but you didn't exactly leave your number. Richard Greene was shot dead in front of his house earlier today."

Henry swore under his breath, but he didn't look particularly fazed. In their line of work, it was easy to get accustomed to death, but he showed no emotion at all. He'd obviously been working closely with Richard for a while, and yet it was as though she'd told him that their dinner reservations were canceled, not that a man was dead. Did he not care at all? Was he completely devoid of empathy, or was he just a terrible person?

"Well, that's another avenue of intel gone," he grumbled. Olivia shook her head at him in disbelief. *Definitely a terrible person,* she thought.

"I checked out the scene. It's got to be ANH, right? They're the only people who would be bold enough to send someone to shoot him in broad daylight just to get rid of him, right? And who else would have a reason to?"

Henry shrugged. "Who knows? Maybe he really wound someone up. But most likely, yes, it's them. Besides, it's not very British to shoot someone in this country. At least, not randomly in a quiet neighborhood. That's gang behavior. You don't get common criminals running around with guns so much here. It screams of ANH, of something bigger."

"So, what's the next step?" Olivia pressed, curious to see how he would respond. After all, if he was truly interested in getting to the bottom of the case with ANH, he would find another mole.

THE **LOCKED BOX**

But Henry just shrugged again as though the conversation was boring him to tears.

"We'll just have to keep trying to find a way to infiltrate the company. Keep pushing, stay on the grind. But we'll get to that tomorrow. I'm knackered."

She blinked. "So, that's it? You're signing off for the day?"

"What more do you want from me? I'm not a robot. I've got to sleep sometime. So, in the politest way possible, get out of my room. I'll see you in eight hours when I've caught up on my sleep."

Olivia wavered. She wanted to grill him some more, but she had to admit that the jet lag was catching up with her. She needed to sleep. At least he was only in the next room over. *Keep your friends close and your enemies closer,* she thought.

She was about to head for the door when her phone rang in her pocket. She looked up at Henry, and he waited for her to pick up the call, his hands on his hips. Olivia took out the phone and saw it was Jonathan.

"Please tell me you have good news for me," she begged as she picked up the call.

"Nothing good. I'm sending you what I have now. There's another video."

Olivia closed her eyes. Of all the things she'd been hoping for, that was by far the least. She had been hoping for an interview with Charlie Evans or at least some sort of lead on Brock's case. But as she opened the file she'd been sent, she felt sick to her stomach. She felt Henry looming over her shoulder to see the video, and she had to resist the urge to shove him away. She also wished she'd gone back to her bedroom before picking up the call. She hated the idea of Henry seeing her at her most vulnerable, with all her feelings being worn on her sleeve. Where Brock was concerned, she couldn't hide how she felt for a moment.

In the video, Brock was tied to a chair once again, but he was no longer on the boat. It was hard to tell what kind of state he was in, but he didn't look as though he'd been hurt too badly. The look on his face was one of pure exhaustion, but he was alive, at least. That was what she needed to know the most. The rest, she could hope to work with.

Once again, a masked man stepped in front of the camera.

"We see you are yet to hand over the money for the safe return of your agent," the man said, his voice distorted by the voice changer he was using. "We are unwilling to negotiate with you on this. You hand the money over, or he dies. And since we are getting impatient… let us up the stakes a little. The ransom cost has now doubled, and you have five days left to supply us with the money. If you don't, you can say goodbye to Agent Tanner."

The man stepped away from the camera again, leaving Brock in the center of the camera's focus. He didn't struggle against his bindings, as though the fight had left his body entirely; but he did look up to stare into the lens, as though he was looking right into Olivia's soul. She felt her stomach twist with anxiety.

Everything had changed.

Five days. That was all she had to take down a company that had been running amok for years without being caught. Five days wasn't enough time. Before she knew it, Brock would be dead if she didn't pull it together.

And she didn't see how she could. There were too many threads to pull and too many questions left unanswered. Already, she had a murder mystery on her hands, an untrustworthy agent at her side, and zero leads to speak of. How was she going to pull this off?

Breathless, she brought the phone back to her ear, knowing that Jonathan was waiting to hear her thoughts. She grappled for something to say, but she could only exude silence.

"I know this is a lot," Jonathan started. "If you need an out—"

"No," Olivia said. "I want to see this through. It's just… it's a lot. We're already running on empty, and there's not much in the way of leads…"

"I know. I understand. We're working like dogs over here, too, trying to figure out a way to find him. There's no way we can hand over the kind of money they're asking for. You understand that, right?"

"Yes," Olivia said meekly. Their demands were far too high. It was almost as though they knew that the United States would

THE **LOCKED BOX**

never pay for Brock's life. Now, with the bounty doubled, it was even more ludicrously out of the question than before.

...which meant that the only option was to find him and bring him home without getting themselves killed. Whatever they did, it would open a whole new can of worms. ANH would never stop until they got what they wanted, even if it meant brazenly murdering a federal agent in cold blood.

And yet Olivia didn't care what they were capable of. She only wanted to know that Brock was safe. The rest was irrelevant.

"I'm pushing for that interview you wanted," Jonathan told her. "Even if it's a shot in the dark, I trust your instincts. Keep going. You always latch on to something good. It's not over yet."

Olivia knew she should be reassured by her boss's confidence in her, but it didn't matter to her in the slightest. Any other time, she would've been touched, but if she didn't succeed now, none of it would matter. Brock's life was hanging in the balance, and only she could rescue him. It was a lot of pressure, and Olivia could almost feel it weighing down her body, her knees threatening to buckle beneath her.

She hung up the call and stood silently for a moment, letting everything sink in. Henry eventually cleared his throat.

"Um, hi. You alright?"

Olivia's head whipped to look at Henry. He didn't look particularly sympathetic, but Olivia was starting to believe he wasn't capable of that kind of emotion. She held her chin high and straightened her back.

"I'm fine. Completely fine."

"You don't seem like it."

"That's none of your business."

Henry raised his eyebrows, folding his arms. "I think it is. If we're searching for him, then I guess I need to know how much your heart is in this. Is he your partner or your *partner?*"

"Excuse me?" she replied hotly.

"You know what I'm asking you," Henry needled her. "Are you romantically involved with this man? Partners come and go in our line of work. You shouldn't be so attached to someone that is essentially just your co-worker. It's odd to see you so invested."

"You're saying that you wouldn't care if your partner was captured? If someone threatened to kill them?"

Henry shrugged. "I guess so. But I work alone, most of the time. It's easier that way. Partners just complicate things."

"Oh, well, of course, big strong Henry Caine doesn't need a partner," she snapped, letting her anger get the better of her. He deserved the lecture though. "*Now* everything makes total sense. Not exactly a people person, are you? I don't think you'd know empathy if it slapped you in the face."

"I don't think I'm particularly bad with people."

"Then maybe I should make you a little more self-aware. Usually, when a person goes missing, you should care. Even if it's someone you don't know that well, you should care. That's the whole point of this job. Trying to put away the ones who hurt others. Because we want to keep people safe. Are we on the same page, or are you just going to slow me down?"

Henry held up his hands defensively. "Easy there. I promise you—I'm trying my best here. I want to find your friend. Boyfriend, whatever. I care about finding him. I just wanted to know a little more background information."

"Yeah, well, you had your chance to play twenty questions on the drive over here. Now we're on the clock, and I don't need you asking your invasive questions and trying to cajole something out of me that you can dangle over my head."

"That wasn't my intention."

"Unfortunately, I don't believe that for a second."

Olivia made it clear that the conversation was at an end and headed straight for the door. Henry sighed behind her, clearly done with trying his half-attempt at diplomacy.

"Alright then. I'll see you in the morning."

Olivia slammed the door shut behind her. Anger was coursing through her veins. Why did this kind of thing always seem to plague her life? Things could never just stay simple, not even for a few minutes. Olivia's chest felt tight as she headed back into her bedroom and closed the door behind her.

She didn't even know where she could begin now. Henry's solo mission had failed, Olivia had only added more stress to their workload by taking on Richard's murder, and they had no time to waste. Every second counted, and yet each one was slipping away from her without furthering their knowledge. She was beginning to believe that she wouldn't find any answers until it was too late for Brock.

Olivia threw herself onto her bed and covered her head with the duvet, sending herself into darkness. She needed sleep to take her. She needed a chance to wake up refreshed with new ideas and a new zest for the case. But she lay there for hours and hours, getting more frustrated with herself as sleep continued to evade her. She could see Brock's face in her mind, his tortured expression staring back at her. He was hurting, and there was nothing she could do about it. He was slipping farther and farther away from her, and she couldn't stop it. How could she ever fall asleep knowing that?

Next door, she could hear Henry snoring soundly.

Part of her wished she could be more like him. He was her polar opposite, so disconnected from his work emotionally that he didn't seem to care that people were dropping like flies around him. He was so far removed that if Brock died the next day, he would probably tell Olivia it was time to move on with her life after five minutes. He was as cold as ice, and it suited him just fine.

But Olivia was glad to have those emotions. She clung to them in her sleepless night, knowing they would be her driving force to finish the case. Her love for Brock would get her through the week and beyond, no matter the outcome. Even if she couldn't save him, even if they lost this war with ANH, she knew that her feelings would keep her alive and keep her moving for revenge.

It was better to have loved and lost than to never have loved at all.

CHAPTER TWELVE

EARLY MORNING ARRIVED, AND OLIVIA STILL HADN'T SLEPT much. She had drifted off a few times, but she was jolted awake by the beating of her own heart, furious and wild in her chest. Olivia found herself rubbing at the spot as though trying to soothe her heart, but it was no use. She felt like she'd drank too much caffeine and was crashing into withdrawal at top speed.

It wasn't ideal, but Olivia decided she would be more useful if she simply embraced her tiredness and got up. She headed into the bathroom and took as cold of a shower as she could bear, scrubbing her body furiously, trying to wake herself up a little. It sort of worked in a distressing way, and so she dressed and sat in

THE **LOCKED BOX**

the chair nearest the wall she shared with Henry, angry at the fact that he was sleeping so soundly.

Her rules for the day were simple. Number one. She wouldn't trust her new partner, not even for a second. He had shown her more than once that he wasn't on her side, regardless of whose team he actually played for, and she couldn't afford for him to mess this up for her. Number two. She would throw her all into the case and beat the clock to get to Brock before they killed him. And number three, the most important of them all...

She would trust her gut. Her intuition had taken her far in her line of work. There were times when people thought she was crazy, that her theories couldn't possibly be correct, and she usually turned out to be right. Olivia was used to thinking outside the box and then throwing the box away entirely. It was the only way she could beat the criminal minds she faced, and she was sure she was about to be faced with her most difficult task to date.

She wasn't going to wait for Henry to catch up to her. She wished she had a car so she could go wherever she pleased, but an opportunity presented itself to her in the form of a phone call, making it unnecessary for her to leave at all.

The name of the person on the other end of the line was none other than Paxton Arrington. Olivia always felt a jolt in her heart whenever she saw his name come up on her screen. Before Veronica had been murdered several years ago, Paxton had been her husband. He didn't call often, and when he did, it was usually to talk shop. Still, speaking to him always reminded her of their shared loss, of the agony they had to endure after her sister had been taken from them. Seeing his name come up now reminded her that she was too close to losing someone else important to her.

She picked up the call.

"Pax... it's good to hear from you."

"Hey, stranger. Heard through the grapevine about the situation you're in. How are you holding up?"

"Honestly?" Olivia replied, rubbing her forehead. "I'm kind of losing it. There's not enough time. I just... I don't know how we're going to get out of this one. I'm... I don't want to lose him, Pax. I've lost enough already."

"I know you have," Paxton told her gently. "But if there's anything I can do to help, just name it. I can get Brody to pry into some Parliament records—"

"Don't—" she sighed, "don't admit to that on an unsecured line, please. I have enough on my plate without having to call Blake to keep you in line or get myself mixed up with hacking into a foreign government's records."

Paxton's laugh was soft and wry. But even he seemed to understand the gravity of the situation, and his voice was serious and sympathetic. "I mean it though. From what I've heard about this case, it seems like you'll need as much help as you can get. I just want to throw it out there—offer up whatever I can. I've got some time, I've got some contacts, and I might be able to help."

Olivia chewed her lip. Of course, he'd somehow caught wind of the case. She didn't want to entangle even more people into this, but time was ticking, and if there was any way she could find a lead, she had to take it.

"To be honest, right now I could use a miracle. Any lead you could find would give me something to work with."

"Lay it on me."

Olivia gave him a brief summary of ANH, their global network, and how they seem to have completely evaded the authorities for years. She skimped on some of the finer details and didn't want to overcomplicate it by mentioning Richard Greene's death, but when the story was done, Paxton whistled low.

"All right. Sounds like a complicated one. I can't say I've ever heard of this company, ANH? But if they're a front for all this, there will be a trail for us to follow. I'll do some digging and see if we can find anything on our end, but to be honest, there's only so much I can do from out here in Seattle."

"I appreciate that, Pax. Every little bit helps."

"What about the money?" he prodded. "Four million dollars is—"

"Absolutely not," she cut him off. Sure, Paxton was a billionaire heir to one of America's largest media conglomerates, but she couldn't ask him to just drop the ransom to get Brock back. Besides, she knew this whole thing had never been about the money at all. She knew that if she did contact ANH to try to arrange the ransom, she'd be walking headfirst into a trap. And then she'd for sure be signing Brock's death warrant—and her own.

"Think about it, Olivia," he pressed.

"There's nothing to think about," she said. "I don't believe for a minute that what these people want is *money*. They seem to have plenty of it with their operation. I really don't want you involved in this in any official manner."

Pax let out a sigh. "Fine. Just know the offer stands."

"Good. Because I'm not sure I can handle any more trouble on my end, But, thank you," Olivia said, glancing at the wall that separated her room from Henry's. She suddenly felt a shiver running down her spine.

And then a thought came to her head.

"Pax…"

"Yes?"

"There is actually one thing you might be able to help me with."

"Why does this request feel so ominous?"

Olivia bit her lip. Did she really want to do this? If Henry knew what she was up to, it could blow up her entire world in a matter of seconds. If he was who she thought he was, then she was putting herself at risk. She stood up from her chair and crossed the room to the far side, the phone pressed to her ear. Was she doing this? Would she put herself in danger to save Brock? To uncover the truth?

The answer was yes.

"I need you to look into someone," Olivia whispered into the phone.

He was silent for a moment, but she could almost see Paxton's cocky grin all the way across the Atlantic.

"Now we're talking," he said. "Who is this mystery person who needs looking into? What kind of a wild theory are you working on?"

"Not so wild from where I'm standing. I need you to look into my partner. He works for MI5, and his name is Henry Caine."

"Your... partner? The guy you're trying to take down ANH with?" he asked skeptically.

"I'm concerned he may be compromised," she explained in a whisper. "And spare me the lecture. I don't care if you think I'm nuts. I'm completely serious. Something about this guy is off, and I don't trust him."

The pause he gave on the other line was interminable. Olivia was sure he was about to fire off some snarky rejoinder.

"Will you do it or not?" she hissed.

"You're so much like Veronica sometimes that it's not even funny," he finally said.

And that dredged up all the emotion she'd been holding at bay all night. She shook her head and tried to shoo it away, but it crested, and Olivia felt a single tear slipping down her cheek.

"Of course, I'll help. I'll look into him," Pax said. "I know better than most not to doubt the intuition of a Knight woman."

That made her chuckle at least. "You're damn right," she said. "I... thank you. And thanks for checking in. You didn't have to do that."

"Of course, I did, Olivia. We're family. Even now, even though Veronica is gone... you know you'll always be my sister-in-law. Which means it's my job to check in, be overprotective, and drive you crazy every once in a while."

Olivia's lips twitched into a smile. "Well, I guess it keeps me humble. Thank you again. I think it has done me good to hear a voice from home."

"Anytime. I'll be in touch. And I'll put some feelers out to see if I can find out more about this ANH. But you might have to be patient. Keep your phone close."

As the call ended, Olivia felt a small twinge of relief. It was a start, at least. Knowing that Paxton was in her corner and was out there fighting for her made her feel a little better. She'd really come around in her opinion of the man since Veronica had first brought him home all those years ago. He was hardworking, fought to find the truth, and always tried to solve the impossible problems. He tried to do good in the world the same way Veronica had. It was why the two of them had connected so well, and Olivia knew the type because she was the same. She could only hope that he could use his resources to find something on this case that the FBI couldn't.

And now, Olivia could focus on what she was going to do next. She felt better knowing that if she didn't have time to do some digging on Henry, then at least someone was. She wanted to find all his dirty laundry. Had he ever botched a case? Has he ever been on suspension or hurt someone he shouldn't have? Was there a single tarnish on his perfect record, even one that had been buried to make him look good?

Whatever it was, she wanted to know. Something about him didn't sit right with her. He was as cold as a killer and as ruthless as one too. He made her uneasy, and her gut was usually right. Now, she could find out if there was any truth to her suspicions. If she was wrong, she'd put it behind her and never think about it again. But if she was right, then at least she wouldn't regret putting his name on Pax's radar. She knew that some of his investigative methods skirted the line of legality, but she didn't have the luxury to choose whom she worked with. Her uneasy alliance with Henry proved that much.

In the meantime, she was ready to get started on the day. She checked the time. It was still before six, but she was itching to continue with the case. Every second wasted was another that she could be searching for Brock.

She headed out of her room and knocked on Henry's door. Since he was the one with the car, she needed him if she wanted to go anywhere. She had to knock several times before she heard him stirring in his room, muttering irritably to himself. It gave Olivia some small pleasure to have ticked him off as much as he had her the night before.

The door opened, and Henry looked a little worse for wear, his hair sticking up at odd angles and his eyes drooping with sleep. He looked like an aggressive dog who had just had its tail stepped on, teeth bared and eyes dulled.

"It's not even six," he snapped. "And you've probably woken up half the B&B."

"Then get dressed, and let's move before we wake up anyone else."

Henry grunted, shaking his head. "You're impossible, American."

Still, fifteen minutes later, he was ready to hit the road. They had no plan, which Olivia hated, but she didn't protest when Henry suggested that they head down to the docks again to see if there was any activity on the *Dynamic Dawn* or any of ANH's other ships. As they were driving over there, Olivia could see the tension in Henry's shoulders, but she ignored it, hoping they were about to have another silent car ride.

But he had other ideas.

"So. You were on the phone early this morning."

Olivia's heart froze for a moment. She hadn't thought that he was awake. How much had he heard? Did he know that she was looking into his past?

Olivia played it cool, shrugging her shoulders at him the way he'd done to her a million times since they met. "I had a long-distance call."

"I see. Your little friends at the FBI?"

"Maybe. Why were you eavesdropping on me?"

"I wouldn't call it eavesdropping. I'd call it having a noisy American staying in the room next door to me."

Olivia felt her cheeks flush with anger. This man really knew how to push her buttons. She didn't think anyone in the world had ever irritated her so much, not even Brock at his worst. At least Brock was funny and charming.

"Well, I guess I'll try to keep it down. Although I spent all night listening to the sound of your incessant snoring, so I don't think you have a leg to stand on."

"Now who's the one eavesdropping?"

Olivia made her decision then. Whether he was good or pure evil, she couldn't stand Henry Caine at all. The smugness that tinged everything he said only made her want to pull her hair out even more. She was having one of the roughest weeks of her entire life, forced to work relentlessly to save her best friend's life.

THE **LOCKED BOX**

So, of course, in swept the world's biggest jerk to make her life even more miserable.

Would she ever catch a break?

It was at that moment that her phone rang. She felt her heart jolt, wondering if it was Pax already calling with urgent information. She really didn't want to take a call while she was right next to Henry. Then she'd really be in trouble.

But fortunately, it was a known number. It was the police officer, Cheryl, who she'd spoken to at the crime scene of Richard's murder. Henry raised an eyebrow.

"Another *long-distance call?*" he asked. She scowled.

"No, actually. It's the police who are investigating Richard Greene's case. So maybe you should shut up for a minute and let me take it."

Henry put his hands in the air defensively as though he hadn't done a thing wrong in his life. Ignoring him, Olivia picked up the call, trying not to let her irritation at him seep into her call with Cheryl.

"Agent Knight speaking."

"Good morning, Agent Knight. Good to speak to you again," Cheryl said politely, which seemed especially British to Olivia. "I just wanted to give you an update on the investigation of Richard's murder…"

"I'm listening," Olivia said eagerly, chewing on her thumb while she prayed for some good news.

"Well, it's not exactly a direct link to Richard himself, but something interesting has come to light. We have a missing person on our hands. Apparently, another employee of the same company, Gareth Dean, didn't make it home last night. He was seen leaving work around the same time as Richard, and camera footage shows him getting into his car and driving off. But he never arrived at his house. His wife called us this morning to let us know that she was worried. I don't know whether this means something, but it seems like too much of a coincidence to me. Two employees of the same company being targeted at the same time? Surely that's related?"

"Yes," Olivia replied thoughtfully. It did strike her as odd. She knew nothing about Gareth Dean, and it was possible that he just drove off on his own accord… but two people from the same company having unusual circumstances on the same day? That couldn't be a mere coincidence—especially since Henry had pointed out that it was common for bad things to happen to those who worked for ANH.

"What else did Gareth's wife say? Anything of interest?"

"She did mention that he'd been out of sorts lately. Perhaps a little jittery, a little paranoid. She was shocked, but not entirely surprised, for him to behave this way. It's possible he'll come home yet, but we're sending out a patrol to look for him. If he's alive, he might be able to shed some light on what we're dealing with here."

"Thanks for letting me know about all of this. I can't imagine this is a coincidence. Are there still officers on the scene at Richard's home?"

"I believe some of them are there this morning, yes. If you'd like to go over there and take a look around, his wife seemed happy for us to take a look around her home. She said she just wants answers."

"I'll head there now and report back."

"Alright. Take care. If I hear anything else of interest, I'll let you know."

Olivia hung up the call, feeling a little strange. She didn't like the idea that low-ranking workers from ANH's legal side were dropping like flies or disappearing off the grid, but the timing was too suspicious to be ignored. It was like the organization was preparing for battle, worming out the traitors before they could turn on them first. Olivia turned to Henry.

"Change of plans. We need to go back to Richard Greene's home."

"Why?"

"Because I think he might be the key to all of this. We have no other solid leads, and he was our only source of intel. Maybe there are things he was keeping from us, things that we can use to get

THE **LOCKED BOX**

insider knowledge of ANH. His wife is cooperative; she's allowing us to look around her home. I think it's a golden opportunity."

"It seems like a waste of time to me," Henry scoffed. "Greene was always just a pawn in their game. He meant nothing to them, and that means he wouldn't have known anything of use. Besides, he was an informant. When he did manage to get intel, he told me about it. That was his *job.*"

"Everyone has secrets," Olivia stated coldly. "I think there's something there."

"And I disagree."

"So, that's it? You'd rather just sit at the docks and hope for a miracle? That was our only hope before, and now we have a direction to go in. Wouldn't you rather be active about this?"

"I'm not interested in going there."

"Then let me out of the car. I'll walk."

Henry glared at her as though she was being impossible. Then he began to veer the car off to the right and toward Richard's residence.

"Fine. We'll do it your way. Watch this crash and burn before your eyes, American. You're grasping at straws."

Olivia narrowed her eyes at him. Why was he so resistant to the idea of visiting the home of his own dead informant? Was it because he felt responsible for his death? Or was it because he knew that Richard had been hiding secrets that Henry didn't want to be leaked?

Anything seemed possible, but Olivia would find out… one way or another.

CHAPTER THIRTEEN

On their drive to the Greene residence, Olivia filled Henry in on the status of Gareth Dean. Neither of them was sure what to make of it except that it seemed more than coincidental.

When they arrived at the Greene home, it was vacant. The police officers on the scene told them that Rebecca had gone to stay with family while she dealt with the death of her husband, but she had left keys for them to investigate whatever they wanted inside the house. Olivia was glad that they could sidestep Richard's widow. As much as she felt for her, Olivia needed to be able to get started on the investigation without worrying about treading on her toes and being insensitive. Time wasn't on their

THE **LOCKED BOX**

side, and they needed to find some connection between this case and ANH before it was too late.

But rather than starting with the house, Olivia started with the car. The door was still left open, just as it had been the night before since the crime scene had been secured. The officers had already scoured the scene for evidence, but Olivia knew that if there was anything to find, it would be hidden somewhere beyond the scope of a normal search. She donned a pair of nitrile gloves and made her way methodically around the car. She opened the glove compartment and found it empty save for a car manual and some old CDs. There was nothing in the side door pockets or under any of the seats. In the trunk, there was a set of golf clubs that were kept shiny and polished. All in all, it seemed like a perfectly ordinary car. Just as the police report said.

"You're wasting your time," Henry insisted. "Why would an informant leave anything of worth in the car? If he was carrying secrets around with him twenty-four seven, he'd be stupid to part with them overnight."

"It's worth a shot," Olivia said, rolling her eyes at him. "In the US, we like to be thorough with our investigations."

"And in the UK, we use our common sense," he shot back. "What are you expecting to find? A manila folder with 'classified' stamped across it in red ink? A file saying 'here are all my secrets' across it? He might have got himself killed in the end, but he wasn't stupid."

"Gotten himself killed?" Olivia nearly sputtered. "He wouldn't have been in this position in the first place if it weren't for you! Have some respect and be quiet. Let me do this."

Olivia got down on her hands and knees beside the car and peered underneath. She couldn't see anything at first, but then she spotted something unusual. A smug smile formed on her face. She knew she'd found something of use.

She slid her slim frame under the car carefully and fumbled for the object she'd found beneath it. With a little rattling, it came off the base of the car, and she emerged, the smell of gasoline clinging to her jacket. She held up her findings triumphantly.

"Bingo," she said. In her hand, she held a tracker not unlike the one they'd placed on the truck coming from the docks—and that wasn't lost on her as she presented it to Henry. His cheeks reddened a little, and he stepped forward to examine the tracker without apologizing for what he'd overlooked.

"ANH, presumably?" he muttered, refusing to look Olivia in the eye.

"Unless it's one of yours," she said pointedly.

He gave her an irritated glance. "It's not."

"They must have known he was spying on them for a while. Maybe they wanted to see who his contact on the outside was. Maybe you got lucky, and they still don't know who you are."

Henry had the sense to look a little concerned, but Olivia wondered whether this was news to him at all. Perhaps ANH had already let him know that they were on to him. Perhaps they'd threatened him and told him that he worked for them now. It would make sense if he really was a double agent. It did seem suspicious to Olivia that after all his years on the case, he'd lost multiple contacts within the company, but they'd never come after him. Plus, he'd seemed peculiarly uninterested in investigating the car… maybe because he'd known what Olivia would find all along.

It was all food for thought.

"Still, it doesn't tell us much," Olivia said, examining the tracker. "I'm not sure if there's any way to reverse trace the tracker back to them, especially not without them finding out. And if they wanted Richard dead, it makes sense that they kept tabs on him secretly. We might be on the right track though. Let's see what we can find inside."

Olivia handed the tracker over to the police—both for them to follow up in a lab and to keep it out of Henry's hands. Unfortunately, as of now, it was a dead end. Unless they could do something with it, it didn't get her closer to Brock. She hoped that whatever they could find in Richard's home would be more useful.

"Do you know what I've been thinking about?" Henry remarked as they climbed up the stairs to find Richard's study. "We know that ANH had figured out that Richard was a mole…

THE **LOCKED BOX**

that much is clear. But how long have they known? If that tracker has been on his car for a while, maybe they didn't see him as a threat up until recently. The things he'd been leaking to me weren't going to get me very far, and they knew that. But then to kill him on his driveway before the sun has even gone down… anyone could have seen the hit man. Anyone could have found a trace back to ANH. Maybe this was a rush job. Maybe Richard was actually on to something big, and they finally decided that he knew too much."

"That does make sense," Olivia agreed. "An organization like this is smarter than to just kill off anyone who betrays them outright. It's too performative. Richard had a false sense of security, clearly. He drove around with that tracker on his car for God knows how long… he was probably feeding ANH more intel than he was feeding you, if only by accident. But if he actually saw something of use to MI5, if he started getting too warm, then it certainly makes more sense to kill him quickly and efficiently, if not in a subtle way."

"Precisely. And there's more to it too," Henry began to explain. "Richard was one of the managers. He was pretty high up as far as jobs on the dock go. Far from the big leagues, of course, but he was well-known. He was the sort of typical participant who knew a little of the corruption, but not enough to snitch, and not enough to benefit from whatever schemes they're pulling. Guys like him… if ANH sensed that he was trying to climb higher, that he was working with us to try and get himself to higher ground, they would want to shoot that down and make sure no one else got the same idea. Such a public death… everyone will hear about it. It's not just an assassination. It's a warning."

Olivia nodded. "Sounds like you can come up with some smart stuff when you apply yourself."

"Sounds like you need to pipe down."

Olivia smiled. It was almost banter, but not quite. She could still feel that he was a little wounded from being proven wrong about the car, and the tension between them was still there. Neither of them really trusted the other. But things felt lighter than they had before, and it made the stress of the day seem a little less intense. Their constant bickering was something that she was glad to do without, especially since they were supposed to be a team. Neither of them had to like one another, but keeping things civil made the day a little easier.

They checked several of the other rooms upstairs as they talked, but it was the study that interested Olivia the most. Rebecca had mentioned that Richard spent a lot of time in there after a stressful day at work. If he was hiding any secrets, it would certainly be in that room.

The door was unlocked, but there was a key in the lock. That in itself was unusual. She didn't often see locks in people's houses unless it was on the bathroom door or for attic and basement rooms. Usually, a lock was installed for the specific reason of keeping something hidden. She pushed into the room and found that it was much messier than the rest of the house, as though Richard's disorganized thoughts had spilled out into his study. Olivia let out a puff of air.

"Man, we have our work cut out for us here. Let's hope there's something in here!"

"If there is, we might never find it," Henry muttered, turning his nose up at the mess. But after a moment, he began to methodically search through the debris, looking for something of interest.

Olivia began to root through the piles of papers on his desk, unsure what she was hoping to find but praying that something might jump out at her. Henry walked slowly, inspecting the bookshelves lining the room. Olivia didn't really want to do this as a pair. If she was right about him being a double agent, then the last thing she wanted was for Henry to get his hands on useful information that he could feed back to ANH. Still, she didn't have much of an option, and having Henry there would speed up the process.

"There's a safe inside this cupboard," Henry reported as he checked out a big wooden cabinet. Inside was a large, box-shaped safe. Olivia's eyes widened.

"I mean, it's a good place to hide things. I wonder if his wife knew the passcode?"

THE **LOCKED BOX**

After a few phone calls made by the police, Rebecca gave up the passcode for the safe. Olivia opened it eagerly, but she was disappointed to find that the only things inside were a stash of cash and an antique gold watch that didn't work.

"Well, that's that," Olivia sighed. She almost felt like it was pointless to keep looking in the study, but she pressed on anyway, not liking the idea that there were stones left unturned. She was very aware of how little time they had, but since Richard's home was their only hope of a lead, she had nowhere better to be. She organized the papers that she found into neater piles, hoping that tidying the desk would eventually unearth something useful.

And it did. She shifted a brown folder on the desk, and as it moved, a scrap of paper floated down to the floor. She bent to pick it up and examined it closely.

It was a five-digit number. A different one to the lock combination on the safe. Olivia felt her stomach clench in excitement. This was the kind of thing she was looking for.

"Check it out. Something useful *did* come out of a manila folder after all."

Henry checked out the number, his forehead creased.

"Maybe it's an old passcode?" he offered.

"Maybe. Or it could unlock something else. His computer? If it is his computer, we'll have really hit the jackpot…"

But the passcode didn't yield anything on his computer, and Rebecca had already told them she didn't know the code. Olivia found a planner on the desk and flipped through it, trying to figure out if there was anywhere else Richard might have to use a combination or keycode.

"Maybe he used it at work?" Olivia wondered aloud, checking out the manila folder. "I mean, these are work documents here. But we can't exactly stroll up to his office building knowing what we know; and besides, I doubt he would keep intel on the company under their roof. It seems too dangerous."

"What about the gym?" Henry said, tapping his finger on one of the pages in the planner. Richard had penciled in a gym class for later in the week. "People have lockers at gyms. Maybe he felt it was a safe place to store things, where no one would expect him to leave something important."

"It's a good theory. Where is his gym?"

They quickly searched through some of the documents on his desk and found a letter from his current gym, dated a month before. In the excitement of following the breadcrumbs, Olivia felt almost as though she was back on an ordinary case, not one that her best friend's life depended on. Still, she was pleased as they noted down the address and headed out together in Henry's car.

Finally, they were in motion.

CHAPTER FOURTEEN

MITCH'S MUSCLES WAS A SMALL BRICK BUILDING NESTLED in a parking lot on a side street off the center of town. At first, Olivia was under the impression that it would be some sweaty little hovel in the wall, but as she and Henry walked in, she was surprised to note the bright lights, high-end equipment, and well-organized nature of the place. She generally preferred running to lifting weights or dealing with the exercise machines, but it seemed like the kind of place she wouldn't mind going to. People of all ages, shapes, and sizes were dutifully pumping away at their various exercises, even though the place had just opened for the morning.

An eager-looking young woman waited for them at the desk, the kind of receptionist who had so much pep and enthusiasm that it bordered on frightening.

"Good morning!" the young woman said brightly as Olivia approached. Her name tag read *Claire*. "Are you here to join the gym? Perhaps you'd like to sample one of our free classes today?"

"Not today," Henry said as they badged her. "MI5, FBI. We're investigating a murder."

Claire's eyes widened, shocked by the blunt admission. "Oh!"

"We need you to help us out with one thing," Henry said briskly, glossing over the fact that he was talking about murder. "Our victim's name was Richard Greene. We believe he had a locker here. His wife has offered us the combination code for it, but we need to find out which locker it was."

Claire wavered, clearly overwhelmed by all of the information that had just been dumped on her. "Well, I don't know… we're not supposed to give people information about the lockers… it's private property, you see."

"Claire, this man was killed last night," Henry pressed coldly. "Whatever is in that locker is evidence now. Besides, he won't miss whatever we find, will he? We're going to need you to show us the way."

As if chastened, Claire was up out of her chair in seconds, looking a lot less chipper than before. Olivia felt sorry for the girl. She was only trying to do her job well. But they didn't have time to waste, and Henry knew that as well as she did. She didn't know offhand what the procedure would be for obtaining a search warrant over here in England, but she was glad to not have to mess with it.

Claire showed them the way into the men's locker room. It was empty save for a few locked cubicles where people were getting changed, and the hiss of several showers filled the air with noise and steam. Claire consulted a clipboard with a list of names and pointed them to Locker 158. There was nothing special about it from the outside, but Olivia knew that the answers they needed might be held within.

THE **LOCKED BOX**

"Thank you," Olivia said to Claire. She hovered around for a moment before realizing that it was her time to leave. As she walked away, Olivia got the note with the combination inscribed on it out of her pocket.

"Here goes nothing," she murmured. She took hold of the padlock and carefully twisted the numbers into place.

7... 4... 6... 6... 9.

The padlock came undone in her hand. With a sigh of relief, she pried open the locker.

There was no gym bag stored in the locker, though it still gave off a stale smell of socks and old deodorant. The only thing that was left in there was a small leather notebook. Olivia reached for it before Henry could, feeling protective of the secrets it likely held. She wished she could go somewhere to read Richard's notes in private, but there was no keeping this information from her partner. Not without raising the tension between them, certainly.

"I guess this is it," Olivia said. Henry nodded.

"We can take a look in the car."

As they headed back out, Olivia could feel herself itching to dive into the book. She was hungry for something to satiate her investigator's appetite. Something to tell her that she was on the right path. And she hoped, at the end of the trail, she would find her friend waiting for her, asking her what had taken her so long.

But the sands of time were still falling far too quickly in the hourglass of Brock's life. The second she sat down, she opened the pages so roughly that she almost tore them. There was a note on the very first page that she opened, and she saw that it was addressed to Henry.

He saw it too and snatched the book from her hands. She couldn't even blame him in the moment. His mouth moved as he read over the letter to himself, and Olivia read over his shoulder.

Henry,

I hope that if you are reading this, I've had the courage to tell you all the things I was scared to reveal before. If not, I guess I'm dead and gone. If ANH ever found out that I was writing these things down, that I was recording evidence of their crimes, they would certainly kill me. But maybe you can use this information for good and be a better man than I was.

Richard.

"He *was* keeping things from me," Henry grumbled. "So much for being an informant..."

"Keep reading," Olivia pushed. "This could be the key to everything."

Henry flicked through a few pages, scanning them quickly and murmuring to himself. Seemingly finding little of interest, he continued on his way until he found something he was happy with.

"There are a few interesting things in here, I guess. Nothing that surprises me so far," he said, stifling a yawn. Olivia folded her arms.

"Read something to me."

"Alright... I guess we'll go with this one..."

Today I handled a gun for the first time. The day I took the promotion, I was issued a simple pistol, which I was told was a gift from the CEO. It seemed like a strange thing to give to an employee, especially since owning a gun for personal use isn't legal here. But I was told that someday it might come in handy to protect myself. Well, I didn't know if that was necessary, but I took the gift anyway and kept it in my drawer at work. I've never had any use for it. I don't even think I'd know how to use it.

But since I became aware of how things are really run at ANH, I guess I've felt less at ease. I've started to believe that it makes sense to have a way of protecting myself. So, today, when I was told that I was going to have an evaluation... I picked up my gun for the first time.

These evaluations are a new thing. It never happened when I just worked at the docks. I get this feeling that the bosses are watching me. Like Big Brother. Even when I'm alone in my office, I feel as though eyes are on me, though I have checked several times for bugs. I don't know why they would be interested in a grunt like me, but I guess I'm moving up in the world. They keep an eye on me so I don't stray from the path.

THE **LOCKED BOX**

And the meeting today made me more nervous than I can express. Perhaps it is because I have secrets from them now. I kept my pistol right next to me, half concealed beneath my lap. The evaluation lasted an hour with two men I didn't know… and I was terrified that I might have to use my weapon on them. When they finally left, I told myself that I would learn to shoot… for my own sake.

"All the managers get a gun?" Olivia wondered as Henry finished reading out the passage. "That's a little overkill, isn't it?"

"I've been putting together a theory that they have some sort of conflict with the security teams at the docks. They've got to have some sort of way of smuggling all this stuff under the radar, don't they? It's a personal security measure—and a way to keep people in line."

"Poor Richard. He must have been so scared."

Henry sighed. "Yeah, I guess so. He was never really made for this kind of thing. He got dragged into it by no fault of his own."

Henry continued reading, and Olivia imagined Richard sitting alone in an office, cradling that pistol in his hands. Sometimes she forgot how common guns were back home. It seemed almost unusual that a gun would seem so foreign to a man in the UK, but life was different in America. Guns meant power, and she could see how that would frighten an average person who was bestowed with a weapon capable of killing someone.

Henry continued to flick through the pages, not offering to read anything else to Olivia. She sat impatiently, tapping her foot as she waited.

"Huh," Henry noted after a long while. "Well, this is certainly enlightening."

Frustrated with how cryptic he was being, Olivia took the book back from him and began to read.

It's been two days since it happened. It's taken me this long to work up the courage to write down what happened. I still feel sick to my stomach, but I will never tell a soul out loud. These pages are my testimony to what happened.

Brian was a traitor to ANH. That's what they told us as we were made to gather in the warehouse and watch what they did to him. It was the first time I've been allowed into their inner circle, allowed to see things firsthand... and now I wish that I hadn't.

I know I won't tell you about this, Henry. Not to your face. I don't want this to happen to me, and I'm sure it will if I tell you anything really of note. I know my cowardice will allow them to keep harming people, but walk a mile in my shoes, and you'll understand. These people terrify me.

They made Brian sit in a chair and pinched his nose until he opened his mouth for them. They stuffed pills in his mouth and made him swallow them. I don't know what those drugs were, or how much was the recommended amount to take... perhaps they were even testing their product on him to see what would happen. I can't be sure.

All I know is that those pills began to have a horrible effect. I have never seen someone act the way he did. Not even the drunkest man I've ever met was like Brian was then. How can I put it other than he came undone?

He was saying things he would never say, stumbling around like he didn't know where he was. And then he seemed so scared. Scared of things we maybe couldn't see, or of his own thoughts. It was hard to decipher what was wrong with him, but the others in the room kept laughing and laughing, as though we were simply watching a play or watching a clown at the circus.

And things got worse and worse. They made him take more of the drugs. He was screaming and begging, clawing at his face. He kept clutching at his heart. And it must have been a few hours later when he finally keeled over and died. They took his body away and we were told to get back to work. Business as usual.

His wife called me and asked if I had seen him last night. She said that he never made it to their book club meeting. She'd made a buffet, which he loved. I couldn't bear to tell her. I told her I had no idea where he was.

I didn't know I was such a filthy liar.

Olivia shuddered at what she had read, but things were starting to make sense. The pills... she was certain that she

THE **LOCKED BOX**

knew what ANH was dealing: the same pills that Charlie Evans had been harboring on his boat; the same drugs that the Grim Reaper had smuggled into the prisons. This stuff was dangerous and almost always deadly, and that terrified Olivia. It seemed that people were being made to think that it was an ultimate party drug, a high like no other... when really it was sending people to their deaths without them knowing that years of their lives were being stolen from them.

One pill would put you in a suggestible trance, almost like mind control. Two were likely to kill you. Three would kill you for sure, and painfully... slowly. It was sickening.

And ANH was profiting from it.

"This... this is next level," Olivia mused, flicking through a few more entries. Richard recalled a few more similar events between the pages, and Olivia found herself even thinking of the cult of Apep that she'd dealt with months and months ago. The followers of the cult had been given similar drugs so they would follow orders unquestionably. She remembered the agent she'd sent undercover, Shelby, who'd been affected with some sort of super-drug and inducted right into the cult. Were they all one and the same? Were these drugs the connecting link between everything she'd seen that didn't seem to make sense?

"What else does it say?" Henry asked. Olivia shook her head.

"These drugs... they're capable of a lot. They lower your defenses, and when taken in the right dose, they seem to make people highly suggestible. Here it says that ANH has used them to make people do their bidding. Richard talks about it in length here. But it seems like overdoses are very common. I guess they haven't quite perfected their formula yet. And it's killing people everywhere."

Henry was silent as he took the information in. He took back the notebook and flicked through the pages.

"This," he said, "is a goldmine. We're going to know so much that we didn't know before. He's even left a list of names and places of ANH strongholds. We could storm them right now and catch them off guard..."

"Except we can't. Because if we do that, they'll kill Brock in an instant," Olivia cut him off. "This stuff is good for figuring out what ANH are up to… and we can scout these locations out, but we have to play it carefully. We don't know what ANH know. Both of us could be on their radar. They might have been watching the house this entire time waiting for us to head to the gym to lead us right into a trap."

Henry nodded. "So what do you want to do? We're running out of time, Olivia. If you want to save your friend, we have to make a move soon."

"Don't rush this. That's how people get killed," Olivia insisted, closing her eyes for a moment. Then she remembered something. Something important. Her eyes snapped open.

"Give me a day. I have someone I need to talk to."

CHAPTER FIFTEEN

THE PERSON SHE WAS HOPING TO SPEAK TO WAS CHARLIE Evans, and she'd been waiting on a call from Jonathan. She knew it could come in at any moment, but when her phone rang and she saw the call was coming from an anonymous number, Olivia frowned. Suddenly she was glad to be alone if it turned out to be Paxton calling back. Henry had dropped her back at her room after their trip to Richard Greene's home, and she was chomping at the bit to know if Paxton already had some information for her.

"Hello?" Olivia said quietly as she picked up the call. She didn't want Henry to hear her talking again, especially when one of the subjects of conversation would undoubtedly be Henry himself. Then he would definitely question her about the whole thing.

But the voice on the other end of the line surprised her.

"Olivia?"

"Blake?" Olivia frowned.

Olivia only knew Supervisory Special Agent Blake Wilder through Paxton, despite both working for the Bureau. They'd come together on a case recently to help rescue Paxton after he'd recklessly plunged headfirst into the organization that he'd discovered was responsible for Veronica's death. Olivia didn't know her well at all, but she respected Blake. She was the kind of strong, capable, fearless agent Olivia wanted to become. Blake's recent takedown of a far-ranging conspiracy that netted several high-profile government officials had turned her into one of the FBI's brightest stars. And it made Olivia respect her even more.

"What's going on, Blake?"

"Pax gave me an update on what's going on," she started. "I'm sorry about Brock. I don't know him well, but we worked together once or twice back when I was stationed in New York a while back. Good guy and a hell of an agent. I didn't realize the two of you were partners."

"Thanks. I appreciate that," replied Olivia. "But I don't get the feeling this is a social call."

Blake let out a soft chuckle. "Intuitive as ever."

Despite the first impression they'd had that had left Olivia feeling pretty intimidated, she found herself grateful that Blake was reaching out. Just from her limited exposure to Blake, Olivia knew she had a tendency to be somewhat firm and blunt from time to time, but she had a genuine sense of empathy at her core that every agent needed. In a way, she was like a mix of Brock and Olivia herself.

"I have some information that you may find interesting," Blake said, "but it's absolutely imperative that you keep this completely under wraps."

Olivia nodded. Cloak and dagger seemed to be the way of things everywhere these days. "Sure. What do you have for me?"

"Well, Pax asked around, and wouldn't you know it, he struck up a conversation with my sister. And now he's got her running on the case, even when I *told* her not to…"

THE **LOCKED BOX**

Olivia hadn't ever met Blake's sister Kit, but she'd heard her name mentioned before. She wasn't sure of all the details, but knew that Kit had suddenly reappeared after a very long time of being thought dead. She'd heard that Kit had been trained as an elite spy and assassin by the Thirteen, the organization that Blake had just taken down. There were so many different stories and plots the Wilder sisters had been caught in that it sent Olivia's head spinning. What could Kit possibly know about ANH? Had she had dealings with them in her former life? Or did she have contacts across the international underworld that could help her dig a little deeper into the organization than even Pax could go? The fact that he'd pulled Kit into this, even though Blake had warned him not to, told Olivia there was a lot more going on there beneath the surface.

"It seems that Kit may have some information that might be of some help you," Blake went on. "I don't know what it is exactly, but she told me she has some contacts and leads she might be able to follow up on that might help you roll up some of ANH's network. She said she'll look into that for you."

"Oh my God, that would be amazing. Tell her thank you for me, please. We're really running out of options here, and I don't know where to turn."

Something about Blake's silence on the other end of the line felt a bit tentative.

"What is it?" Olivia prodded.

Blake let out a long sigh. "Alright. If we're doing this, I have some ground rules, okay?"

"Okay."

"Number one. She makes all of her contact with you remotely, and *she* contacts *you*—not the other way around. Two, I don't want her going undercover and infiltrating ANH in person. She can hack whatever she wants, and she can speak to whomever she wants on her burners, but she will absolutely *not* be going into a danger zone. Are we clear?"

"Absolutely. I wouldn't dream of asking more of her."

"Good. And my last rule is... if anything happens to her, you're going to answer to me. If this blows back on my family in any way, I will *never* forget it. Am I clear?"

Olivia was taken aback by the sudden edge in Blake's voice, but she understood. "Crystal. Look, I just need her to pass along the information for me. I'm on the ground here in England, and I can take the rest from there. I promise I'll do everything I can to keep her out of the line of fire on this."

A long moment of silence passed before Blake finally sighed. "You're right. I'm sorry for getting heated. It's just that... Kit is all I have. After so many years living in the shadows, I finally have her back in my life. She's finally able to live out in the open again. And I don't want to put her in danger. I won't. Not for you, not for the FBI, not for anyone."

"I understand completely. I would feel the same about my sister."

Blake let out a soft chuckle at that. Olivia had forgotten that she, too, had been close to Veronica.

"You two are a lot alike, you know," Blake said.

"I've been hearing that a lot lately," Olivia replied. "I just hope she's proud of me, wherever she is."

"You know she is. Honestly, back in the day, she never shut up about how brilliant you were."

"Really?"

"Really. Always bragging about you. She always used to tell me that once you got older and a little more experienced that you'd run circles around her."

Olivia let out a quiet, sad laugh, still trying not to disturb Henry next door. She didn't want to admit to him yet that she might have some leads through Kit or Blake. She didn't want him poking around until she was sure she could trust him, and she didn't think that would be anytime soon.

"Alright. So, I guess this is going ahead," Blake said, snapping their attention back to the situation at hand. Olivia could hear the anxiety in her voice, and she felt a pang of guilt. She silently vowed to herself that she wouldn't ask Kit to do anything if it wasn't necessary. But it wasn't just about Brock anymore. Yes, her priority was saving him. Yes, she wanted him to make it home safe. But she also had to think about all the lives that ANH was ruining. They were casting a shadow over the world, causing hopelessness and addiction and grief in their destructive wake. Olivia couldn't stand by and watch that happen, and she didn't believe that Blake or Kit could either. They all felt a sense of duty to the ordinary people who were unable to protect themselves. Whether they liked it or not, they had to do the hard tasks that no one else was up for. That no one else could do.

Even if that meant making personal sacrifices.

"It's going to be okay," Olivia assured Blake.

Olivia paused for a moment, thinking about her own family. She thought of her mother and the strange words she'd said to her as she sent her off to England. *Aurora Nova… The New Dawn.* Those words had never truly made sense to Olivia, but now, she felt drawn to them. What if it meant something to someone else? Maybe Kit could decipher what it meant. If she could, then it would be another mystery solved out of the thousands that Olivia seemed to be tangled up in.

"Blake? Can I ask you a favor?"

Blake was quiet for a moment. "Other than loaning out my sister?"

"Well, yes."

"It depends on what it is. I think we might have already reached our quota of serious favors though."

"It's just something I thought of in passing. I spoke to my mom the day before I came to England. She said something to me… the words *Aurora Nova*. I looked it up, and apparently, it means—"

"New Dawn," Blake finished for her. Olivia's heart throbbed a little harder. Either Blake was more familiar with Latin than she was, or she knew something about what those words meant.

"Do you think you could pass the phrase on to Kit when you speak to her? I don't know how useful it might be, but my mom has been working a case with the Bureau for a long time that might somehow connect to this one. If that's the case, then perhaps it's a code word for something. I don't know. Maybe Kit will understand better than I do."

"I'm actually…" Blake paused as though trying to figure out how to word it. "I actually think this might be more of Pax's domain."

"What do you mean?"

"It might be a bit tough to explain," Blake replied. "He would be the one to talk to though. I'll be sure to get it to him."

Olivia felt a little bad that she was asking so much of Blake when they barely knew each other. But she knew she was willing to do anything necessary to find Brock. She'd already caused a ruckus. A little more wouldn't do any more harm.

"Thank you for this, Blake. I know I'm asking a lot of you."

"Anytime," Blake said. "But you should know that I'm not doing this for free. You owe me now. And Kit. If we need you for anything, at any time, you'll come running. Understood?"

The thought made Olivia a little uneasy. She had no idea what she might be called on to do, and she didn't like the feeling of being so out of control. But she also knew that she owed Blake. She was putting her out of her comfort zone too. The least she could do was promise something in return.

"Alright. Understood. I promise," Olivia replied. A small chill ran down her spine, and she tried not to shiver. She didn't know Blake well, but Olivia knew she was a good person and a good agent with a sterling reputation, despite the tension in their phone call. Olivia was sure that whatever favor Blake called in wouldn't be a bad one and wouldn't compromise her in any way.

At least, she hoped.

"Good. Nice doing business with you," Blake said, sounding amused. "I guess Kit will be in touch. And like I said, if anything happens to her…"

"I know. You'll hold me responsible."

"Damn right I will. Good talk. See you around, Olivia. Be safe and good luck."

When Blake disconnected the call, Olivia let out a long sigh of relief. She was glad Blake had agreed to let Kit work with her. It

THE **LOCKED BOX**

wasn't easy to arrange, but at least she was on board. Now, all she had to do was hope that Kit could work a miracle for her.

CHAPTER SIXTEEN

BROCK FELT HANDS GRAB HIS SHOULDERS AS HE SLEPT. As he was yanked to his feet, it felt like he had been plucked directly from his dream and back into reality. As he was dragged roughly through the same concrete hallways as before, he tried to cling to the remnants of the dream he'd been having.

Olivia had been there. It was the first moment of reprieve he'd had from his nightmare scenario since he had arrived. In the dream, the two of them were walking along a beach, their hands locked in one another's. The wind was in her hair, and she looked as though she didn't have a care in the world. He could hear the gentle, shushing sound of the sea lapping on the shore, a sound he'd always found so calming.

THE **LOCKED BOX**

In the dream, Olivia was laughing at something he'd said, and it felt so real to him that he had known that it couldn't be. Happiness wasn't a part of his life any longer. That had been snatched away from him, and there was no chance he was getting it back... not when he knew what fate awaited him.

He had already escaped one beating, and he knew he wouldn't be so lucky this time. They'd tried to do things the easy way, and now it was time for the hard way. But Brock knew that no matter how hard they hit him, no matter how badly they broke and bruised his body, they still wouldn't get the outcome that they wanted. They wanted Walter to crack, to give in to their demands, but that wasn't going to happen. All that was going to happen was that Brock would be beaten until he bled, and then they'd send him back to his cell wondering why the hell he wouldn't talk to them.

Brock had no desire to give up his grandfather anyway, but even if he did, what could he possibly tell ANH that they didn't already know? Anyone keyed into the chatter of the military-industrial complex knew about the top-secret, automated weapon drone project that McCall Defense Corporation had been working on. It was highly delicate information, but the rumors had taken hold.

ANH clearly wanted that technology for themselves, either to exercise dominion over their own holdings or auction it off to the highest bidder—and they'd clearly been hoping that Brock would be the crucial negotiating chip in giving up the technology.

And he'd never do that.

Brock was collateral damage, but he was so much more than that. He wasn't on either side. He didn't support either of them. And yet somehow, that made him the villain on both sides. ANH hated him for not giving up information that he didn't even know. His grandfather hated him for ever leaving his side.

Losers can never win, Brock thought to himself.

His lagging eyes were desperate to pull him back into sleep and into that beautiful dream, but that was never going to happen. Not when his body was being tossed around like a sack of potatoes. He didn't know how far they dragged him through the corridors of their compound, but it was a relief when they stopped, even if only for a minute.

The trouble was, Brock knew it would only get worse from there.

He was tied to a chair in the dimly lit room by the goons who had dragged him there. Brock wondered if the old man who'd interrogated him would come and get his hands dirty, but he doubted it. He was old and frail, built for cunning plans rather than severe beatings. Besides, he didn't want to give that man the satisfaction of watching him crumble.

Because he would. How could he not? He had nothing to give these people. Gritting his teeth and trying to power through wouldn't change the fact that they were going to beat him to a pulp. By the time they were done with him, his body and soul would be crushed into dust. There was nothing that could save him from that fate.

But he forced himself to keep a level face as he waited for the first punch to land. There were several hulking, brutish thugs in the room—all of them watching him in amusement. No doubt they would take turns getting their hands bloody. Brock let a small laugh escape him, though nothing about this was funny.

"Just don't go for my face, okay? Let's keep me looking pretty," Brock said, but his heart wasn't in the joke. There was nothing to laugh about anymore.

He watched as one of the men set up a video camera in front of the chair, and Brock immediately understood what was about to happen. First, they'd hit record and torture him, beating him senseless and hoping he'd beg for mercy. Then they'd send the recording off to Walter, hoping that it might sway his decision. When that didn't work, they'd switch up their tactics. Maybe they'd chop a few fingers off and send them in the mail. They'd start doing things to Brock that couldn't be fixed. And eventually, when his grandfather still refused to do their bidding, they'd put a gun to his head and finish him off.

Brock wanted so desperately to close his eyes and return to his dream. He just wanted to see Olivia's face again. She felt so far away now that it felt impossible that he'd ever see her for

THE **LOCKED BOX**

real again. And if he did, would it be the same? He'd be different. Scarred by the things he'd seen and the things that had happened to him.

Between the two of them, he was the one who had mostly walked through life unscathed. Now that he was about to become damaged goods, how could he be the same as he once was? How could he still be the person that Olivia leaned on? He used to be so strong, but now, as he was preparing to feel the force of a thousand fists on his face, he couldn't be that man anymore.

The red light on the camera blinked on, and one of the thugs, a tall, heavy man, walked toward Brock. The man's face was wide and looked like one of those red-faced soccer hooligans. It took everything inside him not to make some cutting remark.

The worst part was the waiting. He knew he was about to hurt. He knew his life was about to fall apart. But not knowing exactly when the pain would begin was a form of torture in itself.

"Tell your grandpa to give up his weapons for us," the goon growled at Brock in a thick accent. Brock looked directly into the camera, hoping that the fear didn't show on his face. If it was the last thing he did, he wouldn't look weak in front of his grandfather.

"No."

The first punch knocked his face sideways. Brock grunted as the force of it almost sent the chair toppling over. It hurt, but he could handle it, for now. He knew how pain could stack though. The next punch would only hurt more than the first because it was layered on top of the pain he already had to endure. And with each time they hit him, his resolve would weaken a little more.

"Wrong answer," the thug snarled at Brock. "You don't want to mess about with us, agent. We'll beat you to a bloody pulp."

"Oh, of that I have no doubt," Brock murmured. "But the thing is, there's nothing I can do about it, and there's nothing you can do that will get information out of me. I don't have what you want."

"We'll be the judge o' that," the thug fired back with a grin that revealed a gold tooth. His second punch knocked the wind out of Brock as it pummeled into his stomach. Around him, the other goons were laughing at him, taunting him. Brock gritted his teeth. Only two punches in and he already felt like he was going to be sick.

"You're making a mistake," the goon told Brock. "You think this little act o' yours will make us give in? There's not a chance. We'll beat you 'til you tell us *something*. And if you don't, at least maybe this video will make yer granddaddy think twice. But how much are you worth to him? What I heard, he don't care at all. Else wouldn't 'e 'ave given us what we want by now?"

Brock closed his eyes. He didn't need to be reminded of how little he meant to his family. Walter saw him as a disgrace for leaving him and the company behind. When he had chosen to walk away all of those years ago, he was seen as wasted potential, as a traitor to his own family. He'd been entirely cut off. And now, it didn't matter how much he was hurting. Walter would allow him to suffer. Perhaps he thought that by the time this was over, they'd be equal.

The third punch smashed into Brock's nose, and he grunted hard, feeling something snap. A fourth and fifth came quickly afterward in the same spot, and he nearly gagged. Blood trickled from his nostril and over his lip, but he couldn't even move to wipe it away. The blood was coming harder now, spilling into his mouth, almost choking him on the metallic taste.

The men around him continued to jeer and egg his assailant on. Brock wished that he had his hands free, that he'd been given a chance to fight. He was certain that if his hands were free, he could make mincemeat of the man standing in front of him—the coward who was attacking a man who couldn't even fight back.

"Got anything to say to us yet?" Gold Tooth asked, but he didn't wait for a response before he plowed his fist into the other side of Brock's face. *At least the bruises will match on both sides now,* Brock thought to himself bitterly.

The next punches came hard and fast to his gut and his chest. Brock felt like he might throw up from the pain, glad all of a sudden that they'd made him weak with hunger. He had nothing left to throw up anyway.

There was a momentary lapse of relief when Gold Tooth stepped back to egg on his audience, coaxing them to cheer him

THE **LOCKED BOX**

on. Brock managed to steady himself enough to stop his vision from blurring momentarily. His eyes found the camera. How would Walter feel seeing him like this? Would he pity him? Or would he think he deserved it?

"Who has a bet on how long he'll last?"

The men began clamoring out, desperate to get their bets in first. Brock felt sick to his stomach.

"I thought the British were polite people," he mumbled to himself, though his lips were slick with his own blood. These people were crazy. They were taking pleasure in watching him get beat up like they were watching a boxing fight. Except in a boxing match, both men could use their fists.

Well… if they wanted a show of action, then maybe Brock could turn the situation in his favor...

Brock spat blood out of his mouth to the side of him and stared up at the man with malice in his gaze. He had so much hate stored up inside him at that moment that he felt capable of doing anything. He wished he could pummel his fists into the man in front of him. Brock wasn't usually a violent person, but these people seemed to bring out the worst in him.

"Do you really think you're so tough? Punching a guy repeatedly when he can't fight back?" Brock snarled. His voice could barely be heard over the raucous laughter around him, but he continued to strain to be heard. "You think I couldn't kick your ass if I had my hands free?"

Some of the other men began to laugh harder, but this time, it was at the man attacking him. His face turned red with anger, and Brock knew that he'd gotten under his skin. He snarled at Brock, baring his teeth.

"You're not in a position to talk back to me," Gold Tooth hissed. Brock managed a caustic laugh.

"Why shouldn't I? What do I have to lose?"

"Shut up!"

"Fight me if you dare," Brock spat, his eyes alight with fury. "If you think you've got the guts, let's make this a fair fight. I win, you let me go back to my cell."

The men in the room seemed excited by the idea. It was a lifeline for Brock, a way out of the misery they were putting him through. Of course, the goon was too dumb not to fall for it. He didn't want his pride to be hurt by their prisoner. He was sure he would win. So, he nodded to one of the other men.

"Unbind him," he said with a wolfish smile. "And then we'll see who's really boss 'round here."

The men around the room cheered as they untied Brock. He felt hope in his heart. He was sure he could win the fight. After all, this is what he'd trained for his entire life. He glanced briefly at the camera, knowing that if he lost then his humiliation would be sent to his grandfather for him to watch. And he couldn't bear that thought at all.

Which was why he had to win.

As Brock was allowed to stand up, he felt the pain in his body putting him off balance. He was still a little winded, and his face was aching. He could barely see because of the pain, but he could see enough to take down Gold Tooth once and for all.

"Show us what you've got then," Gold Tooth said, grinning at him. Brock knew not to make the first move. He would wait him out. He put his fists up like a boxer, ready to block any attack that came his way.

And when his opponent threw the first punch, he went in for the kill.

Ducking beneath his fists, he thrust an elbow into Gold Tooth's stomach. He heard the wind get knocked from him, and he didn't wait around for him to catch it. Aiming from underneath, he sent a series of quick rolling blows to his stomach. Gold Tooth snarled and lunged forward at him, but Brock stepped to the side and put a knee right into the man's ribs.

The crowd was whooping and heckling now, and it wasn't lost on Brock that he'd have to defeat not only Gold Tooth, but the rest of them in there as well, if he wanted a chance to escape. But escape where? He assumed he was in England, given the men's accents, but he had no idea where on Earth he could possibly be otherwise.

THE **LOCKED BOX**

Gold Tooth got up and reset his fists. He managed to land a glancing blow that Brock only barely deflected onto his shoulder with a block. He grunted and tried to yank his hand back, but then Brock saw his chance.

Before the goon could even react, Brock darted low and landed another punch square into the man's chest—and then he reared back his fist into an uppercut right into his throat. He punched him so hard that he watched, almost in slow motion, as Gold Tooth was lifted off the ground, his mouth agape in shock, blood flying from his battered gums. And then Gold Tooth was no more as the accessory went flying from his mouth and across the room.

The man lay on his back, and the room fell silent. Brock knew that he'd made a mistake. He had defeated him too fast. It was an act of humiliation, and Gold Tooth was never going to let that fly. As he sat up slowly, groaning, he glared at Brock in horror. He was breathing hard, his eyes full of fire.

He wanted Brock dead.

But he'd settle for the next best thing, that Brock was sure of. They'd made a deal, but a deal among criminals was never set in stone. He watched in horror as the other men around the room began to silently advance on him, their circle closing in on him. They were there to protect their legacy, to protect their fellow henchmen, and that meant Brock was dead meat.

He could try to fight his way out, but when he looked around, he saw that there were at least ten men and only one of him. He was grossly outnumbered, and now, he'd poked the bear. They were all angry with him. He'd been too good, and now he was going to pay the price for it.

"Make sure he pays," Gold Tooth snarled. "Make sure he hurts."

One of the men lunged at Brock, and he managed to fend him off with a swift kick to the groin, but the others charged all at once. Brock tried to regain his footing and land a punch, but even as his knuckles grazed one of the men's chins, he felt someone grab him around the middle and tackle him to the floor.

Brock felt all of the air go out of him as his back hit the floor. Before he could even register the pain, a foot kicked him hard in the ribs.

And so, the onslaught began. Brock tried not to cry out as they all zoned in on him, beating him senseless until he could do nothing but close his eyes and pray for it to be over. He kept his arms wrapped around his already beaten face, so his ribs took the worst of it.

And when it was all over, they dragged him away again. He didn't fight. He didn't beg for mercy. He just let it happen to him. What choice did he have? All of his choices had long since been taken away from him. Now, all he had was one last shred of dignity to hold on to. He told himself that at least he had fought hard and fought bravely. At least he wasn't completely broken yet.

When he was alone in his cell at last, he closed his eyes and saw Olivia's face again. He smiled and allowed himself to be tugged under by the sight of her, by the joy of seeing her face one last time.

It was the best he was going to get.

CHAPTER SEVENTEEN

"I NEED TO TALK TO HIM TODAY."

"I've pushed for it, Knight, I promise. But he said he doesn't want to talk," Jonathan told her. "And the DA won't approve any deals for half of a hunch."

Olivia scrunched her eyes closed in frustration. The one person that she wanted to speak with was thousands of miles away in an American prison, trying to figure out a way to play her, and it was driving her crazy. She knew that Charlie Evans would only be willing to talk to her if he thought he could get something in return. But what did she have to offer him? She'd already squeezed as much leverage as she could when dealing with the murder of Darcie Puckett, and somewhere across the ocean, the former CEO of Infinity was laughing at her, fully aware that he had all the power.

"Is there nothing we can do? I just need... I need ten minutes to speak with him. I'm sure I can get something out of him."

"Olivia, he's barely even been in prison for a couple weeks. He doesn't care about what you want to talk about. He's not feeling the strain yet, and he knows he's getting nothing out of it. You knew it was a long shot when you requested to talk to him."

"He knows things—I just know it. These drug connections... the Grim Reaper, the cult of Apep, the *Astoria*... they're all related. And I'm almost certain now that his supplier had to be connected to ANH... so if Evans would just—"

"He doesn't know where Tanner is, Knight. You need to keep your focus. Leave ANH to Caine."

Olivia rubbed her forehead. Henry was still sitting beside her in the car, waiting for her to get somewhere with her chat with Jonathan, but she knew now that it wasn't going to happen. She had tried and failed. Charlie Evans was never going to give her what she wanted, and neither were any of the other crooks she'd dealt with. Why would they, when she had sent them to prison for life? Why would they, when she was fighting people like them, and they were waiting to watch their buddies rise to the top?

"Alright," Olivia said quietly. She hung up the call before Jonathan could say anything else, feeling defeated. She'd needed to get that call with Evans. It was her one hope of solidifying the connections she'd made.

But she wouldn't get another shot now.

"Hey," Henry said, his tone a little softer than usual. "You did what you could."

"It's not enough," Olivia snapped, her fists clenched. "Brock is counting on me. Have you ever had someone rely on you to save their life? Do you even *have* any friends? Are you even capable of caring about anything or anyone besides yourself?"

Olivia knew she'd gone too far, but she didn't say sorry. If Henry was unapologetic all the time, then she could be too. Henry didn't seem to take the comment to heart anyway. He just sighed and shrugged in his usual manner, unfazed.

THE **LOCKED BOX**

"There isn't much you can do to change things now. You should let it go."

But Olivia couldn't. As they tried to draw up a plan of action together in Henry's stuffy little car, Olivia couldn't stop thinking about Charlie. She knew his resistance to having an interview with her had to mean more than just being petty. If he really was involved with ANH, then he would be scared to talk. If only she could find some way to offer him protection, but that hadn't worked out so well in the past for her. In the past year, she'd already lost a few people in prison after they agreed to talk to her. That wasn't going to encourage Evans, or anyone, to talk to her.

And time was slipping away from her far too quickly. She didn't have time to linger on the past. They had to figure out how to infiltrate ANH without getting Brock—and themselves—killed. And what's more, Olivia wasn't even sure she could trust the man sitting beside her. It was making her impossible task seem even more impossible.

They headed back to their B&B in the afternoon when it became clear that they weren't getting anywhere, and Olivia wanted to pick up her laptop. That was when Henry declared that he had to make some calls and disappeared for half an hour, leaving Olivia wondering what he was being so secretive about. She had hoped he might stay in his room so that she could eavesdrop on him, but he seemed to know better now since he'd taken his call outside. It made Olivia's skin crawl. Why would he do that if he had nothing to hide? She saw no reason for them to have secrets from each other if they were working together, and Henry's loner act was getting old. No, she was certain there was more to it. She was starting to believe more and more that Henry was up to something. Something that might derail the case and keep her from rescuing Brock.

She'd kept Richard's notebook close, wanting to be in charge of it rather than Henry. She didn't need him having extra time to study it. She flipped through the pages some more and researched some of the locations that had been mentioned in the book, but it didn't give her much more than she already knew. The problem now wasn't finding them. It was making their move without getting everyone killed.

She pored over it again, frustrated at the lack of progress. Things were piling up now—the disappearance of Gareth Dean, one of Richard's colleagues, meant that the police were too busy following up those leads to be truly useful in assisting on the ANH side of things. She mapped out each location Richard had listed and even tried to find satellite imagery of the locations, but it seemed that they were all legit places from ANH's public properties.

It wasn't quite a miracle, but a breakthrough came for Olivia later that evening when her phone rang. She glanced at the display and saw it was coming from an unknown number. Her heart leaped in her chest. Could this already be the information from Kit? Or could it be Paxton with news of his own?

She glanced at the wall separating her room from Henry's and knew that she'd have to take the call elsewhere. She saw the irony in that when she was so suspicious of him, but if Pax had any dirt on him, then she couldn't risk him overhearing what she had to say.

Olivia pulled on a jacket and left her room as quickly as she could, picking up the call just before it stopped ringing.

"Hello?" she whispered down the line. "Agent Knight speaking."

"Hey! I thought you were going to leave me hanging!" came an animated voice with a laugh that surprised Olivia. She didn't recognize the voice but knew it had to be none other than Kit Wilder. From everything she'd heard about the woman and her long life on the run from dark forces and doing darker things, Olivia wasn't expecting her to sound so… peppy.

"Sorry, just trying to get someplace quiet. How… how are you?"

"Never better," Kit said. "Recovering from a coma isn't all fun and games, but you know. It is what it is. To be honest, though, I wouldn't trade places with you right now. I'm sorry to hear about your friend. These guys are the worst."

"Thanks," Olivia said, stepping out of the B&B and into the cold parking lot. She wrapped her arms around her midsection, preparing herself for whatever Kit had in store for her. "I guess I'll feel better if you've managed to find something."

"Well, strap in tight because I'm about to send you on one hell of a roller coaster," Kit said. Her words were light, but her tone had changed, and Olivia got the sense that Kit was disturbed by whatever she had found. Olivia knew that ANH was capable of a lot of bad things, but she'd been spared the goriest details. Now, she was sure she was going to learn about the darkest side of their operations.

"I should warn you… I don't have any direct leads on your friend Brock. Not yet, at least. But I did learn a lot of things about these guys that are likely to be kept completely under wraps. I'm hoping that what I'm about to tell you might help you build a case against them and maybe help you to bring them down."

Olivia was a little disappointed Kit had no leads on Brock. But she reminded herself that Kit hadn't been digging into everything for very long. She was just grateful that Kit could help her at all, especially so quickly. Kit took a deep breath on the other end of the line, so deep that Olivia almost felt it herself.

"Okay. So, I managed to get in touch with an old contact who used to… let's say, they've done some contract work on and off for ANH. Unofficially speaking."

"Unofficially." Olivia nodded. She had been expecting something like that and wasn't sure how to feel about it. But Olivia knew she couldn't afford to be picky when it came to Kit's underworld contacts.

"So, as I'm sure you know, ANH keeps up a pretty robust public face. They have a massive network of legit operations, major contracts with international corporations and various foreign governments, as well as a huge fleet of actual container ships. They run a very big and very profitable shipping company, but by now you've certainly figured out that it's all a cover for a huge international crime syndicate."

"It's been hard finding evidence, but there's way too much smoke for there not to be fire," Olivia concurred. "I've been tracking a number of shipments of some sort of super-drug as they've crossed into the United States from my previous cases, and I have reason to believe that all of it originates from—or is at least centrally facilitated through—ANH. I don't know what it is, but these drugs they've been pushing are like nothing I've ever seen..."

"According to my contact, the drugs first came on the scene around ten years ago," Kit told her. "ANH has access to several pharma laboratories they use to experiment and create all sorts of drugs, including these ones that they've started pushing. I think they finally perfected the formula in the last year or two. And these drugs act as almost a rudimentary form of brainwashing for whomever takes them."

"That's exactly it," Olivia replied. "They become suggestible. Erratic. Addicted. Almost mind-controlled. These drugs make them act completely out of character. I saw a police officer once succumb to those drugs, and she was almost immediately brainwashed into joining a dangerous cult."

Kit made a sound of agreement. "My contact tells me that's exactly how they're used. They keep the grunts in line and the authorities off their trail with those drugs. That's how they've gone under the radar for so long."

Olivia was pacing around the parking lot, feeling sick to her stomach. It once again occurred to her how much bigger this whole thing was than just saving Brock. ANH was destroying people's lives all over the world. The drugs seemed to be taking as many lives as the guns they sold. These drugs they were creating were deadly, and they didn't even care. They were even experimenting on their own people.

"It's sick," Olivia murmured. Kit sighed.

"You've got that right. But there's so much more to ANH than just the drugs. They're supplying weapons all over the world, selling to both sides in war zones, getting their smaller weapons into countries where guns are illegal. You've probably already seen it yourself, but Britain is facing its biggest gun crime crisis in years. ANH does not play around. And that's why you probably won't be surprised by what I'm going to tell you next."

"That can't be good," Olivia muttered.

"Now, look. I've seen some pretty horrible things in my time. I've done some things I'm not proud of. But this is some of the worst I've ever seen. So just… prepare yourself."

Olivia's heart was hammering against her chest as she waited patiently for Kit to start talking. She sounded like she was preparing herself on the other end of the line, taking big, steadying breaths.

"So, as part of these trials they've been pushing on their people—and as part of their vast network—they've… well, you can imagine the things they've done. But not even I was aware of the scale."

"Meaning?"

"Meaning that ANH doesn't just kill an informant or traitor here and there. When they've been experimenting with these drugs or deciding that their employees are more trouble than they're worth, they make them just disappear. And I'm talking about hundreds of people in the last few years alone. Transients, poor people, immigrants… the kind of people who can disappear and nobody will even notice. They're… disposable people."

"Jesus," Olivia muttered. It reminded her of the way Lomtin Labs had disposed of its test subjects. And that organization had killed her own sister for trying to expose the truth. Yet again, she felt Veronica's presence pushing her forward on this case.

"Yeah. And here's the worst part of it," Kit went on. "I suspect that ANH understands the need to isolate their people from the rest of the world, to ensure they're not missed when they disappear off the face of the earth. But they have to go somewhere, right? The bodies of all these dead people have to be put somewhere. And according to my sources… there may be a mass grave right on your doorstep."

Olivia felt her jaw drop. Her mind went dizzy, and her skin was crawling. "What are you talking about?"

"I'm talking about a place where all these people have been buried. Where the bodies have been dumped for years. Bodies upon bodies upon bodies. I even have a set of coordinates that I can give you. If it turns out to be correct… then you're about to stumble across more evidence against ANH than the authorities can dream of. But it's risky. ANH is still using it as a burial ground, so you might run into trouble while you're there. I don't know if it's a lead to find your friend… but this is the best I could find right now. And all I was able to get was the location. I don't know about how it's guarded or what other operations they have onsite there. For all I know, this place could be a fortress."

"I understand," Olivia said. "But we need this. If we can prove a connection between the mass grave and ANH as an organization, perhaps we can get the support for a big operation against them. The only chance of getting Brock out is to catch them off guard, make sure they're in complete chaos. This could be the moment we've been waiting for."

"Agreed. So, I'm guessing you want the location?"

"Yes. Absolutely."

Kit read out the coordinates for Olivia. Not having a sheet of paper handy, she wrote them down awkwardly on her hand for later.

"Thank you. Thank you, thank you, thank you," Olivia said earnestly. "This could level the playing field for us."

"Anytime. I'll reach back out if I can find anything else that might be useful. But I called in a lot of favors for this one, and this is about all I could find. I hope it helps."

"It really will. I can't thank you enough."

"I'm glad to have helped. One last thing before I go… um, actually, Pax is going to take this one."

"Pax?" she frowned. There was a rustling on the other end of the line, and then her brother-in-law's voice came through.

"Hey, Olivia. It's about your new friend from MI5."

"Hey! Do you have anything good?"

Pax sighed. "I could barely find a thing. Even had to look in some pretty dark corners, but the guy seems clean. No one seems to have any dirt on him. But that doesn't mean you should trust him. I've studied up on this guy, and all I've found is that he's worked alone ever since his partner died on a job seven years ago."

Olivia's eyebrow raised. That was something she didn't know. "How did they die?"

THE **LOCKED BOX**

"No suspicious circumstances, apparently, and foul play wasn't suspected. But I have to imagine that having a partner die changes a person. Especially since he was a young agent at the time. But in the files I read, his performance reviews have all said no one has been able to get close to him since. It's a red flag for me, and I'd say that means you shouldn't trust him. He apparently doesn't know how to be part of a team, and one comment that stood out was that he displays an attitude that says if you're not with him, you're against him. So, keep that in mind and be careful with this guy."

Olivia chuckled. She was more than familiar with that attitude from the man already.

"I will. Thanks again, Pax."

"Of course. But now I have a question for you," he pressed. "Where the hell did you hear the name Aurora Nova?"

Olivia was taken aback by that. She hadn't been expecting the phrase to be so relevant to Paxton of all people. "It's... it's something my mother said. Right before I left. I've been thinking it might have to do with the case that she worked on for years, or maybe this one. I don't know."

Paxton let out a breath. "Before... Before Veronica died, she worked with a hacker by the name of Brian Takahashi. He was helping her take down Lomtin Labs. He was killed before I could get much information from him. But before he was killed, he told me the name of the group that had killed her..."

"Aurora Nova," Olivia whispered at the same time as Paxton said it.

"I don't know if they're connected. I don't know how this all ties together. All this time, I've been thinking it was just a codename for what Lomtin were doing. But this has to be bigger. If this is the same group..."

"I know," was all Olivia could manage to say. "I'll do whatever I can."

"Thank you," Pax said, emotion coloring his voice. "We'll be in touch if we can find anything else that might help you. Be careful out there."

"I appreciate that. Thank you."

"Good luck."

The call ended, and Olivia slid her phone back into her pocket. It was so much to process all at once that it was nearly overwhelming. But she didn't have time to dwell on that. For now, she had to follow the clues where they led her. She read the coordinates on her hand then found a piece of paper and jotted them down before her hand got sweaty and smeared the ink. It had to be worth checking it out. She needed a lead of some sort to work with, and this seemed like a good place to start.

The air seemed to turn colder as Olivia headed back toward the B&B. It took her a moment to realize why.

As she looked up, she saw Henry staring down at her from the window of his room, watching her like a hawk.

CHAPTER EIGHTEEN

BROCK LAY ON HIS SIDE IN HIS CELL, TRYING NOT TO FOCUS on all of the bruises blossoming on his skin. It had been an hour since the punches stopped landing, since they'd turned off the camera and sent the video off to Walter. Now, it was a matter of waiting.

A failed call to Walter had resulted in, what the head of ANH liked to call, "desperate measures." They wanted Walter to see Brock beaten and hurt, hoping it might change his mind about working alongside them. After all, Brock was his only grandson, and they were sure that Walter would hate to see him suffer. They were sure that seeing him beaten would be enough to sway his stance.

But they didn't know Walter like Brock did.

He closed his eyes. The bruises on his body hurt, but not half as much as the knowledge that his grandfather cared more about his company than he did about him. Of course, Brock didn't *want* Walter to do ANH's bidding. Of course, he didn't *want* his grandfather's moral compass to sway toward evil.

But he also didn't want to be lying half dead in a cell, wondering why he wasn't good enough to change his own grandfather's mind.

The pain wouldn't go away. It was like an itch he couldn't scratch. They'd offered him no painkillers, so Brock was forced to just lie there—nose crooked, jaw bruised, ribs cracked—and come to terms with the fact that life wasn't going to get any better for him from this point on. It was only destined to get worse.

The one small mercy was that Olivia hadn't found him yet. That meant she was safe, at least for now. In some ways, he hoped that she wouldn't make it to him in time. He didn't want to throw her into the firing line. He didn't want her to suffer the way he had. Olivia had suffered more than enough for one lifetime anyway. All he prayed for was that she would live, even if he didn't.

He shifted his body and felt every part of him screaming out in pain. It was too much for him to bear. His stomach was empty and grumbling, his head was pounding, and his eyes were almost too tired to remain open.

And when he closed his eyes, hoping that sleep might take him away for a while, he fell into a reverie of the way his life had once been before.

Brock followed his grandfather through the factory, the loud whirring noises of heavy machinery already giving him a headache. The room was stuffy despite the high ceilings, on account of the fact that there wasn't a single window in the tin shack. And yet, Walter watched over the scene like a proud father, observing his workers as they tightened bolts and screws, micromanaged levers, and sliced heavy sheets of alloy into precise configurations for all manner of bullets, bombs, and guns.

"Someday," Walter told him, "this could all be yours."

THE **LOCKED BOX**

Brock forced a smile, but he didn't really see how this life was meant to appeal to him. At eighteen, he was just about to head off to college, and he was sure that his eyes would be opened by the things he saw there. This factory of death and destruction was just about the last thing he wanted.

"Just you wait," Walter said, sweeping his hand out in a grandiose manner. "Big things are coming in this world. You're too young to understand the scope of it, son, but you'll understand one day. This thing I'm doing here… it's going to make waves all over the country."

Brock nodded along, but he disagreed. How was it possible that a man selling weapons around the world could really be proud of his work? Guns in the hands of good men saved lives, but in the hands of bad men, they took them away—and these days, it seemed there were more bad men than good. Brock had never really understood why his grandfather was so proud to work in the weapons industry. He called it his patriotic duty… his mission to serve his country; but all Brock could tell was that it was just another way to get rich. They weren't even a major contractor with the Department of Defense—most of their work was contracted to agricultural manufacturers—but Walter McCall was only beginning to build his empire.

"You wait," Walter told him, almost as though he could read his grandson's mind. "Everything will be different then."

At twenty-one, things were different. Armed with a degree and a new outlook on life, Brock allowed his grandfather to guide him around one of his biggest factories. These places were different now. Gone was the cramped metal shack out in the middle of nowhere, and what had started as McCall Technologies now proudly boasted the name McCall Defense Corporation. The tall, bright room was airy and full of happy chatter from the workers, many of them veterans themselves who could no longer return to active military service but had been granted a second chance to serve their country. The operation was even bigger than Walter had promised, and as Brock walked around with his grandfather, he could taste the ambition in the air.

Brock had left college with only the desire for more. More of everything good: money, knowledge, power. He knew he was full of untapped potential, and he wasn't sure yet what he wanted to spend it on. But walking around his grandfather's factory, he was beginning to see what his life might become.

He could picture himself rolling in money the way his grandfather was, surrounded by pretty women who were happy to spend it for him. He could envision himself putting his feet up after a two-hour day at the office because his only job was to oversee the empire that his grandfather had already built. He could picture leaving behind the drudgery of daily life and replacing it with the life everyone craved, but few achieved. Brock was ambitious in the way that poorer folk couldn't afford to be.

His ambition was to have no ambition at all.

"What do you think?" Walter asked him with a curious smile. "A little different from our last visit, isn't it?"

"You built all of this from nothing," Brock said. There was a tinge of awe to his tone that he couldn't hide, and he didn't particularly want to. He wanted his grandfather to know he was proud of him. "I doubted that you could, but you did it anyway."

Walter laughed, clapping a hand onto his grandson's shoulder. "Well, if there's one thing I've learned from life, it's that people will always doubt what you can do. Then all you have to do is go ahead and do those things anyway. There isn't always going to be someone there to pat you on the back and say 'well done, kid.' Sometimes, you have to go ahead and just make your own success out of nothing. Got no magic beans? You can still grow a beanstalk."

Brock looked around and saw things he hadn't seen the first time. He saw how content the workers seemed to be. He saw how the space was wide open and not claustrophobic in any way. He knew that beyond the warehouses, there were offices filled with people who kept the show running, who had good salaries and holiday bonuses, who left work each day feeling satisfied. It didn't seem like such a bad way to live.

When he'd been younger, he'd had ambitions that stretched far beyond that kind of life. He wanted to travel the world, to speak five languages, to have a house in every country across the world.

And this was the middle ground. The comfortable life where he didn't need to work himself to the bone. Who needed to be ambitious when you had money?

THE **LOCKED BOX**

"Do you think you're ready to become a part of this?" Walter asked him. "Because if you are, I'll teach you everything I know. I'll raise you up to the top, and one day, when I'm gone, you can become the future of this company. You and I can make a lot of money together, son. What do you say? Does that sound good to you?"

In his dreamlike state, Brock realized that he wished he'd said no. He wished he'd walked away at that very moment. Things would have turned out very differently for him if he had. But in reality, he'd smiled. He'd nodded.

"I think I'd like that very much."

Walter grinned at him. "I knew you'd come around. You're just like me. You know what's good for you. Come on, then. Let's explore. I'll show you all the nooks and crannies. And one day, you'll show your own grandson how to play the game of business."

Brock was so caught up in the glamor of it all that he forgot his moral qualms. He forgot that what they really made was weapons to harm and kill others. He forgot how much he'd once cared about world peace. He forgot that there were more important things in the world than money.

And he left all his values behind.

When Brock woke from the dream, he almost felt like laughing at himself. How could he have been so foolish? How had he not seen the dark path he was going down? He was smarter than that. He wasn't stupid enough to truly believe that money would make his life perfect.

And yet, for a while, he'd lived in that fantasy. He'd trailed around after his grandfather, trying to make himself believe that he was building a brighter future for himself, paved by the lost lives that his grandfather's bullets ended.

He had tried to ignore the bigger picture of what he was involved in. He'd tried to justify it by saying MDC was defending their country and protecting their freedoms, but every time he said those words it felt like a lie. He'd tried to forget that his actions had consequences, that each time he sent a shipment off, someone—many someones—would lose a life because of the weapons he sold. And when his conscience finally kicked in and he began to realize what he was doing, it was already too late to save himself.

He had already caused so much death.

It was a long time ago, but the ache of his past was even stronger than the pain radiating inside his body from his beating. No matter how many years passed, he couldn't outrun the life he'd once lived. Everyone made mistakes, and he knew that.

It was just that some people's mistakes were bigger than others'.

CHAPTER NINETEEN

"**G**OING SOMEWHERE?"

Olivia had returned to her room to find that Henry was waiting for her, his arms crossed over his chest. Now, as she was readying herself for her excursion, he watched her packing a bag from the doorway.

"Yes."

"Are you going to tell me about it?"

Olivia chewed the inside of her cheek. The last thing she wanted to do was to take Henry with her. If he was under ANH's thumb, then he could have an ambush prepared for her there in no time. But she needed a ride there, and she also thought it was likely that she was going to need some help once she arrived.

"I've just spoken to a contact that I have who managed to get some inside information for us. She thinks that there is a mass grave not so far from here that is proof of the people that ANH has disposed of over the years. Informants, traitors, but also their guinea pigs—former workers that they experimented their drugs on. If it's true, we have a brand-new set of evidence against them and the means to launch a bigger attack on their company."

"Why is this the first I'm hearing about this contact?"

"I'm telling you now, aren't I?"

"And you've been keeping this a secret from me? Who is this contact? How do you know you can trust him?"

Olivia at least had the sense not to smile that Henry assumed the contact was a man.

"I'm not about to blow my informant's cover. We already have one dead informant on our hands. Maybe you should just trust me. You're not the only agent here who has a lot of experience in the field. I'm not giving away my contact's identity. Not after what happened to yours."

Henry raised an eyebrow at Olivia. "Alright, so what I'm hearing is that you're unwilling to give me any details, but you expect me to drive you to wherever you want in the middle of the night and do as you say, even though this is my case, not yours. Am I hearing this right?"

"Pretty much," Olivia shrugged, managing to keep the irritation out of her voice. "Grab a jacket, yeah? It's cold outside."

Henry looked desperate to roll his eyes at her, but after a moment's hesitation, he went back to his room and donned a coat. A few minutes later, the pair of them filed silently out to the car, and Olivia showed him the coordinates that she'd jotted down. They managed to figure out the location, which according to Henry's map was a large patch of farmland about ten miles away from where they were. He buckled his seatbelt.

"And we're off to the creepy field in the middle of nowhere then," he muttered with a yawn as he drove off. Olivia said nothing. She still didn't like the idea of Henry being there with her, but she was running out of time and out of choices. She couldn't exactly take a taxi out there alone and start digging around in the fields.

THE LOCKED BOX

No, she needed someone to back her up. Even if that person was a snake in the grass.

"You were out there on the phone for a long time," Henry commented, like he was pushing for some kind of confession from Olivia. She narrowed her eyes at him.

"Yes. I guess you noticed that since you were watching me. Haven't you got better things to do?"

"Well, I have to know that I can trust my partner. Can't have you sneaking around and keeping secrets from me, can I?"

You mean I can't act the same way as you do? Olivia thought to herself. *Slight double standards there, pal.*

But what she said was: "I brought you along, didn't I?"

"Reluctantly," he countered. "Is there something you're hiding from me, American? Because if so, I'd appreciate you letting me in on your secrets."

"I don't have any secrets," Olivia said firmly. *Apart from the fact that I think you might be a double agent, so I'm using a private eye to try and figure out who you really are... no big deal.*

"I guess I'll have to give you the benefit of the doubt," Henry said. "Not that you're leaving me much of a choice..."

"Well, you started it. You haven't given me a chance since the moment I got here. Why should I do the same for you?"

They spent the rest of the journey in silence, and with each passing moment, Olivia felt more unsure of the man sitting beside her in the driver's seat. If he was starting to suspect that she was suspicious of him, then it could be a complete disaster—yet another complication in their mission. She needed to keep on his good side, at least for a while longer. That was difficult, considering they'd never been on particularly good terms to begin with, but keeping him happy would at least buy her a little time. Both for herself and for Brock.

As they arrived at their destination, Olivia peered out the window. The field in question had very little in the way of landmarks. It was just plain, flat land that looked like no crops had grown there in a very long time. What particularly caught Olivia's attention was that there were large patches where no weeds had grown. It was just bare dirt that looked like it had been moved around recently. If there was something buried beneath the surface, she was sure to find it there.

Henry parked on the shoulder of the road, and they got out of the car. There wasn't another soul in sight, which wasn't surprising since it was past midnight now. Olivia hopped the distance between the road and the field, feeling the soft soil sinking a little beneath her shoes.

She kicked up a little dirt with her shoe anxiously, wondering what she might find buried beneath her feet. She needed the intel to be true, but that didn't mean she wanted it to be. How many people had lost their lives to this monstrous organization? How many of them had spent years hidden away here, buried beneath the surface where no one could find them?

Well, that was about to change.

"What's your plan here?" Henry asked, folding his arms as he looked down on her from his stance on the roadside.

"I hadn't thought that far," Olivia admitted. "We could dig around a little and see what we find, but it's not exactly subtle. And I don't know about you, but I don't carry a shovel around with me wherever I go."

"I might have something that can help."

Olivia waited patiently as Henry disappeared out of sight. She heard him open the trunk of the car, and then he seemed to wrestle with something heavy. When he came back into sight, he was carrying something that vaguely resembled a lawnmower; Olivia had seen one of them before, and it certainly wasn't used to cut grass.

"What the hell are you doing with a ground penetrating radar stowed in your car?"

Henry let out a low chuckle. "Let's just say that before you arrived, I was doing something similar at an abandoned warehouse. I was following up on one of my leads on the site that had burned to the ground a few days before. I got the kit from headquarters."

"Well, as much as I have more questions, we don't have time to make idle chitchat. Let's get started."

She allowed Henry to handle the equipment, knowing she had no clue how to make it work.

THE **LOCKED BOX**

He glanced around the field. "Where do you want to start?"

"Maybe we should start somewhere where the ground is looser, like it's been tampered with recently," Olivia told him. "We might even find someone who went missing recently."

"Makes sense. Take the lead. I'll follow where you go."

Olivia raised her eyebrows as she began to slowly walk through the grounds. "How generous of you."

"Don't get used to it. This is still my case. But this thing is heavy, and you wouldn't know how to use it if you tried. You're more useful for scouting."

"And here was me thinking you were being nice."

Olivia did as she was asked though. The least they could do was make a joint effort. She tested the ground that she was walking on. She had the same feeling that she did walking on the grass at graveyards… the knowledge that something beneath her was once alive made her legs feel like jelly. She'd seen plenty of dead bodies in her career, so she wasn't squeamish, but something about corpses beneath her feet didn't sit right with her.

"I think this has decided it for me. I want to be cremated," Olivia remarked. Olivia couldn't see Henry, but she heard him make a noise of agreement.

"Tell me about it. The sooner this is over, the better. This whole thing is giving me the creeps."

Olivia almost smirked. At least she knew that there was something out there that could ruffle Henry's feathers.

She tried to gauge his mood as they made their way through the field. He didn't tend to show much emotion at all, which made him hard to read, but she did feel as though he was a little uneasy. Was that because he was innocent of any crimes and he was simply uncomfortable walking over a potential mass grave? Or was he concerned that she was getting closer to the truth… closer to unearthing the organization that he had been working for?

No answers came to her, but she did find a patch of land that seemed like a good place to start.

"Here," she told Henry as he wheeled the equipment to the spot she'd chosen. He nodded and began to fiddle with the control pad on the screen that accompanied the trolley.

"They use these on archaeological digs," Henry said. "If we were looking for something living, we'd be looking for heat signatures. But since we're looking for bodies, it'll be a case of seeing what shapes we can decipher from the pictures."

"How many times have you done this?"

"A few. I used to have a real interest in archaeology. I guess I was kind of a nerd in my college days. I didn't really go out partying or making many friends. This is the kind of stuff I researched instead. I guess you could say I was a loner."

"And yet you turned out so great," Olivia said, a slight edge to her tone. She couldn't seem to help herself. He brought out the worst in her, and she seemed to do the same for him. It wasn't even the fun kind of banter. As pairings went, they were kind of toxic.

Henry didn't seem offended by her comment, but then again, he was always unreadable. Olivia thought of Brock, who never wore his true emotions on his sleeve, but he let the good ones slip through—when he was happy, she knew. When he was excited or pleased about something, it was always obvious; he was open with his struggles with mental health in a way that was downright refreshing compared to most men. Brock might not have liked to show her weakness unless she dug for it, but he was still much more expressive than Henry, whose face was always like a blank canvas. He could be elated on the inside, and you'd never know it.

Maybe that was why she found him so damn hard to trust. He gave nothing away at all, and it made her uncomfortable. No wonder she had suspicions. How could she not, when she seemed to collide with evil more than she did with good? So few people had good hearts. So few people were the kind she could rely on. Even her family had let her down many times in the past. So, it wasn't so strange that a man like Henry Caine could make her feel like he had something to hide.

But in that moment, he didn't seem to be conscious of her doubts. He was too busy working his machinery, frowning as it began to do its job. Olivia didn't know what she was looking for on the screen, but when he paused and took a closer look, he ushered her over to see what he was seeing.

THE **LOCKED BOX**

"I think there's something down there," he murmured, pointing at the grainy picture on the screen. "I think we should take a look at it."

"You mean we should dig?"

"I mean we should try. If there is a body down there, it could give us a lot of the answers we need. Are you afraid to get your hands dirty, American? It's not too deep down. I guess people don't have the time to dig a deep hole when they're ditching a body. And since no one has guessed what lies here anyway, maybe they don't need to."

Olivia felt uneasy about digging on her hands and knees for a skeleton, and yet it was the only option they had. They could call a team out there to do a larger dig, but they couldn't afford to attract ANH's attention.

"Okay. Let's give it a shot."

They began to dig. The earth was soft beneath their fingers, and it moved easily when they scraped away at it. Olivia could feel the dirt settling underneath her nails, a feeling she hated, but she kept pushing through. She didn't want to wait. She didn't want to come back later better prepared. She wanted answers, and she wanted them now.

But the worst part of it all was wondering *who* they might find. The grave was relatively fresh. What if she found Brock's dead eyes staring back up at her? She felt sick to her stomach as she dug like crazy, the earth flying up behind her like a dog trying to find a bone. She needed to know. She needed answers.

And then her nails scratched on something. Her skin went cold and her eyes met with Henry's. He took a deep breath and bent into the hole they'd dug, dusting off the thing they had found with his hand. His face turned pale.

"Oh boy."

Olivia stared down at the man in the hole. He was half decomposed, half still clinging to the likeness of the man he had been. To her relief, it wasn't Brock. To her dismay, it was someone else who could have been in his position. Someone who likely didn't deserve to be lying dead in an unmarked grave.

He could have been an informant, a traitor, a mole. He could have been a random victim of the super-drug, or an employee who started asking too many questions. And now here he was, buried beneath the surface with a bullet hole through his skull. Judging by the condition of his body, he couldn't have been there for more than two weeks, but it was long enough to distort the humanity of him.

"A quick death," Henry murmured as he examined the bullet hole. But something about the leftovers of the man seemed to make Olivia feel like his death hadn't been quick at all. Maybe he'd been tortured before they finally finished him. Maybe the bullet was a blessing to him in the end—a quick end to the suffering they had already put him through. It couldn't be counted as mercy when he was left to rot in a pit.

"There could be hundreds more like him here," Olivia murmured. And then her eyes fell upon something that she hadn't noticed before. A piece of plastic attached to the shirt, still shrouding the man's shrunken body. Olivia reached out and tugged it away, dirt falling away from it. Her eyes widened when she saw what it was.

"His name was Carl Armstrong," she whispered, turning the name badge to show Henry. "And he was an employee of ANH."

Neither of them was able to speak or breathe. This was the connection they'd been looking for. Dumping the bodies here had clearly been designated as grunt work, and they'd gotten sloppy. They'd never expected anyone to find the bodies there, that much was clear. After all, if Kit's intel was to be believed, they'd been using this burial site for years. So far, she'd been right.

And now, they had not only the identity of a man killed and buried there, but also solid proof that he was an employee of ANH. Nothing else mattered. Olivia knew this was going to be enough to prove that ANH was corrupt. She was too excited to even move, stunned into silence by their discovery.

Until they heard the car pulling up.

Olivia's head snapped toward the road. A Jeep was pulling up at the opposite end of the field where they'd left their car. Olivia

THE LOCKED BOX

felt sick. Who else would be here other than someone working for ANH?

And why would they come if they didn't have a body to toss?

"We need to get out of here," Olivia hissed at Henry. "We don't want to be caught."

"They're going to see us from a mile off," Henry replied, his eyes dark. "This flat land doesn't exactly have anywhere to hide. We're busted."

"Then what do you want to do?"

Henry took a gun out of his coat pocket and readied himself without a word. Olivia pulled her own gun from her hip, knowing they didn't have another option. And if they could take someone from ANH down, then perhaps they could get additional intel about where Brock was…

So long as he wasn't the body in the car.

Olivia and Henry crept closer to the parked car, hearing the two men inside talking in low voices. They were moving around to the trunk of the car, ready to unload their cargo. Henry moved so quietly that even Olivia could barely hear him next to her, so she didn't dare even breathe. They needed the element of surprise.

A moment later, they saw the two men lugging a corpse out of the car. Olivia couldn't tell in the dark if it was a man or a woman, let alone if it was Brock.

But she didn't have a chance to keep looking anyway, because one of the men turned on a flashlight, and despite their hiding in the grass, he immediately caught sight of them.

"Hey!" the man yelled. "Who the—"

Henry fired the first shot. It lodged in the leg of the man, and he howled, dropping the body. The other man dropped the legs of the body, too, and it tumbled down the embankment into the field.

And then chaos ensued. Henry fired another shot as the man with the wound hobbled to the other side of the car. The man still standing fired a shot that was so well aimed that it missed Olivia by just an inch, whizzing past her ear. With steady hands and steady aim, she shot for the man's chest, and he recoiled as it hit him, but he didn't go down. He clearly had some kind of protective vest on, and he didn't stick around to see if it would hold twice.

He and the other man were in the car and away before Olivia and Henry had the chance to stop them. Breathing hard, Olivia ran to where the body had dropped. She needed to see who it was. Could it be Brock? Could it be over?

She breathed out as she found the body lying limp at the edge of the field. It wasn't him. It was an older man, a perfect shot made between his eyes and a blank expression coming from his dead eyes. Olivia was sure he was another ANH employee. They were getting sloppy.

"We need to call this in and get back up," Olivia said authoritatively. "This is too big for just the two of us."

Henry nodded and took out his phone, ready to make the calls. Olivia slumped down beside the man's body, exhaustion taking over her.

"I'm sorry," she murmured to the body beside her. "But I'm glad you're not him."

CHAPTER TWENTY

BY THE TIME THE POLICE SHOWED UP AND SET A PERIMETER around the scene, Olivia knew that the men they'd seen in the Jeep would be long gone. She was angry with herself for not managing to detain one of them, but she had to remind herself that they were still closer to answers than they'd been before. They had two bodies to work with already: one of a former ANH employee, and a new body that they had yet to investigate.

The body of the man still lay strewn at the edge of the field, and while the police began to mark the scene and document everything to begin digging, Olivia found the man's wallet on his person to check his identity.

"Preston Anderson," she read aloud as Henry stood a few paces away, listening. She chewed her lip. "He was forty-seven two days ago, according to his driver's license."

"Do you see a work ID on him?"

Olivia fished around in the wallet, pulling out several plastic cards. A credit card, a library card, a gym pass. Then, right at the back of the wallet, she found a work ID.

"He didn't work for ANH," Olivia said, unable to stop disappointment from seeping into her tone. She had been hoping to establish a pattern. Sure, they already had two victims from ANH and one missing person, but a third death from the company would certainly raise suspicions further. She turned over the card and checked out the company logo.

It was one she recognized, but couldn't quite place. She handed the card over to Henry to see if he was any wiser on the topic. "He worked for MDC," she said.

"Ah," he noted as he took the card. "Interesting."

"What do you have?"

"MDC is an American company. McCall Defense Corporation. They're a major arms contractor for the US, the UK, even NATO. They supply drone technology, missiles, guns and bombs and bullets—you name it."

"Could they be the ones supplying ANH with weapons?"

Henry shook his head. "I don't think so. I've looked into that connection before, actually. But from what I've found, it's all above ground."

"You're sure?"

"I suppose you never can be sure. But I haven't found any direct links. What's interesting, though, is that they risked killing someone from a rival corporation. I'd assumed most of these victims would be connected to ANH directly. But they're getting bolder."

"They must have really wanted this guy dead to risk killing him now," Olivia murmured, glancing back at Preston's still frame. "What could this man have had on them that they risked killing him when there was already such heightened suspicion on them?"

THE **LOCKED BOX**

"I guess they never thought they'd be found here. It's taken years to get to this point of the investigation. Without that tip-off, we'd still be fumbling in the dark," Henry said. Olivia thought she could hear a little bitterness in his tone. She could sort of understand that. She'd accelerated the progress of his case more in one week than he had in years. It didn't look great for him, no matter how good of an agent she happened to be.

"Well, the point is, we have some leads now," Olivia pointed out. "Don't you think it makes sense for us to go speak with Preston's wife? I've got her number right here on his phone. I can call her up and explain that we need to know if there was anything connecting him to ANH. I'm sure she wants justice for her husband."

"Alright. Ring her up," Henry said. "Tell her we'll drop by in the morning. We need to head back and get some rest for now. There's not much we can do until then. Don't look at me like that, American. You might be able to live off of caffeine and determination, but I'll be useless without a few hours of shut-eye."

Olivia glared at him, but even as she did, she realized he was right. It was past three in the morning, and she was fading fast.

"We're on the right path now, Knight. There's still time."

Reluctantly, Olivia nodded, hoping Brock still had time. On the way back to the car, she made the call to Preston's wife, doing her best to remain sensitive and offer her condolences. The woman, a sweet lady named Rose, thanked her for her help and offered up her address for their visit in the morning while the police took in Preston's body.

Olivia managed a few hours of sleep before they headed back out again. It was the first time she'd slept without dreaming of Brock, without her mind taking her to the darkest places imaginable. She woke up feeling a little better, knowing that they had a chance to win this race. And if Brock wasn't dead in the pit with all those other bodies, then he was likely still fighting for his life.

Hold on just a little longer, Olivia told him in her mind. *Do it for me.*

Henry drove them to the house that Preston shared with his wife Rose, only a few miles out from the B&B. Henry shook his head as he took in the pretty rows of houses that they passed by.

"Such a small town... and yet so much has happened here," he murmured. Olivia nodded solemnly. It was hard to believe that such a picturesque place was the home of so much horror. And not just the events of the past few weeks, but for years before too. Olivia wondered how many bodies the police would find at the scene, but that wasn't her concern right now. She couldn't concentrate on the murder of Richard Greene, or the disappearance of Gareth Dean, or even the two bodies they'd found the night before. There was no hurry to avenge the dead when they could still save the living.

As they pulled up in front of Preston's home, they found Rose sitting on the front lawn on a bench, hugging her knees up to her chest like a child. She was staring ahead, and it seemed like she might have been there for a long time, out in the cold, but she didn't seem to be affected by it. Olivia could see the stain of tears on her cheeks. She'd just lost so much, and Olivia didn't want to ask anything of a grieving woman, but there were things they needed to know. Things that would make everything clearer to them.

"Rose Anderson?" Olivia started gently as they approached her. "I spoke with you on the phone. It's Olivia Knight with the FBI. Would you like to go inside, or would you prefer to stay out here? I can make you a cup of tea if you like..."

Rose shook her head softly. "Let's stay out here. It was Preston's favorite place to sit. I always said to him, 'Why not the back garden? Don't you want a little privacy?' But he said..." She laughed a little to herself. "He said he couldn't see his beautiful car around the back."

Olivia smiled. "Men and their cars, huh?"

Rose laughed quietly and dabbed her eyes. "You don't say. Anyway... I know you didn't come here to talk about Preston's quirks. You want to know how this might have happened."

Olivia nodded gently. Henry was standing a few paces away, distancing himself from the conversion. He seemed

THE **LOCKED BOX**

uncomfortable with Rose's show of emotions, so Olivia figured it was best that she took the lead.

"I guess we just want to know if this is a surprise to you at all. As I told you… he was shot through the head and dropped off at a location that we now believe to be a mass grave. We also believe that a company called ANH is responsible for killing a lot of people and burying them there. Does that name ring a bell to you?"

Rose nodded slowly. "I… I believe it does. I never really understood much about Preston's job… and to be honest, I didn't want to. I've never felt good about guns and weaponry, so a part of me just didn't want to know what Preston got up to at work. I know it's all legitimate, and I know he brought home a lot of money to give us a lovely life… but in some ways, that always felt worse to me, knowing I was profiting off people's pain."

"I understand…. this isn't the most pleasant conversation in the world," Olivia told her.

Rose nodded. "Anyway… I guess I never really got down to talking to him much about work. But I couldn't tell you if he ever talked about ANH. It doesn't ring a bell." Rose sighed, closing her eyes. "I wish I had paid more attention now."

"Don't worry. Anything at all that you tell us will likely be useful. How long did your husband work with MDC?"

"Gosh… a long time. Fifteen years, perhaps? Maybe more? He liked it there. The salary was good, they got good holiday bonuses, he liked the boss…. he couldn't ask for more, really. But this ANH… *they* killed him?"

"That's the theory we're working with," Olivia said. "Did your husband seem to be acting differently lately? Had you noticed any changes in him that might be described as unusual or erratic?"

Rose chewed on her lip anxiously. "I… yes. There was definitely a difference in his behavior these past few months. But I don't think it was related to work."

"You don't?"

Rose shook her head slowly. "I… I don't want to get into any trouble… but I know that I have to be honest. There's something that you should know about Preston. Something that changed his life recently… and to be honest, I don't think he was ever going to recover from it. Follow me."

Rose stood slowly to show Olivia inside. Henry gestured that he was going to stay by the car, and Olivia sighed quietly. So much for having a partner. She wondered if maybe he would use the opportunity to make some more sneaky calls like he had the past few days.

She didn't have time to really worry about that. She needed to know what Rose was talking about. Inside, the house itself smelled like her name—a floral scent so strong that it tickled Olivia's nose. Rose rounded a corner into the kitchen and began to root through the cupboards for something, which she then hid behind her back like a child. She looked at Olivia with wide eyes.

"Before I show you, I want you to know that Preston was a good man. He just got sick. He got to the point where he couldn't stop himself, and he was like a new person. I didn't know what to do. I tried to make him stop, but he said he'd die without these…"

From behind her back, she produced a bag of pills. Olivia didn't need to look closer to know what she was dealing with. Those damn pills had ruined so many lives already. She could see from the look on Rose's face that Preston was yet another victim of them.

"My Preston had never taken drugs in his life. He didn't even drink, really," Rose said, her voice trembling. "But a few months ago… he started acting strange. He came home one night and was all jittery and couldn't form his words properly. I didn't know what the hell was going on. He just… he wasn't himself. I demanded to know what had happened, what had gone on, but he just sort of… aimlessly shambled around. And the strangest thing was, after an hour or so, it all dried up. It went away and he was back to normal again. He had no idea what I was talking about."

"Did you think he'd been drugged?" Olivia asked.

Rose nodded. "I didn't know what to think. And when the episode was done, he had no memory of anything that had happened. He didn't remember a thing. I was going to just put it behind me, but then it happened again a couple weeks later.

THE **LOCKED BOX**

And then again, and again. Each time, the episodes got longer. Sometimes they would even last for hours and hours."

"What was his behavior like during these episodes?" Olivia asked. "Did he ever become... suggestible? Like he'd just do anything you asked?"

A light seemed to come on in Rose's eyes at the suggestion. "Yes. Yes, I suppose he did. Normally I couldn't get Preston to do anything he didn't want to do. But sometimes, he was like... like putty in my hands. He was willing to do anything he was told. It made him very mellow, in some ways, but he could also be aggressive. Like he didn't know his own strength. It was the most bizarre behavior I've ever seen...." She looked at Olivia, and her shoulders slumped. "You do believe me, don't you? I know I must sound crazy."

"You don't sound crazy," Olivia said gently. "I believe you."

She might not have believed it if she hadn't seen it herself only weeks earlier. Darcie Puckett hadn't even taken a full dose, and it had been enough to get her killed. She'd been out of control, angry, and confused, and Olivia knew that story ended with her being pushed over the side of a millionaire's yacht by accident. Now, she was dead, like so many others who had been subjected to the lethal drug.

"How was he when he woke up from the episodes? Did he ever remember why he'd started? How he'd gotten involved with this in the first place?"

Rose swallowed. "He never knew when he was sober. But one day, he came home with an episode, and he had this bag of pills in his pocket. And I made him talk. And finally, he managed to relay the story to me. He told me that he'd been at the pub and struck up a conversation with an old acquaintance who introduced him to a new friend. He couldn't recall the new friend's name, but he'd had a headache, and the man offered him a pill to ease the symptoms. He took the pill, thinking nothing of it, and came home. That was the first time."

Rose's eyes were distant now as she spoke, like the light in them had dimmed long ago. "Apparently that first pill made him insatiable. He had it put in his drink the next time. Then injected, like some sort of... God. He couldn't tell me the name of his supplier—or his face. Just that he was a friend of a friend. Eventually, this friend of a friend let him come home with his own supply."

Olivia shuddered at the horrific story. This man had been targeted and broken apart just for ANH to test their drugs. "Did you contact the authorities?"

"I told him we should involve the police, but that was the *one* thing he pushed back on. Almost violently. He flew into a rage at the suggestion. It was like any mention of the police made him completely hotheaded. I was going to destroy the stuff. I was going to dispose of it. But he screamed. He wasn't himself anymore. And... and by the end of the day, his craving was so strong that he got on his knees and cried, begging me to let him have a pill. And I didn't know what to do... I was scared. So I gave in to him. Over and over again. And each time I let him have a pill, I felt like I lost him a little more. He was dead long before last night."

Olivia nodded in understanding. She knew how drugs could ruin lives completely, and this drug was the worst of the worst.

"Did he ever say why he felt he was targeted? Or why the supplier had sought him out?"

Rose sniffed. "He didn't like to talk about it. I think he preferred to pretend like none of it had happened at all... as though it was all just a bad dream. But I had my theories."

"Such as?"

"I think... I think they knew exactly who he was when they attacked him. I think they'd been keeping tabs on him for a while and that they chose him to make him suffer. He was being used as some kind of guinea pig. I think that's why they gave him the rest. They didn't care if it killed him slowly. I suppose eventually, they decided they'd seen enough, and now they've put him out of his misery. I... I'm not even sure it makes sense to me entirely, but it's the best explanation I've got for now."

Olivia nodded. It seemed to make sense to her, too, no matter how outlandish it seemed. It was a form of torture, but it was also a way of testing the waters. Their product was faulty, and they knew it. So, while they perfected their craft, they seemed to

THE **LOCKED BOX**

have no issues in using the reject products and the prototypes on any number of targets. Olivia wondered how many others had made it to the mass grave after being subjected to the same things as Preston. How many more would have to die for ANH to be satisfied? Would they ever stop?

"I'm glad his suffering is over," Rose said, her voice cracking a little as she spoke. "I never... I never thought things would end this way. But if you'd seen him... those drugs made him into someone he wasn't. And I'm glad he doesn't have to endure that anymore." Rose stepped forward and took Olivia's hands in her own. "Please say you'll find the people who did this to him. Please say that you'll make them pay."

"I will," Olivia promised. But the more she learned, the more she realized how big a task it was going to be. Even if they managed to save Brock, even if they somehow managed to make some of ANH's walls tumble down, Olivia knew that they were rooted deep into society now. They had made their mark, and it wasn't going to be possible to destroy them all in one shot. The organization was so big that Olivia didn't even know where to begin with picking out the individuals responsible for this huge mess. Even the likes of Charlie Evans, a businessman all the way on the other side of the globe, had been roped in by them—Olivia was sure of it. They were spreading like a disease, and Olivia didn't yet have the cure.

"Thank you so much for speaking with me, Rose," Olivia said. "I promise I will let you know when we find something. In the meantime, the police are also working on this case. You will be able to see Preston today, to identify him and say goodbye."

Rose nodded, seemingly unable to speak. Olivia knew that grief could render people silent, even when there were no tears in their eyes or on their cheeks. She didn't want to leave Rose all on her own, but she had to keep pushing for answers. The pressure was still on, and there was still a lot to do.

She left the house and found Henry leaning against his car in the middle of a phone call. When he saw Olivia coming out, he quickly ended the call, and Olivia felt her skin crawling. What the hell was he up to? Why was he always sneaking around like he had something to hide?

"Did something more important come up?" Olivia asked coldly. Henry's expression didn't shift even a little. He simply opened his car door and slid into the driver's seat.

"I saw that you had things handled. Besides, I thought you liked being in charge."

Olivia was too irritated to give him any sort of an answer. She simply got in the car and readied herself for whatever was coming next. Time wasn't up yet, but she was still very aware of the hours counting down until Brock's death date. Now that they were able to attack with force, they could target ANH with no problem.

But that didn't help them with Brock. They still had no idea where among the ANH empire he was being stowed. They needed more information. And until they had something to work with, they were going to have to keep digging.

CHAPTER TWENTY-ONE

"THE MAIN QUESTION I HAVE IS... WHY NOW?"

Henry frowned at Olivia. They were sitting in his room at the B&B, trying to look through some of Brock's old cases, looking for clues. They were searching for some kind of connection between his old cases and the ANH case, but they had yet to find anything of use.

"What do you mean by that, Olivia?"

"What I mean is that Brock has been tailing these guys for a long time. Something tells me that ANH doesn't actually care that much about that. I mean, they're obviously pretty cocky, given the way they run things. They've had a mass grave just sitting there in the open for God knows how long. They're killing people left, right, and center, and it's like... it's like they know that no one has any way to prove what they're up to."

"Until now."

"Well, yes, but only because of our investigations this week. Before, you were completely in the dark."

"Thanks for the reminder."

"This isn't about your pride, Henry, get a grip. I'm just saying, they're brazen because they can get away with it. Which makes me think that actually, they probably knew all along that Brock was investigating them. And then when he went undercover this time around, they finally decided that the jig was up. So, either Brock found something out that they didn't expect him to... or they had another reason to take him in. What could he offer them that they don't already have?"

Henry thought about it for a moment. "I don't know... perhaps they want to know insider knowledge from the FBI?"

"Like what?"

"I don't know. You blokes have all sorts of secrets that would be useful to criminal masterminds. Or perhaps they were looking for a weak link, someone they could use to their advantage..."

"I'd hardly call Brock a weak link. He's the best of the best," Olivia said defensively. She knew logically that Henry was only theorizing, that he wasn't personally attacking Brock, but she still felt as though she wanted to defend his honor, somehow.

Henry ignored Olivia's protests. "Or maybe he has connections that they want to know about. It's certainly not about the ransom money. I think that's just a bonus while they're toying with him."

"Agreed. It's a power trip. They're more interested in getting us to bow down to them than they are in getting the money. But I guess Brock isn't giving them what they want to hear. That is, if he's actually still alive..."

"If you're right about them and they actually do know that they're being investigated... then maybe they're trying to buy themselves time. By now, those meatheads who were dumping the body at the grave have likely already told their bosses all about it. Maybe they're hoping that while they're dangling Brock in front of us, we'll keep at bay. They know as well as we do that we can't go in all guns blazing if we want to find him alive. Maybe that's what they're counting on."

Olivia nodded, chewing her lip thoughtfully. It still didn't explain why they needed Brock so badly. If he wasn't important to them, then why would they draw so much attention to themselves by kidnapping him? It had only accelerated their investigations of them, so ANH were the ones losing out in the end. Once Brock was dead, they had no collateral to work with, and then what would they do?

"Maybe they're bluffing about killing him," Olivia offered. "I can't see a scenario now where they can kill him and get away with it. They must realize that the second they do that, they lose all of their leverage. We can just hit one of the locations that we know of and start taking them down, piece by piece. They need him now. I think they made a mistake when they took him… I think they thought that he would be more important to them than he has been. And now, they're stuck between a rock and a hard place, with us on their backs and a useless captive."

"So, you don't think Brock has talked?"

Olivia blinked in shock. "Of course not. Brock is the strongest man I know. There's no way he's giving up anything for them."

"Are you sure about that?"

"Yes, I'm sure," Olivia said irritably. She folded her arms over her chest. "You don't know him. Brock is tough as nails. I know they're beating him around a little, but it's nothing he can't handle. He's trained all of his adult life for this, just like any of us have. We know how to withstand torture if we have to. At least… at least for a while."

"It's one thing saying we could do it, and another thing entirely to actually do it," Henry pointed out. "How do you know that Brock hasn't told them everything they want to know? Maybe *that's* their leverage now."

Olivia shook her head, but she didn't have anything left to say on the matter. Because maybe Henry was right. Maybe they had broken him. They'd had him long enough to make him feel the sting of suffering. Had it become too much for him? Had he given in to the pain and told them what they wanted to know?

Olivia shook her head again, like she was trying to shake off her own negative thoughts. "No. He just wouldn't."

Henry sighed, leaning back in his chair. "Olivia, how well do you actually know this guy?"

"Excuse me?"

"Come on, now. I know you've worked together for some time… but how much do you really know him?"

Olivia could feel rage flaring up inside her, raw and hot. "I lived with him for months, Henry. We spent every single day together. We worked together, ate together… spent our spare time together."

Henry shot her a knowing look, and Olivia couldn't stop the blush from spreading across her cheeks.

"Stop it. It's not like that. I know him pretty damn well is what I'm saying. I don't know why you're suddenly poking around in my business like this, asking me if I *know* him… you're grasping at straws."

"It's a valid question. You have no idea what he might be involved in."

"Are you trying to suggest that this is all some kind of ruse? That he's actually *with* them?"

Henry held up his hands defensively. "Don't shoot the messenger."

"I will if he keeps making up his own message. Where is this coming from?"

"Nowhere in particular. It's just our job to think outside the box, isn't it? And I don't know this guy, but I've checked out his files. He's got a lot of experience, has a lot of skills… you seriously don't think that he's the sort of guy that these places would want to recruit? And maybe they offered him a lot of money to play on their side…"

"Brock isn't like that. He's not materialistic in that way. He wouldn't care about how much money they offered him."

Henry fixed her a stare. "That you know of."

Olivia threw her hands up irritably. "This is ridiculous. You're just looking for a way to toss blame around, to make it seem like he walked into this. I've told you: he's not like that."

THE **LOCKED BOX**

"So, you know everything about him? You know all about his family, his friends, his life before he met you? You're an expert on this man, are you?"

Olivia opened her mouth to argue back, but Henry's words were like an ice pick to her heart. Henry had no idea how hard it had been to get Brock to open up about his past. He had no idea that he was actually sort of right about Brock. His bright smile and easygoing manner had always been cover for the parts of him he didn't want to share. Just beneath that pleasant surface, he was secretive and hard to understand, and he kept to himself. Now he had Olivia questioning why that was.

She knew he'd been through some tough times in his career. She knew some of the stories that made up his past. But it was also true that Brock knew much more about her than she did about him. It had always frustrated her, but now, she was wondering if there was more to it. Was he keeping secrets from her deliberately? Was he hiding away because there were things he couldn't tell her—things that proved he wasn't the man that she thought he was?

Henry leaned forward in his seat, examining Olivia's face closely.

"You can never really know a person," he said quietly. "Not if they don't want you to know them. Is it possible that you've been played this entire time, Olivia? Is it possible that Brock is a double agent?"

Olivia's eyes snapped up to look at Henry. Now she was torn again. She'd been so suspicious of Henry from the start, and now here he was, trying to turn her against the one person she trusted completely and cared about most deeply. What did Henry gain from all of this messing with her head? Was he trying now to cover his own back and turn her anger toward Brock instead?

"You think he could be?"

"I'm asking you to consider a very real possibility. I'm saying you might have overlooked some things about him. Maybe you can't trust him as much as you think you can."

"So, I should trust you over him?" Olivia said coldly. "I should just abandon the months of companionship he and I have shared and believe some lie you came up with about him?"

Henry rolled his eyes. "You're taking this way too personally. I'm not trying to *tell* you anything. I'm just theorizing."

"Well, you're wrong. I don't care how much Brock has kept from me. He has a right to his secrets. That doesn't make him a bad person. That doesn't mean he's working with the enemy."

"So, you admit he keeps secrets," Henry said. He wasn't looking at Olivia now. Instead, he was typing away at his computer. "And you've never wondered what those might be?"

"Of course, I have. But that still doesn't mean he's betraying me or his values…"

"Look, I hate to break it to you, but just because you care about someone, it doesn't mean they're not capable of doing things that disappoint you. I know he means a lot to you, so I'm going to break this to you gently. I think I've found something about him. Something that might change the course of this case."

"What?" Olivia snapped. She stood up and moved behind Henry to see what he was doing on his computer. He'd pulled up several files about Brock, and he pointed at the screen.

"You see this? This is Brock's grandfather. His name is Walter J. McCall. Did Brock ever mention him to you?"

"No," Olivia replied, a defensive edge to her voice. "What does his grandfather have to do with anything?"

Henry sighed, typing Walter's name into an internet search. "A little light research can get you a long way, Olivia. Look at this. Look at what his grandfather owns."

Olivia stared at the screen for a moment. Shock filled her inside as she read the content on the screen.

Walter J. McCall is the founder and CEO of McCall Defense Corporation, a leading defense contractor in the research and development, engineering, manufacture, and supply of military-grade weapons and technology.

Olivia stared at the words again. *McCall Defense Corporation…*

"MDC," Olivia breathed. She thought back to Preston's work ID. MDC was the company he worked for.

THE **LOCKED BOX**

And it was all owned by Brock's grandfather?

"Now do you see?" Henry asked. "Brock used to work for MDC. If they're in cahoots with ANH, then this might make sense. Either that, or MDC is their rival, and ANH is working to bring them down. That could explain why Preston wound up dead. Olivia, are you even listening to me?"

Olivia wasn't listening to him. She was too wrapped up in what she had just discovered. Henry was right. It was like she didn't even know Brock at all…

She had no idea that he had once worked for an arms company. In fact, she had always believed that he was against them. And now she was finding out that his grandfather was the head of one of the largest weapons dealers in the world?

If MDC and ANH were working together, then Brock could easily be on their side. But if they were at war, then Brock was in more danger than she'd even thought before. ANH might be selling Brock back to the government, but it was really Walter's attention they needed…

None of it made sense to her. She felt her knees about to buckle and lowered herself back into her chair, feeling nauseous. How had she missed all of this? How had she been so blind to Brock and his past?

Could she still trust him?

Did he really need saving at all?

Whose side was he on?

CHAPTER TWENTY-TWO

BROCK HAD AN UNEASY FEELING IN HIS STOMACH. HE SAT opposite his grandfather in his office as Walter detailed the blueprints of a brand-new, cutting-edge drone targeting system. He had been working with his grandfather for just over a year, and he was already beginning to doubt the things they were doing there.

And now he was finally being let in on the company's biggest secret project. Walter had certainly kept these plans under wraps for a long time, and now Brock understood why.

"What do you think, son?" Walter asked him eagerly. "The world's never seen anything like this. We'll be doing a great service for our country—and making a pretty penny while doing it."

THE **LOCKED BOX**

Brock couldn't find the words to speak. A year ago, he thought that he would do anything to be a rich man. He thought that was all he cared about. And for a while, it had felt good. His starting salary had certainly been upped by the fact that it was the family business, so he bought himself a flashy car and his first apartment. He'd spent months partying, spending all of his money on women and booze. He had more money than he knew what to do with, and he was sure that the phrase "money can't buy happiness" had to be a lie.

But the deeper into the company Walter led him, the more he began to feel sick at the things he was seeing. He'd seen missiles being shipped off to war-torn countries, ready to land devastating blows on innocent people. He'd seen drones and other new tech being tested and then used for planning the deaths of hundreds of people without a second thought. He'd seen the MDC company logo printed on boxes filled with items capable of ending lives without a second thought.

And he was beginning to have doubts.

"Grandfather... these plans... they're impressive," Brock began. Walter raised an eyebrow.

"But?"

"But... but you can't be serious about this. It's so... personal. People are going to use tech like this to do awful things."

"Brock, don't be getting all soft on me now. People kill each other, no matter what. If we took away everyone's guns and bombs, people would still go after one another with swords and knives. That's just man's nature. It's a dangerous world out there, and someone has to make money off of that. This weapon would make death quick and merciful. Isn't that a good thing?"

Brock continued to stare at the plans in front of him. Plans for a drone device capable of facial recognition to target specific enemies only. This special drone would also be capable of cloaking itself in any environment, able to blend in wherever it might need to go and avoid radar or any detection technology. Brock had to admit that the idea itself was genius. There was no denying that the weapon would be effective and impressive—if they could get it to work.

But there was also no denying that a weapon like that would change the way that wars were fought. It would sell to the highest bidder and allow global superpowers to eliminate anyone they wanted. It would change politics and war forever.

"I don't know about this. It's impressive, don't get me wrong, but—"

"Think of the lives that would be saved," Walter cut in. "With the use of facial recognition, people can really go for the jugular. They can kill just one person instead of hundreds. They can take down the root of the problem without so many casualties along the way. One shot and you can kill a dictator. One shot and you can hunt down the leaders of extremist groups without having to worry about collateral damage. I don't understand how you can't see the potential in that."

"I see the potential," Brock admitted. "I see the potential all too well. That's what worries me about this. If a weapon like this gets into the wrong hands…"

"You know that I'm very careful about who I sell to," Walter said, crossing his arms. "I don't deal weaponry like this with just anyone."

"Anyone with a weapon like this would go mad with power. You're right, it will change the world. And not in a good way."

Walter scowled at Brock. "What on earth has gotten into you, son? I thought we were on the same page. I thought we both wanted to look into exciting new ways to use our products. Was I wrong about you? Are you telling me you don't have the guts to see this through?"

Brock so desperately wanted to be the kind of man that could look past the dangers and just focus on making money. But what he really wanted was to be the kind of man who walked without a footprint. The kind of man whose impact on the world wasn't so big that it could make waves. He didn't want to be known as a man who supplied the most dangerous weapon in the world's history. And he knew that if Walter's plans ever came to fruition, that's exactly the kind of man he would be.

"I can't support this," Brock said, sliding the plans back over the desk toward Walter. "And if you ask me to, I'll have to leave."

THE **LOCKED BOX**

Walter stared at Brock in disbelief. It was like he couldn't understand how Brock could bring in a moral obligation—not now, not after all they'd built together. He studied Brock as though he were seeing him for the first time in his life.

"If you walk away now," Walter growled, his voice low and venomous, "don't expect to come back. If you don't have the guts for this now, then you never will. Don't do this, Brock. You know it's a mistake."

"Maybe," Brock said, rising from his chair. "But I won't play a part in this. I'm sorry. And you're wrong, grandfather. It takes more guts to walk away than it does to stay and be obedient. You taught me that."

Brock didn't look back as he stood and left the office. He could feel the anger radiating off of Walter, his disappointment so obvious to him that it felt like a slap. But Brock had made up his mind. He didn't know where he was going or what he'd do next, but he knew one thing.

He'd never work for his grandfather again.

⁓

It was ten years before Brock even thought about his grandfather again. He had managed to put him out of sight and out of mind, which was the only way he could make peace with what had happened.

But now, as an FBI agent, he was faced with his past once again. He watched as Jonathan James slid him a large file across his desk. On the front of the file were the initials of Walter's company.

"*I am aware that this might be uncomfortable for you,*" Jonathan told him, "*but your family connections could prove useful to us. Intel from a private source has suggested to us that your grandfather may have been contacted by ANH to make a deal. Your mission is to see whether your grandfather took the deal or not. If he did, then it might be our chance to uncover what's really going on there.*"

Brock agreed to take on the task but quickly discovered that his grandfather was innocent. At least, he was innocent of working with ANH. Brock knew that was a slight blow for the case, considering that it didn't give them an in for ANH's operations, but he was secretly glad that his grandfather had stayed on the right side of the tracks, such as they were.

The trouble with his grandfather, Brock knew, was that he was always so certain that he was right. He had been born and raised as a patriot, a man who stood by his values and did whatever he thought was best for his country. In his eyes, selling dangerous weapons to his government was an act of patriotic service, and the same went for American allies. He didn't care beyond that. He just wanted to do what was best for the people he described as "his people."

And that was where he and Brock differed. Brock loved his country, but he didn't always believe that Americans were right. He didn't believe that they were perfect. He didn't believe in the American Dream when so many Americans could never achieve it.

He loved his country, but he understood that there were cracks beneath the surface. He knew that his grandfather had caused a crack so big in the underbelly of America that it could split the country in half. Ten years ago, Brock had walked away from all of that, but Walter remained a stubborn man, determined to see his plans through.

And that meant, somewhere out there, Walter's brand-new weapons were being made.

Ten years ago, the technology would have been considered too advanced, but now, Walter's dreams of his killer drone were coming to life. Brock had discovered that much in his investigation, and he wondered if that was why ANH was so insistent to make a deal with him. They likely wanted a weapon that was discreet and powerful to do their dirty work. In their hands, the weapon could make important politicians disappear from the face of the earth. It could take down rival CEOs or be sold to the next highest bidder, just to cause chaos.

But the one thing that put Brock's mind at ease was that he knew it was unlikely that his grandfather would sell to them. At least that much was a comfort.

So, Brock put them to the back of his mind and moved on with other cases. It was only later, when he was forced to return to

THE **LOCKED BOX**

investigating ANH, that he discovered just how long of a grudge they could hold against someone who had wronged them…

Brock hadn't had a visit from the boss in a while. He also hadn't been given any food or water in some time, and the effect had made him sluggish and weak. He closed his eyes, the pain in his body had dulled to a quiet ache.

He knew he was running out of time.

He lay in his cell, unable to stop thinking about his grandfather and the weapon that had changed everything. It was that weapon that had made Brock a target for ANH. They had been desperate to get their hands on it ever since they'd heard the rumors of its existence. And now, even years after Brock had chosen to walk away, he was paying for his involvement with MDC.

And ANH wasn't getting what they wanted. Walter wasn't interested in cutting a deal, and the FBI hadn't coughed up the ransom money for him either. Brock knew it must be pissing ANH off. He knew they weren't used to failure. And when all of their other plans fell through, he would no longer be of use to them.

They'd kill him, just like they had promised.

And Brock was almost ready for it. He sometimes felt like the past had been chasing him for years—that it was always going to catch up to him eventually. He knew that someday he'd have to pay for those poor choices he'd made at twenty-one.

And now the day of reckoning had come.

He only prayed that they would make it quick when they ended him.

Brock knew better now than to think that ANH didn't have this whole thing planned the whole time. They had planted the evidence of their human trafficking themselves to lure Brock back to the case. They had been keeping tabs on him for months, maybe years. They had taken the time to figure out how to hit him where it hurt.

And that was how they used Olivia against him.

The first thing they'd done when they captured him was to show him photographs of her. The two of them together, more specifically. They were making it clear to him that they understood what she meant to him. All those pictures of them showed them laughing together, smiling, and having the best time because they were in one another's company.

They'd captured tender moments too. Brock comforting Olivia in his apartment, the photographs taken from right outside. Olivia discovering that her home had been ransacked months before. It became clear to Brock then that it had all been the work of ANH. He hadn't known it at the time, but they were dead set on destroying him, destroying his life, destroying everything.

They'd invaded his home too. They'd been looking for anything that he might know about operations at MDC, but they never found a thing. They certainly never discovered his lockbox. Brock wondered if Olivia had managed to find it, to decode the puzzle he'd left for her. He was sure she had—she was too smart to overlook something like that.

But none of it really mattered much. Because Brock lost his use to ANH the second Walter told them that he'd never cut a deal with them. Walter had signed his own grandson's death warrant.

And now it was only a matter of time.

CHAPTER TWENTY-THREE

OLIVIA FELT A LITTLE NUMB AS SHE LET EVERYTHING sink in. The fact that Brock had kept such a big secret from her. The fact that she might never get to find out what else he'd been hiding from her. The fact that maybe he wasn't on her side after all.

"Olivia... hey, I'm sorry," Henry said, looking apologetic for once. Maybe he actually meant it. "I wasn't trying to stir things up...."

"You weren't? Because it sure feels that way."

"Yeah, well... I guess I don't come across very well sometimes. I just wanted to explore every avenue with this case. We're running out of time, and I just hoped that you would consider every possibility. And this... this is a big deal."

Olivia closed her eyes and nodded. She knew that. She knew that she might be on a mission to save someone who didn't need saving at all. She knew she might be sticking her neck out for a traitor, for someone who had spent months faking everything just to get to this point.

But that didn't matter to Olivia. It hurt her, but it didn't mean she was going to give up—not when Brock meant so much to her. If he had played her for a fool, then she was at least going to see it through to the end and see him put away for it. If he really was a part of ANH in any way, then she was going to look him in the eyes and ask him why.

She still had to see him. She still had to be sure.

"You're right. We can't leave any stones unturned," Olivia said with a decisive nod. "And if that means asking myself difficult questions, then so be it. I'm not giving up on this case. We're still going to find him before time runs out. We have to."

Henry's expression was gentle as he nodded. Olivia had never seen him look so considerate, and she wondered if that was what finally unleashed the tears locked behind her eyes. It was all so much that she could barely handle it. She huffed to herself as she wiped tears from her cheeks.

"I bet you're loving this," she said, even though she didn't mean it. She felt the need to lash out, to make someone hurt the way she was hurting. But that wasn't possible, and Henry knew her heart wasn't in it. He shrugged at her.

"Not really. Believe it or not, it's not my mission in life to make people miserable. I just happen to be quite good at it."

Olivia choked out a laugh, trying to compose herself. She knew she didn't have the time for tears or letting her emotions take over. She needed to focus and get to the bottom of things as soon as she could.

"I need some sleep," she said quietly. She checked her watch and saw that it was past midnight. They only had a few days left to figure everything out, and the stakes were more complicated than ever. "I'll be ready to go again in a few hours."

"Take your time. Rest. It'll be good for you. And Olivia… I really am sorry. I hope we can prove that he's a good man."

THE **LOCKED BOX**

Olivia let out a deep sigh. "Me too. Me too."

When Olivia woke, it was to the sound of her phone ringing. She checked the time and was shocked to see that it was almost nine in the morning. She couldn't believe she'd slept so long when there was so much to do. Usually, the stress of her problems woke her up right when it was necessary.

Bleary-eyed, Olivia grabbed her phone and answered the call. "Hello?"

"Hi, Agent Knight. It's Cheryl here from the Newhaven police. I wanted to ask you a favor."

"Um… well, things are kind of hectic on my end, Cheryl. I'm sort of on a timer," Olivia said, all while trying to pull on some clothes.

"I know, and I don't want to add to your stress levels… but I think it might be of interest to you. We've found traces of the nasty drug you mentioned to us in Richard Greene's system. We used the sample to run through some previous cases and found that the test results appear to be identical to some we've found in the local homeless community. It appears these drugs have been pretty rampant."

"Could that be where he got his supply?" Olivia thought back to Preston Anderson, who'd been sent home with a bag of pills. If ANH were trying to push these dangerous chemicals, using the homeless community would be an easy way to do it.

"We haven't confirmed if that's where Richard was drugged. He wasn't a user according to his wife, and there was no evidence that seemed he'd been a long-term user of the substance. Just that it was in his system the night he was killed."

Olivia shivered. The local police might not know the significance of that, but she did. He'd been drugged, made completely pliable, and then *ordered* to drive home, where he'd been killed in broad daylight. ANH was truly getting bold.

"Any update on the killer? What about that missing man, Gareth Dean?"

"Still working on that, I'm afraid. But I wanted to forward you that information about the homeless community. It might be of use in your larger investigation."

Olivia wavered. On one hand, she was keen to learn more about the drugs that ANH was pumping out, but she also had to think about Brock. She couldn't see how going to poke around with some drug addicts was going to get her any closer to finding him.

Yet her gut told her to follow the lead.

"Alright. I'll check it out and see what I can come up with. But I can't spend much time there. I've got things to do."

"Great, thank you, I hope you find something useful."

As the call ended, Olivia pulled on shoes quickly and threw on a hoodie, then mussed up her hair a little. She didn't want to walk into a homeless community looking like police. That would only spell trouble.

Olivia knocked for Henry quickly, bouncing on the balls of her feet to get rid of some of her nervous energy. To her surprise, he was up and dressed for the first time. He gave her a once over, looking a little amused at her disheveled state.

"You've seen better days," he remarked, the corners of his mouth twitching. She scowled back at him.

"I see you're back to being an asshole. Come on—the police tipped me off to a lead on the drugs. I said we'd spare an hour to check it out."

"You think this is a good use of our time? What about Brock?"

"I think sometimes looking in the places you don't expect to find answers leads you to hidden treasure. Besides, if ANH is feeding drugs into the homeless community, then we might be able to get a lead somehow. Maybe someone saw or heard something about him. Let's do this."

"Alright," Henry said with a lazy shrug. "You're the boss."

They drove into the town together, past the colorful houses and the marina, past the cheerful docks into the more sordid parts of town. The pretty little town had been such a nightmare that Olivia couldn't even really enjoy the sights that she passed by. All she wanted was to leave this place behind and for things to go back to the way they were.

But given that wasn't an option at the moment, Olivia hoped that their lead might yield something useful. They parked a decent distance away from their destination, and Olivia was suddenly glad of her hoodie as the biting wind from the sea nipped at her face. Henry motioned for her to follow him, so she did.

They headed toward a large parking garage, and Olivia could see immediately that it wasn't in use anymore. There were no cars inside, and the building seemed to be crumbling bit by bit. As they ducked under the barriers, no longer in use, Olivia saw that groups of people were huddled around a makeshift fire. There were several tents set up, too, and a single car was parked in the center of the lot. Someone was rooting around inside it for something, and it seemed to be filled to the brim with random things that others had stored there. Olivia guessed it was almost like a storage unit for the group.

She felt cautious upon her approach. She could understand why these people wouldn't want two agents sniffing around in their business. Their life was already hard enough without being poked and prodded with invasive questions.

But if what Cheryl had said was true, these people's lives were being plagued by life-threatening drugs. Olivia thought that was a good enough reason to get involved. She approached the group slowly, and Henry followed suit.

Everyone gathered around and looked up as the two strangers infiltrated their camp. Olivia could tell that they weren't feeling warmly toward them, but she forced herself to keep pushing forward. She couldn't leave without speaking to at least one person about the things she had heard.

After a few moments, a young man stood up and met Olivia in the middle. He was wearing a beanie hat and had several tattoos crawling up his neck. He offered her a smile, but she could see the tiredness in his eyes.

"The hell you want?" the young man demanded.

Olivia and Henry traded a glance. "My name is Olivia, and this is Henry. No one is in trouble here, but we would like to talk to you about some things. We're working with MI5 and the FBI—"

"Bugger off, coppers," the young man spat, turning his back on her so suddenly that Olivia was taken by surprise. She stepped forward.

"Wait, please. We just need a few moments of your time. What's your name?"

The young man paused and turned back to her. "I said bugger off," he replied. "We ain't done anything."

Olivia sighed, knowing she needed to lay it all out there. "I promise, we're not going to get you in trouble. We just need your help with an investigation. We're trying to track down a dangerous drug that's been circulating the streets—something beyond your typical street stuff. But you know about that, don't you? It was given to the people who live here. It makes people completely compliant. Like they've been mind-controlled."

At that, the man frowned. "How did you know about that?"

"It's not just you. I've heard of a few other people being handed the drugs freely. Some of them were even forced to take them," Olivia explained. "The company we're investigating… we believe they're using vulnerable people as guinea pigs for their products, which is why they're being handed out like free candy. I know you don't want to talk about it… but I'd like to know how it's been affecting the people living here. I promise, we're not interested in arresting any of you. We want to find out who's done this to your community."

The light of irritation in the man's eyes wavered for just a moment. Olivia could see his hands twitching as he decided how best to answer her. After a moment, he looked back at his friends, and then nodded to the other side of the parking lot.

"Let's talk over there. The name's Dan."

Olivia nodded in understanding and allowed Dan to lead them away from the others. She noticed that many of the people around the campfire looked sickly, jittery, and tired. Olivia knew that many of them must have been dealing with the effects of the drug.

Dan stopped them on the opposite side of the car and folded his arms over his chest, shivering a little away from the warmth of the fire. "Okay, I guess I can answer a few questions. What do you want to know?"

"When did these drugs first appear in your community?" Henry asked.

THE **LOCKED BOX**

"Man, I'm not sure… couple months ago? I wasn't around when they first came. Some of the guys were so excited. They said a dealer in a black hoodie just came and offered them a bunch of pills for free. Living with addicts… you learn that drugs come first and sense comes later."

"Did you ever take them?" Olivia asked.

Dan shook his head. "No. I'm sober and always have been, so I didn't take an interest. Which is why I noticed the changes in those that did. First, the sickness and withdrawal. Then, the more they took, the weaker they became. They lost their appetites, their minds, their mobility. I don't know what the hell is in those drugs, but some people reckon it's some crazy government scheme to rid the streets of homelessness."

Olivia held back a sigh. She didn't have much time for crazy conspiracy theories, and she wasn't hearing anything she hadn't heard before about the drug. Was she wasting her time?

"I know, it sounds nutty," Dan went on. "But that's the other thing. These drugs have made people a little crazy around here. Half of the group is drugged up on it all the time now. Things are going downhill fast." He closed his eyes for a moment. "We lost two people already. They just… died. No warning. I think one had a heart attack. Not even an overdose. I can deal with an overdose. But I've never seen anything like this."

It was unusual that the man who'd seemed to be so aggressive was suddenly so helpful. But there was a confidence in his pose that showed that he must have been a leader of sorts for the community, helping them when nobody else would.

"The dealer who brought the drugs here… did anyone recall what he looked like?" Henry asked. Dan shook his head.

"Not really. It was hard getting sense out of the people who had met with him. They were high by the time I got back. And then it was like they forgot all the details and they only knew the basics. Like amnesia or something. But maybe he wasn't like an ordinary dealer. I've never heard of a dealer giving it out for free."

Olivia chewed her lip. "Does the word ANH mean anything to you at all? That's the company we're investigating. I wondered if maybe it had been mentioned at any point."

Dan's eyes widened. "Well... there was a bloke who showed up a few days back. He had clearly been on the same stuff, and he must have run into some trouble because there was blood on his suit, on his face... and it didn't belong to him. He looked like some corporate guy, you know? Deffo didn't belong here. Anyway, he said he needed somewhere to stay. We let him in. It was obvious that he'd been in a pretty terrible spot. He was waffling on, saying he had to leave his old life behind..."

"Did he say anything else about his life?"

"Yes. He mentioned that he worked for ANH. But he said he couldn't ever go back there. Not after what he'd done. He was pretty off his rocker, more than some of the others. He had such bad withdrawal that we thought he might die in the night, so we gave him a dose to keep him going. He spent a while here... but he actually left this morning."

"He did? Why?"

Dan shrugged. "Not sure. Never got much sense out of him at all. But he said something about making up for his past mistakes. He'd done something terrible to someone, and now he needed to make amends. He said he needed to go back to where it all went wrong... so I guess he felt like he had something he had to do. I never did find out what though."

Dan hung his head, rubbing at his neck. "I hope he's doing okay. This stuff really messes you up. He won't last long out there without a dose."

Something went off in Olivia's brain like a bolt of lightning. She dug around in her pocket and pulled out the photo of Gareth Dean that the police had given her during the search.

"Was it this man?"

Dan's eyes went wide, and he nodded. "Yes. Yes, I'm sure. He was in a state, but that's got to be him."

Olivia's heart was racing. Could Gareth be their killer? He worked for ANH, for one, and he'd been so hooked on their drugs that he was capable of almost anything. Maybe that was why he'd agreed to end Richard's life. Maybe their killer wasn't as cold-blooded as he seemed.

THE **LOCKED BOX**

"Thank you for your help," Olivia said. She grabbed Henry's arm. "I think we need to go."

"Where to?"

"To where it all went wrong... to Richard Greene's home. If Gareth is our killer, and he's trying to atone for his sins, isn't that the first place he would go?"

They piled into the car together, and Henry started driving off before Olivia had even buckled her seatbelt. It felt good to have some kind of a lead, but she was dreading what she might find when she arrived on the scene. She knew that these drugs made people into monsters, into people they had never been before. She just hoped that no one else would get hurt.

But when she saw the man on the lawn where Richard had died, all she felt was pity. He was wearing a soiled suit, his once white shirt covered in dried blood. He was shaking so hard that he almost looked as though he was having a fit. The man was crying loudly and staring into space, his eyes glassy with tears and fear.

On the porch, Richard's widow was begging the man to leave, but he wouldn't go. Olivia got out of the car cautiously and brushed her gun at her side, hoping she wouldn't need it. She approached with her hands in the air.

"Gareth?" Olivia shouted. "Gareth Dean?"

But the man didn't respond.

"Please, sir, you're scaring this poor woman," Olivia told the man. "Step away from the lawn."

But the man didn't move. He just crumpled further into himself, his face wracked with misery. He shook his head fervently.

"I did it. It was me. I killed him. It was my fault," the man sobbed. "But I didn't want to do it... I didn't mean to do it..."

Olivia felt a sigh leave her body. She hadn't expected a confession. But then she recalled that those taking the drugs said what they meant. They couldn't hold it back. This man, whoever he was, had been betrayed by the drugs in his system.

"Please, just take me away," he begged. "I don't want to live this way anymore... make it stop..."

193

Olivia looked up for Henry's assistance. Henry moved behind the man to cuff him, and the man didn't resist. He was completely broken.

"Sir, can you tell us your name?" Olivia asked him gently. She had a feeling she knew exactly who he was, but only he could confirm it. He sniffled loudly.

"G-G-G-Gareth. Gareth Dean."

Olivia nodded to herself. Another mystery solved. The second missing person from ANH.

Their missing person and their killer.

CHAPTER TWENTY-FOUR

Olivia and Henry immediately took Gareth in cuffs and brought him to the police station for questioning. Since he'd confessed, there was no need for them to waste time investigating the murder when Cheryl and the police could handle it, but Olivia was still left with so many questions. What had happened to Gareth to make him go so crazy and kill a man? Was he doing it on the orders of a boss? Could the drugs really be used to manipulate an innocent man into becoming a cold-blooded killer?

Olivia couldn't hide the fact that she was shocked by the outcome of the investigation. Gareth didn't seem like a seasoned killer to her, and yet the murder had been such a bold move.

Olivia knew that he was feeling loose-lipped, and she hoped that the more he talked, the more everything would make sense.

Olivia and Henry took Gareth to a quiet room. He had stopped sobbing, though Olivia thought it was more due to exhaustion than anything else. He had clearly once been a handsome man, but his cheeks were sunken, and he looked as though he hadn't slept in a week. Perhaps he hadn't, given that his entire life had turned upside down.

His brown hair was thick with grease, and he was covered in dirt and blood. Olivia tried to catch his eyes, but they seemed vacant, like nobody had been there for a very long time.

He was trying to control his breathing as Olivia and Henry sat down to speak with him. He took big breaths, in and out, staring at the table in front of him. Henry seemed unimpressed by the whole charade, but Olivia felt for the man. She often had empathy for the people she came across in her work. Sometimes, they really were just down on their luck, and she felt that Gareth might be among them.

"Mr. Dean... we'd like to talk to you about what happened, please," Olivia started calmly. "I know you're feeling out of sorts right now, and we understand that you're under the influence of some pretty strong drugs, so take your time. We just want to know what happened and why. Why did you kill Richard Greene?"

Gareth let out a small whimper, which had Henry rolling his eyes, but Olivia ignored him, keeping her eyes focused on their killer.

"Come on, Gareth. You've already told us that you did it. I'm sure you want a chance to explain yourself."

Gareth nodded a little shakily. He swallowed, still unable to look Olivia in the eye, but he began to speak after a long while.

"A few weeks ago, I got offered a bonus," he said. "But it wasn't money. It was a drug. They told me it would make me feel good and make me more productive. I thought I was going to be fired that week. I guess I'd been slacking a little at work. But when they told me they were giving me something, I thought, *great!* I've dabbled here and there... I thought it might help with some of

THE **LOCKED BOX**

the stress I've been under. But everything... everything changed after I took it."

"You felt completely suggestible. You felt like you had no choice but to do anything you were told," Henry said.

Gareth nodded. "Exactly. I... I've never experienced anything like it. And it didn't really feel good... but the next day, I needed more. I knew I had to have more. I practically crawled on my hands and knees back to work to ask them to supply me with it. And they did."

Olivia felt exhausted by the whole thing. How many lives were they willing to ruin with their little drug experiment? One of their workers had been slacking a little so they decided to ruin his life entirely?

"I got to the point where... where I couldn't function without a dose," Gareth told them. His hands were trembling on the table, and his palms were slick with sweat. "I went into work high every day.... and Richard... he was my boss. Well, he was in charge, and he saw that something was up. He asked a few times if I was okay. He tried to be really nice about it all. But I was feeling cranky and aggressive, and I kept telling him to back off. So, he did, for a while... until he caught me taking pills at work."

Gareth shook his head, fresh tears spilling on his cheeks. "I tried to tell him that they were prescription, but I think he knew something that I didn't. I think he knew that the company was giving them out as... well, they called them incentives. So, I guess I thought he'd try to help me out. But... it didn't work out that way."

"What do you mean?"

Gareth took an unsteady breath. "He told me I was fired. I was so angry with him. I was shouting at him in his office, asking what the hell was going on. I was too high to think logically—to know that anyone on Earth would be fired for taking drugs on the job. But he kept saying it was for my own good. That I was better off this way. I couldn't understand how that was possible."

"Did he explain his reasons for letting you go?"

"It's hazy. I think he was trying to tell me that it was my one chance to escape. That being fired meant I could still have a life...

maybe. But I was so angry. I've got a wife and kids at home. Hell knows they were already suffering because of me. Because of the drugs. So, the last thing I needed was for him to fire me, leaving me penniless and without the drugs to keep me going. I knew... I knew I wouldn't make it."

"So, you killed him?" Henry pressed, his voice level and cold. Gareth's eyes drooped.

"I... yes. I didn't feel like I was in control of my emotions. It was like something was forcing me to move. Like a switch had gone off in my brain, and I was acting completely outside of my own will. At first, I was going to just dig around in his office, but then I found his gun. And the moment I picked it up, I had no choice but to comply with the thoughts in my head."

"The thoughts told you to kill him?"

"I didn't know how to say no. My mind was so mixed up with all the drugs. It was like I was being ordered around and I couldn't stop. My body was moving without my mind. I crushed up one of the pills in his water bottle and then took the gun back with my things. I went back inside and told him there were no hard feelings, and that made him feel at ease. I could tell he was already getting a little high, like me. But he didn't have a lick of tolerance. I don't know if he knew what was going on. So, I followed him home. And then..."

Gareth pressed his fingers against his eyes, like he was trying to rid himself of the image of what happened next. He shook his head violently.

"I killed him. I had to kill him," Gareth groaned. "It was the only thing left to give me some control. He'd taken... he'd taken everything away from me! So, I left the car running. I got out and I just... I pulled the trigger. I barely even felt myself do it. I didn't see the bullet go into him. I still don't know where I shot him. But there was blood all over me, and I just... I got in my car and drove away. I was on autopilot. It felt like the only option."

Olivia and Henry were silent as Gareth began to sob again. Olivia still felt somewhat sympathetic, but she could tell that Henry didn't feel the same. He leaned forward across the table.

"You shot that poor man through the head. He didn't stand a chance. And then you scurried away like a coward."

"Henry," Olivia said in warning, but Gareth was nodding along to what Henry had said.

"I know. And I hate myself. I hate myself! I would never— you've got to believe me, I would never hurt a fly before. I've never… I've never gotten into trouble before. I've never been in a fight or wanted to cause trouble. I don't have violent impulses. But I just… I'm different now. And I'll never be the same. I'll never be the same."

He was crying so hard now that he was bordering on hysterical. Olivia nodded to Henry, and they stood to leave the room. They needed him to calm down if they were going to get anything useful out of him, and that wasn't about to happen with two agents staring him down.

"I need some coffee," Olivia told him. Henry nodded.

"Finally, something we have in common."

They trudged off to the coffee machine, and Olivia sighed as the hot liquid touched her lips. She looked at Henry.

"What do you make of all this?"

He shook his head. "I don't know. Won't people say anything to make you feel sorry for them? At the end of the day, he's still a killer."

"You don't think these drugs are capable of changing people? Of altering brain chemistry so dramatically that they become a different person?"

"You clearly do."

"Well, we've seen a lot of evidence to suggest it. And I bet if we asked any of his family or friends, they'd back him up. They'd say he's a perfect gentleman, a credit to society, all of that stuff."

"Of course, they'd say that. People said that about Ted Bundy, but it doesn't make it true. Killers only let you see what they want you to see. That is, until they get caught."

"But Gareth gave himself up willingly," Olivia pointed out. "He returned to the scene of the crime to try to make things right. You don't think his remorse says something?"

"Does it matter? He's going to prison either way, and we're still no closer to finding Brock. None of what he's told us is of any use, is it? We need him to tell us where the leadership of ANH is."

"You think a grunt like him would know that kind of thing?"

"He said they supplied him with the drugs," Henry replied.

Olivia rolled her eyes. "Yeah, like the CEO is really going to be handing those to him directly. No, I don't think he'll be able to help us with that. He was lower in rank than Richard, and he didn't have anything he could tell you either."

"So, what then? We ask him if he's seen Brock waltzing around lately?"

"Let's be honest, he's probably a dead end. He went missing a few days after Brock did. He was never going to be able to clue us in on that. But maybe if we press him with some more questions, he might be able to enlighten us in other ways."

Henry drained the last of his coffee from his cup. "Let's hope you're right. Otherwise, we've just wasted a few precious hours."

"I wouldn't call catching a killer a waste," Olivia said, but she felt anxiety clutching at her heart, knowing that Brock was only losing time. For a while, it had felt like they were closing on answers, but the answers to all of her biggest questions had only left her with a desire to know more.

They headed back to the room where they had left Gareth. From outside the door, he sounded like he had calmed down. But when Olivia pushed the door open, she gasped in horror.

Gareth was slumped in his chair; his head was flopped to the side, and there was white foam coming from the corner of his mouth. Olivia put a hand over her mouth. The only explanation was that the drugs had finally finished him off. His eyes were vacant, staring ahead as though there had never been any life inside him. A single tear rested halfway down his cheek.

Another man was lost to them because of ANH.

CHAPTER TWENTY-FIVE

As chaos ensued in the local police station, Olivia and Henry took their leave. Gareth's death had left Olivia feeling both numb and angry simultaneously. It should have hit harder, knowing another man was dead because of those drugs, but Olivia could feel herself getting used to it, like it was the status quo that couldn't be changed.

And that made her angry.

Henry's irritation mirrored her own. "You know what we have to talk about, don't you?"

Olivia nodded. There was a strong possibility that they weren't going to find a lead on Brock in time. Every time it seemed like they were getting close, they came to another dead end. And now, they were going to have to accept the fact that it was now or never. They needed to strike before it was too late.

Even if that meant putting Brock in danger.

"I know we have to do it," Olivia began. "And I know that if he's a double agent, then saving him won't be the issue. But what if he's the man I've always believed he is? What if our actions are what get him killed?"

Henry nodded solemnly. "I know. I know."

But he didn't know. He didn't know how it felt to be put in a position of having to choose between doing what was right and doing what her heart told her. Olivia was in an impossible situation. She almost wished she'd stayed out of the whole thing entirely, but then she would have hated herself for waiting around for someone else to save the man she cared about so dearly. How could she ever choose to abandon him like that?

Henry let out a long sigh. "You know… one of my partners died on the job once."

Olivia's heart squeezed. She had forgotten that Paxton had told her about that. She nodded slowly, and Henry ran a hand through his hair, looking anxious. "He was one of my best friends too. And it tore me apart when I couldn't save him. We were tailing a killer, and he got shot. It could have been anyone, but it wasn't just anyone. It was him. I didn't have time to prepare myself for it to happen. I didn't have time to grieve because I had to do my job. And so, I was just left with this… numbness. And it never really went away. I think to this day, I've still never cried over losing him. Something just… broke. It broke inside me, and it never got fixed."

Olivia stared at Henry. Even now, his face was level, as though he was just listing off his grocery list to her. He shrugged slowly. "And it sucked. This pain has been trapped inside my chest for so many years, and I don't know what to do with it."

Henry turned to Olivia. "I know that your pain right now is agonizing. If you lose him, it'll be worse. But at least you can say you did everything you could for him. And who knows? We might get lucky. We might still find a way to get him out."

THE **LOCKED BOX**

Olivia didn't know what to say. Her throat was tight after hearing Henry's confession. All this time, she'd spent her energy on not trusting him, not wanting to believe there was a shred of goodness inside him. And now, she knew how wrong she'd been.

All this time, it was like she'd been looking in a mirror. Because they were too similar. Because she was living the reality that he'd been through for so many years. They'd both had enough trauma for a lifetime. Olivia had taken one look at a broken man and seen herself without knowing it.

And she had hated him for it.

And now, it was obvious to her how wrong she'd been. This man wasn't a double agent. He wasn't a traitor. He was just a man trying to do his job while shoving all his emotions to the side in the process. Olivia, of all people, knew how it felt to live that way, even if she never truly succeeded in keeping her heart tucked inside her chest.

"I know I've been hard on you since you arrived," Henry said. "But I was just trying to keep you tough. I saw strength in you that I wish I'd had back then, when I needed it the most. I've been blunt to keep you down to earth, to make sure your expectations stay realistic. But I guess I should have been facing the fact that I was scared of reliving my own past. Scared of screwing up, scared of working with someone else again. When you're alone in our line of work, you only have to worry about yourself. I've chosen to be alone all this time, thinking it was easier. But it gets lonely." He offered Olivia a small smile. "You've been lucky.... to have a partner you care about so much. No matter how this thing ends, you're blessed to have had this at all. I know that might sound condescending, but it's true. You formed a connection that I could only dream of. And all I want to do now is try to help you. I don't want you to lose what I've lost."

The silence that followed wasn't the tense, difficult silence they'd become used to. It was like they finally had learned how to trust one another, and now they could just allow each other to breathe.

"You know... I never thought to ask about your life," Olivia said. "I just assumed that you were a bad person. I jumped to conclusions about you more times than I'd like to admit. And... while we're being honest... I thought maybe you were working as a double agent."

Henry stared at her in horror. "What?"

"I know. I know. It's just... you kept to yourself so much, and then you kept heading off to make sneaky phone calls..."

"Says you. I was calling my sick mother. I've been taking care of her these past few years, and she's been anxious about being apart from me. What else did you suspect of me?"

Olivia chewed her lip. "Well, your attitude toward me made me think that we weren't on the same side. And there were times when we weren't on the same wavelength..."

"And you thought that made me a double agent? Damn, American. You really are off your rocker."

Olivia sighed. "Maybe. There was more to it than that. But it's like I said... I never got to know you. You didn't want me to, and I stayed back because of it. You made assumptions about me too. There are things you don't know about my past that made me the way I am. My sister was murdered several years ago by a company not unlike ANH. She'd been working on the story to blow them open and expose their criminal behavior, and they had her silenced. And then not long after that, my mother up and disappeared without a trace. For years, I thought she was dead. Then when she reappeared, she told me that all that time, she'd been working for the FBI. She'd lied to me my whole life. And since then, I've been targeted by cults, serial killers, and plenty of messed up people. So, I know what it's like to have a... turbulent past."

Henry blinked. "Well, you win. Your life is like a freaking soap opera."

Olivia laughed, a real laugh that made Henry smile in return. She offered him a sheepish smile.

"We're all a product of our pasts, right? I guess some of the crazy things that have happened to me have made me more than a little paranoid. These things change who we are, and now that I know what you've been through, I feel like I understand you better."

THE **LOCKED BOX**

Henry nodded solemnly. "Same here."

"This has been the craziest week of my life," Olivia continued. "I guess it's made me act a little off. Since Brock was taken, I've had my whole life swept out from under me. But now I know we have to put our faith in each other and try to get this done. We have to find the truth without getting each other—and everyone else—killed. I know I haven't been easy to work with…"

"Well, I haven't been an angel either."

"That's entirely true. I can vouch for that. But I guess my emotions have kind of driven me to a bad place. I'm trying my best to hold it together… but I'm terrified of losing Brock. I'm scared that I'll lose the one person who has finally made my life mean something. And I need to bring him home, if only for my own sake… because I need to get the chance to tell him about the way he makes me feel."

Henry nodded slowly in understanding, a warmth entering his eyes for the first time since Olivia had met him. "I understand. You must really love him."

Olivia's heart skipped a beat. Love… that was never a word she'd used to describe her feelings for Brock. But she knew it was true. Ever since they had met, her feelings had been growing stronger and stronger. He wasn't just the annoying, cocky agent who ground her gears anymore. He was the most caring man she'd ever known, the funniest man she'd ever spoken to, the most loving person she'd ever come across. And when all was said and done, yes. She was in love with him.

"I think I do," Olivia said gently. The car was quiet for a moment as they let that sink in between them. Olivia hadn't expected to confess those feelings to anyone, much less to the man who had made her difficult week seem even harder. Henry wasn't exactly the kind of guy that made you feel like opening your heart, even if he did have a good heart buried somewhere deep inside him. Olivia was surprised at herself, and she felt almost embarrassed that she had made such a deep confession.

Then, Henry sighed.

"Well, that's a shame."

Olivia blinked. "It is?"

"Yeah. Because I was just starting to warm up to you. I was even considering asking you out for a pint. We'd be a great couple, don't you think?"

It took a moment for Olivia to hear the sarcasm buried deep in his tone, but then she laughed. She laughed so hard that her sides hurt. It wasn't even a good joke, but after the week she'd had, it felt good to laugh for the first time. He smiled in return, shaking his head.

"See? I can be funny on occasion."

"I can see that," Olivia said, calming down enough to wipe tears from her eyes. Strangely, she felt better than she had since leaving Belle Grove what felt like ages ago. Even though nothing was promised, even though her world was still upside down... she finally had a moment of relief to fall back on. And she owed that to Henry.

He cleared his throat with an awkward smile, clearly not quite comfortable with their meaningful moment. "But now that we've got all of that out of the way... perhaps it's time to talk about what we're going to do. I can have an elite MI5 team on standby to make a bust. We can pull this together in a matter of hours, if that's what you'd like to do. But the question is where and when? How close are we willing to cut it?"

Olivia sucked in a deep breath. Just like that, she was placed back into her impossible scenario. If she waited, she might be able to find something else to save Brock, despite their run of bad luck so far. But if she waited too long, they wouldn't have a shot at all. Their timer would run out, and he'd be killed before she even had a chance to attack. She knew she had to make a choice. It was now or never.

"I guess we have to strike," Olivia said firmly. "The FBI isn't going to pay the bounty... and when they don't, I'm sure that ANH will not try to negotiate again. If we have any chance of saving him, we have to hit now."

"And where do we want to lead the assault?"

Olivia shook her head. It was impossible to know where was best. Richard's secret diary had given them several important places that they could hit, but Olivia had no idea which of them could be holding Brock captive.

"I guess it's a roll of the dice," Olivia said quietly. Henry nodded.

"You still have a little time to decide today. But tomorrow, early in the morning… I think that's our best bet. We can maybe catch them by surprise."

Olivia nodded, feeling her heart rate ramping up. The whole thing was beginning to feel too real. She didn't want to do this. She just wanted Brock to appear out of the blue and tell her that everything was fine. That he didn't need saving, and he wasn't going to disappear on her again.

But Olivia knew all too well that in life, there wasn't always a happy ending. Henry's tale was a testament to that. She'd seen so much suffering in her life, and she'd had her one miracle when her mother returned from hiding. She didn't think she was about to get another shot with Brock. She was sure that their story was about to come to an end.

But she had to try at least one more time.

CHAPTER TWENTY-SIX

It was the middle of the night when Olivia received a call from an unknown number. She had not been asleep. In fact, she had spent most of the evening pacing back and forth in her bedroom in the B&B, unable to rest. She knew that the next morning was going to be all or nothing. Either Brock came out of it alive, or he wound up dead the moment they launched their attack.

The thought terrified Olivia.

And the thought of an unknown number calling her in the middle of the night did not bring up positive thoughts. She recalled when The Messenger had called her at 3 a.m. and told her to meet him. That night, she had almost died. She didn't want

THE **LOCKED BOX**

to go through that ordeal all over again. What if the call was to tell her that she was too late? That Brock was already dead?

But still, she cautiously approached the phone and picked up the call. Her hand was shaking a little as she brought it to her ear.

"Hello?"

"Nothing to worry about, Olivia. Just me again," Kit said on the other end of the line. Olivia let out a sigh of relief. It was good to hear Kit's voice.

"Tell me you have something, Kit. I could really use some good news."

The other end of the line was silent. Olivia held her breath, hoping that Kit was just preparing to speak. But after a long while, Kit sighed.

"Look… I tried my best, but I couldn't get a location on your friend. I've found out all sorts of background on ANH, and I'd be happy to fill you in… but I know that's not what you want to hear right now."

Olivia was shaking. She leaned her back against the wall to steady herself, feeling as if she couldn't keep herself upright. She had been counting on a lead. She was sure that if anyone could find something, it would be Kit. Now, she felt as if everything she'd been hoping for was lost.

"I'm sorry, Olivia. I wish I had been of more help."

"Don't say that, Kit," Olivia replied gently. "I asked an impossible task of you. ANH is a monster, and we all knew that this wasn't going to be easy. Please, don't beat yourself up about this. It's not your fault. It's just the way things are."

"I know. I just wish I had something. Anything. You deserve a happy ending to this."

Olivia closed her eyes with a tired smile. "I guess sometimes happy endings just aren't in the cards."

"Don't give up," Kit said gently. "I know that's not like you. Paxton told me all about you, Olivia. He told me you're like a bloodhound when you get a lead. Nothing and no one can stop you from doing what's necessary."

Olivia felt her heart warm at the comment. She couldn't imagine her brother-in-law saying those things about her. Sure, their relationship was better these days than it had been before, but they'd never really been close. And now, knowing that he had such positive things to say about her, it made her feel just the slightest bit better.

"He really said that?"

"Of course, he did. We're all rooting for you. I hope you know that."

Olivia felt a tear slide down her cheek, but quickly wiped it away. She didn't have time to be emotional, and she didn't want to break down in front of Kit—not even now when everything felt like it was falling apart.

"I appreciate that. I guess this is it, then. But hey, next time I'm in Seattle, dinner is definitely on me. Thank you so much for trying. I know you did your best."

"Ah, you're welcome. It kept me occupied for a few days at least. Now it's back to the drawing board," Kit replied, weariness in her voice. "I'll pass on the info I've found to Blake and the others. Thanks for bringing me along for the ride; it's been an experience. Hey, maybe our paths will cross again someday."

"I hope so. Thank you, Kit."

When the call ended, Olivia was left feeling helpless. She slid down the wall to sit on the floor, her head throbbing hard. She was so tired. Tired of everything. She was ready for it to be over, with a solution one way or another. She needed answers, she needed truth, and she needed hope.

Kit had been that one last shred of hope for her. She had been so certain that she was the key to getting answers. But now, she felt ridiculous, knowing that it had really just been a shot in the dark.

But why had she not relied on herself? Kit was incredible, but so was she. There was still time. There was still time for them to get a lead and follow it to the end. If only Olivia could find something else, she'd be back on track. Olivia sat up a little straighter, wiping tears from her face. She could break down tomorrow. Tonight, she had to give one final push. She had to see if she could resolve this mystery once and for all.

Olivia found herself reaching for Richard Greene's journal once more. It was the most solid piece of evidence they had

THE **LOCKED BOX**

against ANH, and the most detailed and honest recollection of time within their presence. Olivia was sure that had to be valuable in some way. In any other case, that kind of information would be worth more than gold.

But this case had always stood out for its complexity. Olivia knew that there had to be something of use between those pages, but what, she didn't know. She had read it through a hundred times, thumbing through each page and hoping that something new would jump out at her, but it never did.

This time, she flipped through the pages listlessly, praying for something. She watched the crisp white pages whiz by, but as they did, she saw several markings in the corners of some of the pages. Olivia paused and went back to the beginning of the book.

She stared at the right-hand corners of each page. Some of them were blank, but about halfway through the book, numbers began to appear in the corner of each page. Olivia's first instinct was to assume that they were simply page numbers, but when the two adjacent pages jumped by nineteen numbers, she knew it had to be something else.

Taking out a pen, Olivia noted down the numbers in order, scribbling them down as quickly as she could. She could feel her heart racing hard in her chest, sending her whole body into overdrive. As soon as the numbers in the corners of the page ran out, she observed them in order.

50
79
82
74
, -
00
25
41
7

"What the hell is this?" she murmured. Right there in the middle of the number sequence, there was a comma and a dash, which made Olivia certain that she was looking at some kind of code… no, not a code.

Coordinates.

50.798274, -0.025417

When placed in a row, it became obvious to Olivia. The only thing that made sense was a set of coordinates. She typed them into her search engine on her phone, her heart squeezing painfully in her chest as she did. She knew she had to be on to something. Richard had left those numbers there for a reason. Perhaps it was even one of the last things he did. And now, perhaps he was about to save a life.

The coordinates weren't far away. In fact, they were just outside of Newhaven in an industrial district—not even a ten-minute drive away. It made total sense for a place like that to hide a dark secret. Like Brock, their fugitive. It wasn't one of the addresses listed in the notebook, but Olivia was certain this had to be their location. Richard had hidden this spot from even the list of addresses he'd found. Something had to be there.

Would it be Brock? She didn't know, but she was out of options. And this might be her only shot.

Olivia got herself up off the floor and rushed to Henry's bedroom, knocking loudly on the door. She didn't care who she woke up in the process. Some things were more important. Henry made a gruff noise from within the room and shuffled to answer the door, his eyes drooping with sleep.

"This had better be good, American. I know we're on slightly better terms now than before, but I really hate being woken up… What are you still doing up, anyway? We have an important operation to run in a few hours."

"I know. But there's been a change of plans."

He raised an eyebrow at her. "There has? Great. Fantastic. As though this whole thing wasn't sketchy enough anyway. What's happened? Have you finally just lost your mind?"

"Not at all," Olivia told him. "I think I might know where Brock is being held. I figured out a clue from Richard Greene's journal." She took the page and showed him as she frantically flipped the pages. "You see these numbers? They look like page numbers, but they're out of order. So, I put them together and look at this… they're coordinates. This could be an important site for ANH—so important that even Richard had to keep it a secret—and that's likely where they'd keep Brock, right? I know that we had intended to target a warehouse further out, but I think this is important. This could be it. We might really have found him."

Henry finally looked like he was getting on board. "Why didn't you lead with that? This is good. Really good. I'll make some calls and make sure our team is ready to head out to the new location. And then I really want to get a few hours of sleep, if you don't mind. I don't want to go into this like a zombie."

"Absolutely. And hey… if this goes well, you won't have to put up with me anymore," Olivia said brightly. She was already feeling much better about the operation. Even though they were woefully underprepared, she still liked her chances better now that they had an idea of where to find Brock.

"Let's not jump to conclusions," Henry replied with a weary smile. "But I'll admit, it's good to see you so positive. Now please, get some rest. It would be a shame for you to get shot because you're sleep-deprived, wouldn't it?"

Olivia didn't even mind his sarcastic comments. As she headed back to her room, she felt like she could slip under the covers and close her eyes for a bit. She had more hope in her heart than she'd managed to muster for a long time.

"I'm coming for you, Brock," she murmured sleepily. "I'm coming."

CHAPTER TWENTY-SEVEN

THE ROAD WAS DARK, AND THEY DROVE WITHOUT headlights. Olivia and Henry had opted to arrive in an unmarked car to drive by the warehouse and check the security first. The rest of Henry's team from MI5 were due to follow them, a team of eight operatives who Henry claimed were the best of the best. Olivia wasn't sure she entirely trusted Henry's taste given that he was the biggest loner she'd ever met, but she hoped that he was right about the people he'd enlisted. They couldn't afford a single mistake, or Brock would be dead already.

"What do you see?" Henry asked as they cruised by the warehouse. It was situated far from any neighboring buildings,

THE **LOCKED BOX**

surrounded mostly by fields and woodland. Olivia peered closely at the warehouse as they went by.

"It doesn't look like security is tight. I guess they're not really expecting guests. There's a light on in the building, but I don't see any patrols."

"I can't decide if that's a good thing," Henry muttered, tightening his grip on the steering wheel. "Either they're overconfident, or it's a trap that we're just waiting to walk into. If only we had more time to scout it out…"

"Well, we don't. We both know it's now or never."

Henry nodded, taking an uneasy big breath. "I know that. I'll call in the others. We'll make our move as soon as they arrive."

As planned, they stopped their car at the side of the road, a few hundred meters from the location. Olivia checked her gun while Henry called in his troops with a hushed call to their captain. Then, sliding his phone into his pocket, he took a deep breath.

"Well. This is it," he said. "I've got to admit… I've been waiting for this a long time."

Olivia nodded. For years, Henry had been keeping an eye on ANH, trying to figure out their next move, analyzing them as closely as he could. Now, everything he'd been working toward was about to come to a head. In only a week, their investigation had surged forward, and for the first time in forever, he had an open shot of taking them down. He glanced over at Olivia with a smile.

"This wouldn't have been possible without you, Olivia. I hope you know that."

"I believe that's the nicest thing you've said to me all week."

"Well, if this is a success, there will be plenty more where that came from. I'll be a changed man."

"I'll believe that when I see it. What's the ETA for the others?"

"Five minutes. Then it's go time. Are you scared?"

Olivia took a deep breath. "I think I'd be a fool if I wasn't. There's too much on the line to even consider failing."

Henry nodded, his face turned serious again. "I know. But if he's in there… I promise we'll get him out alive. I won't let you down. I'm giving this my all."

Olivia almost wanted to reach out and hug him. Henry was starting to feel like an ally, if not a friend. It hadn't been an easy ride for either of them, and it was a wonder they'd made it this far without killing each other, but Olivia could now see his true colors, and she had to admit she liked them. She thought it wouldn't be so bad if they ever had to work with one another again. At least together, they got things done.

The sounds of a car approaching behind them made Olivia's skin tingle with nerves, but she calmed down when she saw the eight operatives unloading from the back of the van, double- and triple-checking their gear. They looked like good people to her—sharp, focused, and armed to the teeth. It gave her confidence that they could get through it.

Half an hour. That's how long she suspected they'd be, at most. They'd storm the entrance and take down everyone they could to get to Brock. That meant only half an hour more of agony. Only half an hour before she could let her walls come down. Only half an hour before she finally got answers to the questions plaguing her. Was Brock still alive? Was he on her side or not? Did he really care for her? She knew it would all become clear when she saw his face.

Just thirty more minutes.

"Everyone, listen up," Henry whispered to the other eight operatives. "We still have the element of surprise. We need to get in there and be ruthless and quick. Anyone we come across is likely to be armed, so deadly force may be necessary. We don't know much about the layout of this place, given the short notice of this, but we're likely looking for some kind of holding place where ANH might be keeping the kidnapped FBI agent. We will have to keep our eyes peeled and hope for the best. Any questions?"

The operatives all shook their heads. These men knew what they were getting into. They were putting their lives on the line for someone they'd likely never even heard of, and they were doing it willingly. In a way, they were doing it for service to their country—to the people that had been destroyed by ANH.

Olivia was so grateful for them all at that moment, and she hoped that she would make it through to thank them for their

THE **LOCKED BOX**

service. Her heart was thudding hard beneath her bulletproof vest, and she was keen to end this thing once and for all.

"Are we ready?" Henry asked the group, but he looked at Olivia when he said it. She silently nodded, feeling nauseous at the thought of going in there. There was so much to gain if they found Brock, but so much to lose if they didn't. Olivia had never been so afraid to embark on a mission. The stakes had never been so high for her. But her hands were steady as she readied her gun and prepared to lead the way inside.

"Follow me," she whispered.

The group of ten crept up the road. The moon was the only light to guide them on their way, so they moved slower than Olivia would have liked. But the last thing she wanted to do was blow their cover too soon and send the whole place into a frenzy. They were only a small team, and she had no intention of blowing up the whole operation by striking too soon.

When they reached the dirt path leading up to the warehouse, it occurred to Olivia that it wasn't a particularly secure location. There was no gate guarding the warehouse, and no guards were outside. She knew that ANH liked to hide in plain sight, however, and looking at it then, it just seemed like any other warehouse, not a torture room where an FBI agent could be held. In some ways, that made it the perfect hideout.

As they'd been briefed, the team split up: three men went left, three men went right, and two stayed with Olivia and Henry to lead the charge. There were a few lights on inside that might indicate that someone was there, and it made Olivia's heart speed up even further. She had no idea how many people they might be met with. It might not be a fair fight at all. Perhaps they didn't stand a chance. But she had to try, and the poor souls who had come along with her had nowhere to run to now.

It was all or nothing.

Olivia listened for the sound of voices as they approached the entrance, but the night was eerily quiet. A quiet click of the intercom let her know that the backup teams were in position at either entrance.

Henry lifted his gun to shoot at the padlock keeping the front entrance closed, ready to unleash hell on the place, but Olivia held up a hand to stop him. She took a pin from her hair and carefully began to pick the lock, a trick she'd learned long before she joined the FBI. When she finally heard the click of the lock, she eased the door open slowly and looked inside.

They were met with a dark corridor. Clearly, there was no one around in that part of the warehouse. As Olivia stepped inside, her footsteps on the stone floor echoed around the metal walls. She winced, but there didn't appear to be anyone around to notice their noisy steps. One by one, the others followed her lead, weapons raised in preparation for crossing paths with ANH guards. She signaled with her intercom for the teams on the left and right to enter, and they, too, stepped inside and regrouped as Olivia pressed forward, shining her flashlight into the dark, shadowy corners.

But there was no one. As Olivia led them through the building, her nerves were frayed, expecting to see someone with each door she opened or each corner she turned. She almost wished for someone to show up, just so that she could be sure that there *were* enemies to fight. It was worse not knowing if they were alone or not.

But the torture continued. There wasn't a soul in sight. Olivia's breathing became a little heavier, and it was so quiet that she could hear it as she walked. She could sense the nerves of the others behind her too. This wasn't the scene they'd been told to expect. They had expected men to be firing at them left, right, and center.

But they were alone.

Up ahead, a closed door had a light shining from beneath it. The room on the other side had the lights on. Olivia glanced back at the others and held up her hand to keep their pace slow. She snapped off her flashlight and crept forward to investigate, pressing her ear to the door lightly. There was no sound from the other side. Olivia didn't like that at all, but they had no choice. They'd come this far. They had to see what was waiting for them on the other side.

She turned to the others and held up five fingers. She was counting them down. They all readied their weapons, prepared for anything they might face.

Five…

Four…

Three…

Two…

One…

Olivia kicked the door open and cocked her gun, her heart leaping in her chest. She expected some sort of a welcome party, but all she was met with was an empty room.

Well, almost empty.

Straight ahead of her, a single chair was placed in the middle of the room. There was a note propped up on it.

"Cover my back," Olivia whispered to Henry. She inched forward, looking for any signs of movement, but none came. She was almost certain that they were alone.

She had a bad feeling in the pit of her stomach as she approached the chair. She knew nothing good could come from a setup like this. She felt her heart drop to her stomach as she picked up the note and read the words on it.

Nice try.

Olivia looked around her once more and saw the camera in the top corner of the room. In her pocket, her phone buzzed with a message. Haunted, she took her phone out and saw a video had been sent from an unknown number.

She opened the message.

The man in the mask was standing before the camera once again, for a third and final time. He shook his head at her, tutting at her.

"You should have followed the rules, FBI," the distorted voice said. "But I'll give you one last chance. You now have twenty-four hours to bring us the money in exchange for Tanner's life. Don't try any funny business, or you know what we'll do. We're being generous here. Don't disappoint us."

The video ended. Olivia fell to her knees, unable to stop herself. She felt like she wanted to scream and scream to let out all the anger and fear and misery inside her.

But as she fell to the ground, all she could manage was a whimper.

EPILOGUE

Brock was forced to watch the video from the warehouse over and over again. It was a new form of torture, seeing Olivia fall to her knees in the abandoned warehouse where she had hoped to find him. She had been so ready to fight for his life, so ready to save him from the clutches of the people that didn't care if he lived or died. But she'd been just a little too late. A few hours earlier, and maybe he'd be with her right now, holding her close, thanking her for saving his life.

Now, that was even further out of his reach than before.

"Good thing we moved you when we did, isn't it, Brock? Or maybe this whole scenario wouldn't be playing in my favor so well."

Brock closed his eyes. Olivia had been so close. She had found the location where he had been held for most of his stay in the UK. She had tracked him down out of dozens of warehouses, only to find it emptied out.

When the boss had forced drugs down one of his employee's throats, he'd confessed everything. He'd confessed to being a mole. Confessed to feeding information to MI5. Confessed to wanting to make ANH pay for who they'd become by ending them for good. He'd been so close.

And then he'd paid for his disloyalty with a bullet to his brain.

The worst part was, they'd framed and manipulated another man into doing their bidding. Gareth Dean drugged Richard Greene and pulled the trigger, of course, but not even he could remember the way that the suggestion had been implanted into him from the beginning. It was the perfect crime. One that could be replicated the world over.

"You see what happens when you cross us?" came a murmur in Brock's ear, breath stale on his cheek. "Your grandfather should have played nice with us when he had the chance."

"I told you it was never going to happen," Brock replied. "It didn't have to come to this. You could have just let me go."

"You know that's not true. You know far too much now, Brock. In fact, your friend has done us a favor. She's given us a reason to speed up the process of disposing of you. Now that we've been uncovered, we'll have a war on our hands." His papery face crumpled into a cruel smile. "And since we have some of the world's finest weaponry... this is a war we're likely to win, don't you think?"

The thought terrified Brock. The idea that every single loyal employee of ANH would unleash hell on MI5 and the FBI... they'd be in a lawless land. With weapons like theirs, nobody would be able to stop them. And with the drugs they could slip into anyone, anywhere, to control their thoughts and desires... nobody would even want to.

The boss chuckled to himself. "You'd better hope that your precious Olivia finds the money quickly, Brock. Or you *shall* be dead in twenty-four hours. Not that it'll make much difference anyway... the second you get out of here, it's all fair game. They

THE **LOCKED BOX**

can take you and die alongside you later. I don't mind waiting. I'm a patient man."

"My life isn't worth this," Brock growled. "I don't care if you kill me. I don't care about your petty wars. Just leave her be. Kill me if you must—I don't care. Just don't drag her into this."

"She was told the rules, and she didn't play by them. And now, she will pay for it. I'm sorry that it had to be this way, Brock. Truly, I am. But winners don't bend the rules. They punish the losers."

The man laughed in his ear. "And I have never lost before."

AUTHOR'S NOTE

Thank you for reading *The Locked Box*, book 6 in the *Olivia Knight FBI Series*.

We enjoyed taking this adventure outside of the US and had fun doing our research!

Our intention is to give you thrilling adventures and an entertaining escape with each and every book. However, we need your help to continue writing this new series. Being indie writers is tough. We don't have a large budget, huge following, or any of the cutting edge marketing techniques. So, all we kindly ask is that if you're enjoying the books in the Olivia Knight series, please take a moment of your time and leave us a review and maybe recommend the book to a fellow book lover or two. This way we can continue to write all day and night and bring you more books in the Olivia Knight series.

We cannot wait to share with you the upcoming thrilling adventures of Olivia and Brock!

Your writer friends,
Elle Gray & K.S. Gray

P.S. If you want to read more awesome books while you wait for the next Olivia Knight book. Please, checkout *Pax Arrington Mysteries and Blake Wilder FBI Mystery Thrillers*

P.P.S Feel free to reach out at egray@ellegraybooks.com with any feedbacks, suggestions, typos or errors you find so that we can take care of it!

ALSO BY
ELLE GRAY

Blake Wilder FBI Mystery Thrillers

Book One - The 7 She Saw
Book Two - A Perfect Wife
Book Three - Her Perfect Crime
Book Four - The Chosen Girls
Book Five - The Secret She Kept
Book Six - The Lost Girls
Book Seven - The Lost Sister
Book Eight - The Missing Woman
Book Nine - Night at the Asylum
Book Ten - A Time to Die
Book Eleven - The House on the Hill
Book Twelve - The Missing Girls
Book Thirteen - No More Lies

A Pax Arrington Mystery

Free Prequel - Deadly Pursuit
Book One - I See You
Book Two - Her Last Call
Book Three - Woman In The Water
Book Four - A Wife's Secret

ALSO BY
ELLE GRAY | K.S. GRAY

Olivia Knight FBI Mystery Thrillers
Book One - New Girl in Town
Book Two - The Murders on Beacon Hill
Book Three - The Woman Behind the Door
Book Four - Love, Lies, and Suicide
Book Five - Murder on the Astoria
Book Six - The Locked Box